Insidious Attack!

Lieutenant Duncan Hunter heard booming sounds in the distance. Moments later they heard the whistle of incoming shells. Huddling in the bottom of the trench, they knew what would happen next. The big German 155 shells began crashing to earth, smoke and debris blocking out the sun. The ground heaved and men held onto their helmets. The men hadn't had time to build an extensive network of bunkers, so all they could do was crowd beneath their unfinished fortifications and hope a shell wouldn't fall down on them.

Duncan crawled up the side of the trench and peered through his binoculars over the top. He could see nothing through the smoke and haze. An explosion nearby made him duck.

He got down in the trench with the rest of the doughboys. The Germans evidently thought they could win without an artillery bombardment. *This time the Krauts are wrong,* he thought. Duncan suddenly became aware there was something noxious in the air. He felt giddy and powerless. It was as if a gigantic hand had seized him by the throat and started choking the breath of life from him.

Bayonets
in
No-Man's-
Land

Jonathan Scofield

A DELL/BRYANS BOOK

To be able to say, when this war is finished, "I belonged to the Second Division, and I fought with it at the Battle of Blanc Mont Ridge," will be the highest honor that can come to any man.

Major General John A. Lejeune
United States Marine Corps

1

1

THE BAND PLAYED "Stars and Stripes Forever" as the doughboys marched through Paris. It was July 4, 1917, and the boulevards were lined with Frenchmen anxious to see the soldiers whom they hoped would win the war for them. The doughboys had arrived only six days before and many had still not recovered from their sea voyage, but they held their heads high, marching proudly to the beat of the drums as they made their way through the cheering throngs.

The doughboys were from all over the United States, from all walks of life. Two-thirds of them were green soldiers who'd been civilians only a couple of months before; the rest were grizzled old regular army men who'd served with the cavalry on the Mexican border, and some of the old sergeants and officers had fought in the Spanish-American War.

The French tossed garlands of flowers at them and held out bottles of champagne, but the doughboys kept their eyes straight ahead and continued to march. Their wide-brimmed campaign hats were slanted low over their eyes and their high-buttoned collars were tight around their necks. They carried their Springfield rifles at right-shoulder-arms and their boots beat a steady tattoo on the street as they marched toward Lafayette's Tomb.

Fifty yards in front of the doughboys, in the rear seat of an open automobile, sat Major General John J. Pershing, their commander, and beside him were French General Ferdinand Foch and Field Marshal Joseph Joffre, with M. Raymond Poincaré, President of the French Republic, in the front seat. Pershing waved and smiled to the crowds. He was astonished and touched by the enthusiasm shown for him and his men. He looked back at the advancing columns of doughboys. With all the blooms and confetti showering down on them, they looked almost like a moving flower garden.

Poincaré leaned toward Pershing and touched his shoulder. "The people are indeed happy to see you," he said.

"We shall not fail them," Pershing replied, although he knew his doughboys were not yet ready for war. America had only two hundred thousand men under arms when she declared war on the Central Powers, and that many could be killed in a week on the western front. It would be a tremendous job to build an army that could defeat Germany. Pershing figured he would need around three million men to do the job.

A garland of blood-red roses fell into Pershing's lap. Field Marshal Joffre chuckled and picked them up to place them around Pershing's neck. The crowd roared its approval, and the limousine advanced down the Champs-Elysées.

While Pershing was waving to the crowds, General Foch studied him, trying to size the man up. He knew that Pershing was the most famous officer in the American army, a fearless fighter and a close friend of the former president, Teddy Roosevelt. Pershing was tall and broad-shouldered with superb military bearing, obviously a born leader of men. But Foch knew that Pershing had never commanded a unit larger than a division in combat. Could such a man mold and lead an army to victory against the most devastating war machine the world had ever seen?

People leaned out of tall buildings and waved at the doughboys. Gendarmes struggled to hold the crowds back, but little boys broke through and ran alongside the Americans, touching their uniforms and gazing at them in awe. The girls in the crowd blew kisses. Old men and old women waved tiny American flags on sticks.

Pershing's staff officers marched behind his car in two solid ranks. In the middle of the second rank was Second Lieutenant Everett DeWitt of New York City. Tall and slender, with fair skin and blond hair, he looked through the corners of his eyes at the fabled buildings of Paris as flowers and confetti rained down upon him. Twenty-two years old, a member of one of the most distinguished families in America, he knew this was a momentous day in his life, a day he would talk about to his grandchildren, for he was keenly aware that he was marching across the stage of history.

"You're out of step, Ev," muttered the officer to his right, Captain George S. Patton from Virginia.

DeWitt looked down and saw that he was indeed out of step. He'd been daydreaming and had forgotten the soldier's most elementary task, to stay in step. He skipped once and got into step with the others.

The doughboys marched into the Picpus Cemetery, where a platform had been erected behind the white marble tomb of the Marquis de Lafayette, who had fought for America during its Revolutionary War. The open car stopped beside the platform, and French soldiers rushed forward to open its doors as the doughboys marched into battalion formations in front of the tomb. Poincaré, Pershing, Foch and Joffre got out of the limousine and ascended the steps to the platform. They were followed by Pershing's staff officers, and greeted by various dignitaries of the French, British and American governments. Tens of thousands of French pressed against the gates of the cemetery, wanting to see everything, to hear every word. A battalion of bearded French combat soldiers stood to the side, wearing blue uniforms and helmets, holding rifles with long bayonets, examining the American doughboys who were in turn examining them.

The sun shone brightly on the platform, and General Pershing shook hands with the dignitaries as the crowds shouted and cheered. Paul Painlevé, the French Minister of War, took Pershing by the arm.

"You must speak now," Painlevé said.

Pershing shook his head. "I'm not much of a speaker, sir. I've designated Colonel Stanton to speak for me."

Painlevé's eyes widened. "I'm afraid that is impossible, *mon Général*. You are the commander of the American soldiers here. You are the one who must deliver the address."

"But I haven't prepared anything."

"Surely you can say something."

Pershing looked to the American ambassador, William Sharp, for help, but received a stern look in reply. "I think you'd better say something," Sharp said quietly.

Pershing knew he was on the spot, but he'd been in tighter spots than this. He advanced to the podium, with no idea of what he was going to say. A hush fell over the crowd, and everyone listened eagerly. Pershing looked down at his doughboys and then to the French soldiers to the side of the tomb. Behind them he could see crowds of French people and the skyline of Paris in the distance. Everyone was waiting for him to speak, and still his mind was a blank.

Pershing looked down at the tomb of Lafayette. He cleared his throat, and then, suddenly, like gifts from God, the words fell into his mind. Holding the sides of the podium, he gazed solemnly at the tomb and said in his deep, booming voice, "Lafayette, we are here!"

2

IT WAS LATE afternoon and the sun was setting over the western front. High in the sky, in the cockpit of a Spad S.13, Sergeant Blake Langley Hunter looked down at the battlefield on which hundreds of thousands of men had died since 1914. The earth was brown, interlaced with thin black lines that Blake knew were long coils of barbed wire. He saw the deep scars of trenches and the men moving around inside them.

It was quiet down there; there had been no heavy action that day. He'd taken his Spad up in the hope that he might find a lone German observer plane or a fighter trying to make its way back to German lines. Four of his confirmed kills had been on late afternoon patrols, and he hoped today would be another of his lucky days.

He was an American, twenty-four years old, from Virginia. His squadron was the famous Lafayette Escadrille, composed entirely of Americans flying for France. His Spad had an Indian head painted on both sides of the fuselage, the insignia of the escadrille.

A speck in the distance caught his eye. Squinting between the struts of the wings, he saw that his Spad was not the only aircraft in the area.

Blake pushed the stick to the side and banked his Spad so that it would head west. He wanted to get the sun behind him so that it would be difficult for the pilot in the other plane to see him. The Spad's 210-horsepower Hispano-Suiza engine roared as the biplane angled to the side. Blake continued staring at the lone plane in the distance to see if it altered its course or behaved as though it knew it was being stalked. It continued unswervingly toward German lines, and Blake knew it must be a German plane; no Allied plane would be heading toward Germany at this time of day.

Blake maneuvered his Spad so that it was behind and above the other plane, at the same time searching the skies around him to make sure he wasn't being lured into a trap. The cold windstream whistled through the struts of his wings and washed his face. His heart always beat faster and his perceptions seemed finer when he was closing in for a kill like this. He was slowly gaining on the other plane. Soon he would know whether or not it belonged to the Germans.

It reminded him of when he was a boy, hunting squirrels in the forests of Virginia. He'd crept up on them the same way, gained a favorable firing position, and aimed carefully. Hunting was the same whether the prey was a small forest creature or a lone airplane in the sky over France.

He looked around him again, then checked his compass, airspeed indicator and radiator thermometer. His cockpit was fitted with a Camel joystick and he'd rigged up an apparatus so that he could fire both of his Vickers machine guns with one trigger. He was drawing closer to the other plane now, and he pushed the stick forward so he could dive down and get a better look.

The front of the Spad angled downward, and Blake began his dive. He smiled as the black crosses of the German air force came into focus on the wings of the other plane, for he'd found what he'd been looking for. Then he noticed that it was a two-seater, with a machine gunner behind the pilot; it would be deadly to try to take them from above and behind as he was doing.

Blake pulled back his stick and angled to the right. His Spad climbed into the air and rolled out, its Hispano-Suiza engines snarling through the night. He heard machine guns beneath him. The German gunner had seen him and was trying to bring him down, but Blake was speeding toward the earth at a terrific speed, rolling to the side at the same time. The wind rushed into his cockpit and he held his stick tightly with both hands, feeling the sick, empty feeling in his stomach as he plummeted to earth upside down. He heard machine gun bullets whistling through the air, and one of them shot through the fabric on his upper wing, but he was a fast-moving target and it would take a tremendous stroke of luck for the German to disable him.

Glancing to the side, he looked at the German plane and saw that it was a Halberstadt, which was used as a fighting plane and a scout. He dived below it and pushed his stick all the way to the right. His Spad rolled over and came out upright again. Blake was underneath the Halberstadt and heading toward it at an angle from the front. Aiming his twin Vickers, he gave the Spad some top rudder and took off a bit of aileron. He climbed toward the Halberstadt, aligning it dead ahead. Unconsciously clenching his teeth, he pushed his trigger button, and lightning darted from twin Vickers mounted on the Spad's cowling. The machine guns chattered and Blake saw his tracers making long red lines that disappeared beneath the fuselage of the Halberstadt.

The German plane tried to climb, but that only exposed more of its belly. Blake held his trigger down and sprayed hot lead into the Halberstadt. He was closing fast with it but kept his Vickers firing until the last moment. Then he pushed his stick forward and dived underneath the plane. Looking behind him, he saw a trail of smoke underneath the Halberstadt. I got him, Blake thought. He's hurt.

But now Blake was exposed. The rear gunner on the Halberstadt swung his machine gun down and fired at the Spad. Blake eased off his throttle and banked to the left. He turned around and went at the Halberstadt from below again. The German gunner in the rear seat continued firing down at him, and the Spad twitched as bullets ripped through its fabric. The Halberstadt had slowed considerably and Blake streaked underneath it, turned again, and attacked beneath the

front of the Halberstadt again. The Spad rattled with
the fire of the machine guns, and Blake saw bits of
material fly into the air underneath the German aircraft. The smoke became blacker and more voluminous.
Blake roared under the Halberstadt and looked back at
it. It seemed to be going into a dive.

Blake turned the Spad around and climbed into the
air. Bullets zipped around him as the German rear gunner opened fire. Blake levelled off and looked down.
The Halberstadt was steady in the air but it had evidently lost power and was gliding to earth. It would
crash within a minute or two and Blake would have
another kill to his credit if the kill could be confirmed.

Glancing down, he thought he was over French territory, but wasn't sure. He leaned out of his cockpit
and saw the Halberstadt coasting toward the ground.
Blake thought it might land safely and be damaged
instead of destroyed. He decided to make one more
pass and finish it off. Turning to maneuver underneath
the Halberstadt again, he heard a German machine gun
bullet ricochet off one of his machine guns. You son
of a bitch, he thought to himself.

He pulled back the stick, the wings and struts of the
Spad straining as Blake climbed into the sky. The sun
was sinking toward the horizon behind him and the
brown earth below glowed with the color of gold. He
looked at the stricken Halberstadt and saw black smoke
trailing from its tail. "So you want to trade bullets with
me, eh?" he muttered, pushing the stick forward and
to the side.

The nose of the Spad lowered and dived out of the
sun at the Halberstadt. It wasn't considered wise to
take a two-seater from above this way, but Blake had

the sun behind him and knew the rear gunner couldn't
see him well. Moreover, the Halberstadt was in trouble
and its crew was under a deadly strain. The German
gunner fired valiantly at Blake, who smiled as he fixed
his angle of descent and pressed his trigger button.
The twin Vickers chattered loudly and he smelled
gunpowder as the bullets streamed down at the Halberstadt. The German rear gunner fired back but his aim
was wide. Blake's bullets stitched up the fuselage of
the Halberstadt, and he saw the German rear gunner
fall away from his weapon and clutch at his chest.
Blake's bullets tore up the Halberstadt and the German pilot turned around fearfully to see what was
behind him. Blake was close enough to see the German's face transformed into a mask of blood, to hear
the Halberstadt's engine whine as it went into a tail-
spin. Blake followed it down, still firing. He didn't
want any confusion over whether it was a damaged
plane or a kill.

The Halberstadt disintegrated in midair as Blake
continued firing his machine guns. Bits of the wings
and fuselage flew away, and the Halberstadt turned
belly up, then rolled over again and continued rolling,
its broken struts screaming in the wind. Blake pulled
his stick back and began to climb as the Halberstadt
continued its last dive and crashed into the ground.
Its gas tank exploded in a fiery red burst and the
wreckage was covered with flames.

Blake's Spad climbed into the sky and he raised his
right fist high as he screamed victoriously at the setting
sun.

An hour later he landed at the aerodrome near Chaudun, taxiing to a stop at the end of the rank of other

escadrille planes. He unbuckled his straps, then climbed out of the cockpit and dropped to the ground.

He took off his long-eared flying hat and the silk skullcap he wore underneath it, revealing thick, wavy black hair. He had large hazel eyes set into a lean and handsome face, and he was six feet two inches tall, long-limbed, with wide shoulders and muscles that were taut and hard. Carrying his map case and canteen, he started walking toward the headquarters building just as the mechanics and a pilot left the big hangar and headed toward his plane.

"How'd you do?" asked the pilot, a skinny, mustached fellow named Pierre.

Blake held up one finger. "A Halberstadt."

The mechanics crowded around him and slapped his shoulders, offering their congratulations. One of them took a flask of cognac from inside his service blouse and handed it to Blake, who unscrewed the cap and took a long swig.

Blake sucked in air through his clenched teeth against the burn of the cognac. The mechanics laughed and continued to surround him, for he was one of the squadron's aces and pictures of him appeared from time to time in newspapers. He handed the flask back to them, waved, and continued to make his way toward the headquarters of the escadrille.

The top of the sun was still visible on the horizon, and it cast long red shadows on the tarmac of the runway. Stopping, he took a cigarette from a gold case and lit it with a matching gold lighter. He stared at the elegant new gold pieces. His previous case and lighter had been promised to two fellow pilots, Franklin DeWitt and Bulldog Teeter, in the event anything happened to him during the war. But they had gone before him. He had seen them both gunned down over enemy territory—had perhaps been partly responsible for their deaths, though he would never know for sure. As he flew over the spots where the two men had gone down he had dropped the case and lighter in tribute to their friendship and to what could only be described as heroism. . . .

He shook his head and pocketed the case and lighter, closing out the uneasiness the memories brought. Inhaling deeply on his cigarette, he opened the door to headquarters and went inside.

Major Dubois looked up from his desk as Blake entered. "I know what you're going to ask me, so I might as well tell you the answer. It's been confirmed."

Blake smiled, for now the Halberstadt was officially his. "Who reported it?"

"Our artillery observers in that sector. They said it was quite a little fight."

"It was."

"Any damage to your plane?"

"A few holes."

"The report said you continued to fire at the German aircraft as it was going down."

"I wanted to make sure. I've had too many of them get away."

Dubois shrugged. "They said you fired from above. You should know by now that you never attack a two-seater from above."

"I attacked from beneath. It wasn't until he was going down that I fired at him from above. I came out of the sun and he didn't have much fight left in him by then anyway."

"The report said he was firing at you as he went down."

"He was."

"A few lucky shots might have got you."

"He was finished. He didn't have a prayer."

Dubois smiled thinly. "Some day you're going to push your luck too far."

"I know what I'm doing, Major."

"I hope so, Sergeant."

Blake noticed a newspaper lying on a file cabinet. Angling toward it, he read the headline: AMERICAN SOLDIERS ARRIVE IN PARIS.

He picked the newspaper up and saw a photograph of American soldiers marching down the Champs-Elysées. Another photograph showed General Pershing speaking at a podium.

"Looks as though your countrymen are finally arriving in force," Dubois said.

"Looks that way," Blake replied, scanning the rest of the newspaper article.

3

GENERAL PERSHING sat in his office at the new American Expeditionary Force Headquarters in Paris. On the other side of the desk sat Lieutenant Everett DeWitt, with a stack of papers in his lap. Everett was neat as a pin in his tailor-made uniform, Sam Browne belt and polished boots.

"My impression," Everett was saying, "is that the Allied armies are tired and demoralized, especially the French. The huge losses sustained in their spring offensive have evidently taken the fight right out of them. Therefore, if the Germans ever mount a major full-front attack, we cannot expect our allies to hold. In view of that possibility, I think we ought to have an independent communications system that we can safeguard ourselves. We can't be certain that our allies will be able to defend their own communications, never mind ours."

Pershing nodded and wrote on his pad. "Good point. Anything else?"

"One last thing, sir. If we have our own communications system, we'll need personnel to operate it. I recommend that instead of spending time to train soldiers to be telephone operators, we bring in some experienced telephone operators from the States."

Pershing raised his eyebrows. "You mean women?"

"Yes, sir," Everett replied, "and before you say no, let me point out that women perform a lot of important tasks in the British army, from chauffeuring their officers around to performing important administrative functions."

."I wasn't going to say no," Pershing replied. "If the British use women in that fashion, so can we. I'd just like to think about it a bit. Do you have anything else?"

"Not at the moment, sir."

"I'm still waiting for the report on machine gun availability."

"I'll have it for you by noon tomorrow, sir."

"Very good, Lieutenant DeWitt. You may return to your office."

"Yes, sir."

Everett rose, tucked his papers under his left arm, and saluted smartly before he did an about-face and marched out of General Pershing's office.

He walked down a corridor in the huge mansion at 73 Rue de Varenne, which had been loaned to the AEF by a wealthy American politician named Ogden Mills. There was a beautiful garden in back of the mansion, and DeWitt glanced at the roses and peonies as he passed a window.

The corridors were crowded with officers of all ranks, and Everett was still somewhat surprised to be among them, with direct access to General Pershing. But the American army was expanding quickly, and talented men were being brought into the general staff as rapidly as they could be found. If Everett were older they might have made him a captain or a major right off the bat.

Everett occupied a small office midway down a corridor in the basement of the mansion. Several other officers occupied similar offices in the corridor, and opposite them was a large open area where clerks typed and filed correspondence.

As Everett neared his door, Private Madden rose from behind his desk in the clerical area, waving his arm and dashing toward him. Everett stopped to see what he wanted.

Madden held his forefinger over his lips. "There's someone in your office, sir," he whispered. "He said he's a friend of yours. He told me his name and I wrote it down, but I lost the piece of paper."

Everett sighed in exasperation. His regular army clerks were always losing things and sending correspondence to the wrong places. It was a miracle that the army functioned at all.

"What was his rank?" Everett asked.

"He's a sergeant because I saw three stripes on his sleeve, but I don't know what kind of uniform he was wearing. I don't think it's a French uniform, and I don't think it's British. Maybe he's from Belgium?"

"I suppose I'll find out for myself in a few moments,"

Everett said sardonically. "Thanks for the information."

"Yes, sir."

Everett took the final few steps to his office door, opened it up and saw a man in his mid-twenties sitting in front of his desk. The visitor was wearing the uniform of the French Foreign Legion, and when he stood, Everett could see the silver wings awarded to French pilots pinned to his breastpocket.

The pilot smiled, showing straight white teeth, and held out his hand. "Hi," he said, "I'm Blake Hunter. I was a friend of your brother's."

Everett shook his hand and recalled who he was. The Hunters were an old American family just like the DeWitts, and Blake was one of the aces with the Lafayette Escadrille, as Everett's brother Franklin had been. Franklin had been killed in action in April of that year.

"How do you do," Everett said. "Have a seat."

Everett walked behind his desk and sat, while Blake returned to the chair where he'd been sitting.

Blake smiled genially. "I hope you don't mind my barging in here like this."

"Not at all," Everett replied. "What can I do for you?"

"I read your name in a newspaper article about Pershing's arrival in Paris and thought I'd come to see you about a little problem I'm having. I've decided that since America is in the war now, I'd like to enlist in one of the American air squadrons. Do you think you can help me?"

"I can introduce you to someone in the air service," Everett replied. "I imagine they'd love to have an experienced pilot like you. We don't have much of an air arm yet."

"Air superiority will be the key to victory in this war," Blake said, reaching for his gold cigarette case. "Do you mind if I smoke?"

"Not at all. I think I'll have one, too."

Both men took out cigarettes and lit them up. DeWitt looked at Blake and thought him a very impressive-looking man. He wanted to ask Blake about Franklin, but decided that might be too painful for both of them. Everett recalled his one meeting with Brooke Madigan DeWitt, who had met Franklin in France and been widowed so shortly after her marriage. Their grief over Franklin's death had been so raw that neither had been able to get past the pleasantries. Everett had consciously avoided seeing her again, although he hated himself for his weakness.

"There's one other thing that I'd like you to help me with," Blake said. "I think that my older brother is over here, and I'd like to find out where he is. I haven't heard from him for awhile, but I figure he's either on his way here or is here now."

"Do you know what branch of the service he's in?"

"Infantry," said Blake. "He came to France with me in 1914 and became an ambulance driver. Then he tried to get into the escadrille, but he washed out of pilot school and joined the French Ambulance Corps again until President Wilson declared war. The last I heard he had returned to the States and got a commission in the army." Blake smiled indulgently. "I guess you could say he moves around a lot."

"What's his name?" Everett asked. He wasn't sure what to make of his late brother's friends, and was unwilling, for now, to be drawn into Blake's open friendliness.

"Duncan W. Hunter." Blake told him Duncan's serial number.

"I'll check the rosters," Everett said, rising to indicate that the meeting was over.

Blake Hunter eased his foot off the accelerator of the Renault as he neared the little village that lay ahead. He shifted down and squinted at the sign at the edge of the village. SOULAUCOURT.

This is it, he thought. He drove slowly over the cobblestoned street, seeing old men, old women and little children on the sidewalks, along with a scattering of American soldiers.

"Hey there," he said to one of the soldiers. "Where's First Battalion headquarters?"

"Y'all take a left at the next intersection, and you'll see it straight ahead. You won't be able to miss it because it's got a big regimental flag in front."

The soldier's shoulder patch had an Indian head on it, Blake noticed, just like the planes of the Lafayette Escadrille, and the background was a white star. Blake shifted into gear, rolled down the street, and turned left at the intersection.

It was a tiny village, with a population probably under five hundred. All its young men were either in the French army, in hospital, or killed in action. Its young women had been shipped out to live near the munitions factories where they worked. A big pile of manure was in every front yard, and he knew that the farmer with the most manure was considered the richest man in town. Blake saw flags flying in front of a building halfway down the street. He parked his Renault behind one of the military vehicles in front of the building and got out, placing his kepi on his head and walking toward the building. Climbing the steps, he opened the door and found himself in an orderly room.

A sergeant sat behind a desk on one side of the room, and a private was seated behind a desk on the other side. The sergeant looked up from a piece of correspondence that he'd been reading. He had sandy hair and wore the Indian-head patch on his right shoulder. A wooden sign on his desk said Sergeant Major William Larraby.

"What can I do for you?" the sergeant asked.

"I'm looking for my brother," Blake replied. "He's an officer in this battalion."

"What's his name?"

"Duncan Hunter. I don't know what his rank is, but I imagine he's a second louie."

The sergeant looked at Blake, his uniform and the wings on his breast, and his face lit with recognition. He pointed at Blake and stood up, saying, "Hey—I know who you are! You're Blake Hunter, the flier!"

Blake held out his hand. "How do you do."

"It's a real pleasure to meet you, sir."

"I'm not a sir," Blake pointed out, shaking the man's hand. "I'm only a buck sergeant."

"You're still sir to me. I've heard all about you. I'll bet Colonel Foster would love to meet you. Let me go get him."

The sergeant turned and walked through a door at the rear of the orderly room. Blake turned and looked at the private, who gawked at him shamelessly. Blake waved at him. "Hiya."

The private stood up and mumbled a greeting, still staring.

The rear door opened and the sergeant came back

with a group of officers, led by a man Blake assumed was Colonel Foster.

"Blake Hunter?" the man asked.

"Yes, sir."

The colonel held out his hand. "I'm Jack Foster—pleased to meet you."

Foster introduced Blake to the other officers, and then said, "We've heard a lot about you."

Blake didn't know what to say, so he simply smiled.

"I don't mind fighting with my two feet on the ground," Foster said, "but I'd sure as hell hate to fight way up there in the sky. It must take a lot of nerve."

"I don't know," Blake replied. "I'd say it takes more nerve to charge a German trench and fight face-to-face."

"At least when we charge we have the ground underneath us."

"But you can't fly away from a fight, like I can."

"You haven't flown away from many fights, young man, from what I've heard."

Blake smiled in reply. It was true: he hadn't run away from any fights.

"Care to have a drink with us?" Colonel Foster asked. "I know it's duty hours, but I'd say this is a special occasion. Wouldn't you agree, gentlemen?"

His officers nodded and said yes, but Blake looked at his watch.

"I'm afraid I don't have much time," he said. "I've got to get back to Chaudun by midnight, and I want to spend some time with my brother."

"Perhaps you can join us at mess tonight, with your brother."

"That sounds like a good idea. Where is he, anyway?"

"I'll have somebody take you out to him.. He's train-ing with his company in the field."

Blake chuckled. "Since he's an officer, I guess I'll have to salute him. Is he a second louie?"

"First," Foster replied. "The army is expanding rapidly and rank is being made very quickly. You ought to think about wearing an American uniform, Hunter. They're liable to make you a general."

"I'm working on it," Blake replied.

Blake walked into the fields north of the village, ac-companied by Second Lieutenant Walker, who wore the crossed cannons of the field artillery on his lapels. They came to a sign that said:

WELCOME TO VALLEY FORGE
BRING YOUR OWN POTATO

Walker smiled. "Something the men put up," he said.

In the distance, Blake could see networks of trenches facing each other across a simulated stretch of no-man's land. Massed formations of soldiers charged from one network of trenches to the other in long skirmish lines, with officers behind them shouting directions. Blake could hear the voices echoing across the fields. The skirmish lines were ragged and he wondered why the doughboys were practicing that kind of charge; four years of war had made the tactic obsolete. There'd been a mutiny in the French army during the spring because of charges like that. The soldiers refused to attack again, because the losses had been so great.

"I hope they're not going to do that when they get to the front," Blake said.

"Do what?"

"Attack like that. The German machine guns will cut them down and German artillery will rip them to shreds."

"We know, but old Black Jack believes that the only way to defeat the Germans is in open warfare."

Blake shook his head. "But it doesn't work."

"Don't underestimate the American soldier, sergeant."

Blake decided not to argue, but he thought there'd be a bloodbath if the doughboys ever charged that way. And most of them were green troops. They'd probably break and run when the carnage began.

"I think I can make it the rest of the way by myself," Blake said. "You can return to your duty if you like, unless you'd rather get away from headquarters for awhile."

"I do have a lot of work to do," Walker admitted. "I'll see you at mess?"

"Sure thing."

Walker turned and walked back to Soulaucourt, while Blake moved toward the trenches. The skirmish lines charged and then flopped down on their bellies, while other doughboys got to their feet and continued the charge over them. Each wave was learning how to cover the other as they slowly moved to the enemy trenches. Officers shouted orders and noncoms cursed at the soldiers who'd made mistakes. Blake reached the edge of the battlefield and stood with his hands in his pockets, watching the maneuvers.

As the doughboys ran back and forth, he gave thanks that he didn't have to be among them. It seemed so repetitious and boring, and he knew they did the same thing over and over again day after day—just as he had when he'd first joined the French Foreign Legion.

At night they slept in barns and attics, and when they moved to the front they'd sleep in the dirt. How nice it was, in comparison, to fight high in the clear blue sky, man-to-man, in a test of skill. If you were killed in the air, it happened fairly quickly and usually you were to blame. It wasn't like those poor fellows out there, who could be sleeping peacefully in their filthy little holes in the ground and suddenly have a German artillery shell land on top of them.

The doughboys made it across the field to the opposite trench, and a break was ordered. Blake strolled toward the trench, his hands in his pockets, when he saw a soldier climb out of a trench and walk toward him. Blake realized that the soldier was his brother. Smiling, Blake stepped over the stones and mud of the mock battlefield to meet him. They came together on the field, embraced awkwardly and looked into each other's faces. Duncan was older than Blake and had lighter hair, but he too was tall and lean. He wore his helmet low over his hazel eyes, and on the helmet was painted the Indian head insignia of the Second Division. Duncan's face had always had a more serious cast to it than Blake's, but when he smiled it was the full, open smile of a little boy, more winning than Blake's smile because Duncan was less conscious of its effect.

"Why didn't you tell me you were here?" Blake asked when they separated.

"We've only been here two weeks. I wrote you a note as soon as I arrived, but I guess you didn't get it."

"It's probably easier for you to get a letter through to the States than to somebody in the French Foreign Legion stationed in France. How are mother and father? And Allison, of course?"

"All right last time I saw them. But I haven't heard

much from Allison," Duncan replied. Their sister, the most outgoing and lively of the three Hunter children, had all but withdrawn from the family after the death of a soldier had left her as an unwed mother. It had all been hushed up, of course, with a "proper" cover story concocted to save the family reputation. Duncan sometimes felt that Blake knew more about it than he let on—after all, he and Allison had seen a lot of each other in Paris at the time she'd met the soldier—but it seemed best to leave matters as they were and allow Allison her privacy. Besides, Allison was nothing if not resilient. She'd be all right in time.

They walked off the battlefield to a patch of trees nearby and sat in the shade. Blake lit up a cigarette, not bothering to offer one to Duncan, who didn't smoke or drink.

"I'm trying to get into the American air service," Blake said.

"Sounds like a good idea. They'll probably make you an officer."

"But nothing will ever make me a gentleman," Blake said, grinning.

They laughed, for Blake had always been the bad boy and Duncan the good one. Duncan had graduated *summa cum laude* from the University of Virginia, while Blake got through by the skin of his teeth. Duncan had been the churchgoer and teetotaler, while Blake had never set foot inside a church and came home drunk at all hours of the night. Duncan's wife had been one of the few women in his life, while Blake had got at least two girls pregnant that the family knew about.

Blake flicked some ash off the end of his cigarette. "I went to see Franklin's younger brother, Everett, who works as an aide to old Black Jack. You ever meet Everett?"

"No."

"Well, he's a rather elegant type, a bit stiff, but he knows a lot of people. He sent me to see a Major Bishop in the Signal Corps, which is where the AEF aviators are right now. I think I'll be able to make the switchover without too much trouble."

"Those DeWitts usually are good at pulling strings," Duncan said.

Blake looked over his shoulder at the battlefield. "I was watching your company practice massed charges as I was walking across the fields. I hope you don't intend to do anything like that when you get to the front."

"We intend to do precisely that," Duncan replied. "You can't win victories sitting in a trench. We'll have to wage open warfare and capture ground if we want to beat the Fritzies."

Blake looked at him. "Do you know there was a mutiny in the French army last spring?"

"A *real* mutiny?"

"A real and very widespread mutiny. It happened because the French *poilus* refused to continue attacking. The losses were so staggering it was simply too much for them. I saw some of those offensives from the air, and the battlefield was literally covered with bodies for miles. If you were walking out there you couldn't put your foot down without stepping on a dead soldier. The AEF has to realize that it can't charge machine guns. Jesus, you must have seen a lot of it when you were an ambulance driver."

Duncan nodded. "I wasn't on the battlefields but I saw them come through the dressing stations. It was an endless procession of men covered with blood, and I'll never forget it. But machine gun nests can be silenced; they're not sacred, you know. And artillery can be bombarded until it can't fire. The Americans have to win this war, Blake. The French and British are on their last legs. And if we don't attack the Germans and drive them back, we'll be fighting here in these muddy fields for the next hundred years."

Duncan's voice was low with a determination that surprised Blake, but he only nodded in agreement. Duncan might be the older of the two, more intellectual and serious, but that hardly meant that he belonged in the military or understood what fighting was really all about. And so far, he thought, Duncan hadn't exactly distinguished himself. Washing out of pilot school, serving as an ambulance driver and now defending these insane charges with the doughboys. . . . Well, when the war was over, Duncan could go back to his wife and two kids, and maybe he'd find something more suited to him.

4

THE CARAVAN of vehicles stopped in front of the War Ministry, and French guards rushed forward to open the doors. General Pershing got out of the lead vehicle, along with several of his aides, and the rest of his staff emerged from the other vehicles.

Pershing towered over most of his aides, and his square shoulders, erect posture and stern features made him appear indomitable. He climbed the steps to the War Ministry, followed by his aides and the guards. They entered the building and traversed its wood-paneled corridors until they came to a large conference room.

The door was open, and they walked inside. Orderlies took their hats, and they proceeded to the large map table. Marshal Joffre, who had been standing in front of the table, stepped forward to greet them, followed by General Foch, General Mangin, and several other French officers. From the other side of the table came Field Marshal Edward Haig, commander-in-chief of the British troops in France, and General Sir Julian Byng, along with a contingent of British officers. They all shook hands, exchanged pleasantries, and then gathered around the map table and got down to business.

General Haig had a thick white mustache and the sad eyes of a bloodhound. "Tell me, General Pershing," he said, "how many troops do you have in France as of today?"

Opposite Haig, General Pershing rested his hands on the table and said, "Around seventy-five thousand, with more arriving every week. I expect to have at least half a million here by the end of the year."

"You've been following the events in Russia, I take it?"

"Yes."

"Then you know that Russia may conclude an armistice with the Central Powers any day now. When that happens, the kaiser will be able to concentrate all his troops here on the western front. Therefore it is imperative that you put your men into the line as soon as possible. When might we expect you to do that?"

Pershing was aware that the eyes of the leading soldiers in the world were on him, and most of them had shouldered far greater military responsibilities in their careers than he had in his. Yet he stood there as representative of the United States of America, and knowledge of that duty stiffened his resolve.

"I can't say for sure," he said. "My troops still have a great deal more training to do. I would guess that we wouldn't be ready until spring."

"Spring?" said Haig, aghast. "That long?"

"I'm afraid so."

Marshal Joffre cleared his throat. "But that may be too late, General Pershing."

"I'm not sending my men to the front until they're ready," Pershing said firmly. "It won't further the Allied cause to have them slaughtered. You know as well as I do that the kaiser will certainly take advantage of our first appearance on the line to strike a blow at American prestige and Allied morale. I want my soldiers to be prepared for that."

"But," said General Foch gravely, "we had expected you to help us out long before spring."

"I'm sorry," Pershing replied, "but I cannot say that my men constitute an army yet, and it would be irresponsible to send them into combat now. Only a very small percentage of them are combat veterans; the rest are basically civilians in uniform. The Germans, on the other hand, are a seasoned and highly effective fighting force. I repeat, I will not send my men to fight until they're ready."

Marshall Haig folded his arms and sat back to peer at the American. "But that might be a fatal delay for the Allies, General Pershing."

"I can't do more than I'm doing right now."

"I disagree. There is something you can do," said Haig. "You can funnel American soldiers into British and French units to serve as replacements. They can be trained as they're serving, and God knows we need them. Many of our divisions are down to half strength, and some are even lower than that. We're scraping the bottom of the barrel for manpower. The appearance of your husky boys in our ranks would give our men heart. And they could be trained, as I say, by combat veterans skilled in the tactics of this war."

Pershing looked Haig in the eye, then Joffre, and then Foch. "I want you gentlemen to understand something very important," he said. "American soldiers did not come here as replacements for your armies. They came here as part of the American army, and that's the only way they'll fight. I think it would be very bad for *their* morale to have them fight under French or British officers, just as it would be harmful to the morale of French or British soldiers to fight under American officers. My men are proud of what they are, and I will not permit them to fight under any flag but their own."

Haig gazed steadfastly at Pershing. "We're in a rather difficult situation here, General. I think our common struggle should override the concerns of individual nations."

"I do not consider this the concern of an individual nation, sir. I'm talking about maintaining the fighting effectiveness of my men, and you're talking about diminishing their fighting effectiveness. That is the long and short of it, from my point of view. My men are not here to provide replacements for your armies, and I must ask all of you to respect that point of view."

The discussion over the use of the doughboys continued throughout the afternoon, with the British and French officers raising new arguments, and General Pershing refusing to be budged. Finally, at five o'clock, the meeting was adjourned. Salutes and more subdued pleasantries were exchanged, and Pershing left with his American officers, leaving the French and British alone around the map table.

Marshal Haig sighed and put his hands in his pockets. "Well, he's certainly stubborn, isn't he?"

Joffre nodded in agreement. "Too stubborn, I'd say."

"Now I understand," Foch said, "why the American soldiers call him the Iron Commander."

"They also call him Black Jack," Haig said. "Anybody here know why, by any chance?"

Foch and Joffre looked at each other and shook their heads. In the back of the room, a young British sub-lieutenant raised his hand.

"They call him Black Jack because he used to command all-Negro cavalry regiments," he said.

The men in the room received the explanation in silence and slowly gathered up their papers to leave, none of them feeling encouraged by the American military presence.

5

THE BAND PLAYED a waltz, and the gentlemen danced their ladies across the floor. It was a ball given at the British Embassy, and all the leading diplomats in Paris were there, plus numerous military men and hordes of ladies. The ballroom was immense, with white columns surrounding the dance floor. Crystal chandeliers hung from the ceiling, providing support for a vast network of brightly colored ribbons.

Lieutenant Everett DeWitt leaned against one of the columns and watched a young lady dance with a British officer. Everett had noticed her a half-hour before, and hadn't been able to take his eyes off her since. He'd been following her at a safe distance, watching her chat with people and accept dance after dance. She appeared to be flirtatious and high-spirited, but he thought she was delightful and couldn't take his eyes off of her.

Now he was debating with himself whether to ask her for the next dance. He was sure she wouldn't refuse him—she hadn't refused anyone else all evening—but he was afraid that he might do something foolish, and more than anything else he hated to behave foolishly. He was so taken with her that he knew it would be difficult to be completely self-possessed.

Well, he thought as the dance came to an end, I might as well ask her. Faint heart never won fair lady. Placing his glass of champagne on a nearby table, he straightened his Sam Browne belt and glanced at his reflection on one of the mirrored walls. His uniform was immaculately tailored and pressed, his tie was perfectly centered and not a hair on his blond head was out of place. Taking a deep breath, he marched onto the dance floor. The girl and her officer were applauding the orchestra with everybody else. Everett stopped in front of her and bowed slightly.

"May I have this dance?" he asked, trying to keep his smile from collapsing.

She started and looked at him as though he was a ghost. Then, confused, she looked at the officer she had been dancing with. "Were we going to dance again?" she asked, her English softly accented with French.

"I hadn't really thought that far ahead," the officer said. "If you care to dance with the gentleman, there's really no reason you shouldn't."

She turned to Everett and smiled, but he thought her smile was a little forced. Perhaps she knew her lips and teeth were pretty, and had gotten used to displaying them to their best advantage. Or perhaps smiling was her way of covering her embarrassment.

"All right," she said brightly. She held her arms up.

"Perhaps we should wait until the music starts," Everett said ,suppressing a grin.

She blushed and laughed. "Yes, of course. One can't dance without music, can one?"

Everett shrugged. "I imagine one could if one wanted to."

The British officer took a step backward. "I think I'll leave you two to your dance. Have fun." He turned and walked away, leaving Everett alone with the girl.

"Well," she said, "I knew you'd ask me to dance eventually." She looked at the ceiling, then gave an airy wave of her hand as she levelled her blue eyes on his. "Lord knows, you've been following me around all night."

Everett stood erectly, with his hands clasped behind his back, one leg stiff and the other bent slightly at the knee. "I haven't been following you all night. It's only been half an hour. Exaggeration is the sign of the sloppy thinker."

"Well," she said huffily, "evidently I haven't been watching the clock as much as you have, but it has been quite a while. Even you have to admit that."

Everett nodded.

"So you finally got up the courage to ask me to dance?"

"One might say that."

"Does one know how to dance?"

"One does."

"Good, because I believe the band is about to play. They're quite good, don't you think?"

"All these bands sound pretty much the same," Everett said.

"Oh? So you go to parties quite often?"

"Yes."

"That's strange—I haven't seen you before."

"Perhaps you have seen me, but I didn't register on your mind. However, if I had seen you, I'm sure I would have remembered."

"Why?" she asked.

"You know very well why."

She pursed her lips. "I'm afraid I don't."

"Yes you do. I should think people have been telling you how pretty you are ever since you were born. Anyway, that's why I would have remembered you."

She wrinkled her forehead, and beneath it were sparkling blue eyes. "I don't know whether that was a compliment or not. Was it?"

"Yes." Everett saw the conductor bring down his baton, and the sound of violins filled the ballroom. He took the girl in his arms and swept her across the floor.

"My," she said. "Such drama."

He felt her strong young body against his, and smelled her perfume, which reminded him of roses. "What's your name?" he asked.

"Danielle Giraud."

"How do you do, Danielle," he said. "I'm Everett DeWitt, from New York City."

"Oh, I've been there," she said. "Filthy place. Terribly noisy."

"I love Paris," he replied, ignoring her impertinence. "Where do you live?"

"With my father and mother."

"Where's that?"

"On the Rue St. Fauberg."

Everett knew that the Fauberg was the most fashionable street in Paris. This girl evidently came from the highest strata of French society; perhaps that explained why she was so impudent. But impudent or not, he was completely captivated by her. "Is your father in the French diplomatic service?"

"No, in the army. General Hercule Giraud. If you're a staff officer here in Paris you've probably never heard of him. He's a front-line commander in the Twentieth Corps."

"I've heard of the Twentieth," Everett said.

"Of course you have. It's one of our most famous."

Everett knew she was not exaggerating. The Twentieth had been nicknamed the Iron Corps because it had held the Germans on the Marne.

"Your father must be an outstanding officer."

She nodded. "He is. If you ever meet him, you'll know that immediately."

He held her tightly and twirled her through an opening between other dancers. "Will I be able to call on you sometime?"

"I imagine," she replied.

"How about tomorrow? Perhaps we can have lunch?"

She shook her head. "I have a dance class tomorrow."

"Are you studying to be a dancer?"

"Not a professional dancer, but I love to dance. I think it's a beautiful art form, perhaps the most beautiful. You dance very well, by the way. You probably could be very good if you studied."

He looked at her face, and couldn't find one single flaw. "You're really quite beautiful," he said, the words coming out before he could stop them.

"I believe you told me that before," she said wryly,

"and as you pointed out already, people have been telling me that all my life. Have you always been a soldier?"

"No."

"I didn't think so."

"Why not?"

"You're not like most soldiers. You seem more like a very well-behaved civilian in uniform. I've been around real soldiers since I was a child, and I know what they're like."

Everett frowned. "I don't know whether to be insulted or not."

She squeezed his shoulder. "It wasn't intended as an insult. There just happens to be a very big difference between a man who has trained all his life to be a soldier, and a man who interrupts his real career to put on a uniform and fight for his country. What was your real career, by the way?"

"I didn't have one," Everett said. "I was in my last year at college when we declared war, and they graduated all of us early so we could enlist. I'd intended to go to law school and then work in my uncle's law firm. He's a partner in one of the major law firms on Wall Street. Do you know what Wall Street is?"

"I don't live on the moon," she replied. "Everyone knows what Wall Street is. It's the center of business life in your country, isn't it?"

"Yes."

She wrinkled her nose in thought. "I think you'll make a very good lawyer. You're very persuasive."

He laughed. "I mustn't be very persuasive if I can't even convince you to have lunch with me."

"I didn't say you could *never* have lunch with me," she retorted. "I only said you can't have lunch with me tomorrow, because I have my dance lessons. But I don't have a dance lesson on Wednesday."

6

IT WAS EVENING in the village of Soulaucourt and Duncan Hunter sat behind the desk in the small attic room where he slept and did his paperwork. In front of him sat a wiry little private who'd arrived in the company that day and had been assigned to the platoon. The private was leaning forward expectantly, waiting for Duncan to say something.

Duncan read the private's records with great interest. The private's name was Samuel William Bell. He had been a sergeant only two months ago, but he'd jumped ship in New York and gone AWOL and was finally picked up by the MPs and thrown in the stockade. He was court-martialed, busted, and then shipped to France because experienced men were needed so badly. Bell had been in the army since 1916, and was from New Bedford, Massachusetts, where he had been a waiter.

Duncan thumbed through the pages, and then looked up at Bell, who was smiling at him. "Why'd you go AWOL, Bell?" he asked.

Bell had curly black hair and his eyes twinkled amiably. He pointed at Duncan and said loudly, "I'm glad you asked me that, sir, because some people have said that I'm yeller. And although I might be a lot of bad things, I damn sure as hell ain't yeller."

Duncan nodded. "Why'd you go AWOL, Bell?"

"Well, I'm coming to that, sir. You see it was like this. They shipped us from Texas to New York City and put us right on that damn tub. We was in that damn tub, floating out in the Hudson River for ten days, and they wouldn't let us off it because they were afraid we'd tell somebody where we was going, as if everybody in New York and New Jersey didn't know where the hell we was going."

"The problem wasn't where you were going," Duncan pointed out, "but *when* you were going. If the German u-boat captains could find out when you were leaving, they'd intercept you in the middle of the ocean and put a few torpedoes in your boat. You wouldn't like that, would you?"

"No, sir, but I wouldn't tell anybody where—I mean when—I was going. Do you think I'm a blabbermouth? Well, I ain't. I might be a lot of things, but I ain't no blabbermouth."

"But you've got to understand," Duncan explained, "that the army can't take any chances, and that's why they wouldn't let you men go ashore. Somebody might've got drunk and said something he shouldn't have said."

Bell shook his head. "I don't get that drunk, sir."

"But how's the army supposed to know?"

Bell squinched up his eyes. "You mean the army doesn't trust me?" he demanded. "After all I've done for the army?"

Duncan sighed. It was impossible to reason with them. "Why'd you go AWOL, Bell?"

"That's what I'm trying to tell you, sir," Bell said, frustration in his voice.

Duncan looked at his watch. "Go ahead and tell me. I don't have all night."

Bell placed the palms of his hands on his thighs and leaned forward. "Well, it was like this, sir. I was sitting down in that smelly hold of the ship, thinking about my half-sister who lives in Brooklyn. Now I love that half-sister of mine, I really do, sir. When I was little she used to give me food to eat, because her mother was my stepmother and her mother didn't like me and I usually got less than the others. I used to tell my father but he wouldn't pay no attention because he used to love that bitch. And besides, everybody always thinks the worst of me anyway—that's why I'm in trouble all the time. Well anyway, sir, I just wanted to go see Tessie—that's her name, Tessie—so bad, and I thought if I got killed over here I'd never ever see her again, so I thought I'd just go and see her, and then come back to the ship and nobody'd be the wiser. But on my way back the MPs got me, sir, and put me in the hoosegow."

"Where you belonged," Duncan said sternly. "You're lucky you weren't shot for desertion in time of war."

"But I didn't desert, sir," Bell protested. "I just went to see my half-sister Tessie, who was so good to me when I was a kid."

"How are we supposed to know that?"

Bell blinked. "Know what?"

"That you went to see your sister? And how do we know you were going to come back?"

"Because I said I would!"

"Why should we believe you? How are we supposed to know you weren't lying?"

"Because—"

Duncan held up his hand for silence. "Shut up and listen to me. This is the army and not the Boy Scouts. You should know that by now. We have rules in the army, and if you break any more of them I'm going to court-martial you. And don't you ever come in here asking me to trust you. I don't trust anybody until they've proven themselves. According to your record, you're just another AWOL. Is that clear?"

Bell looked crestfallen. "Yes, sir," he said softly.

"Good. You may return to your squad now."

"Yes, sir."

Bell shot to his feet and saluted smartly. Duncan returned the salute and Bell marched out of the office, closing the door behind him. Duncan sighed with relief and closed the folder that contained Bell's records, wondering if he'd been effective with Bell. He often found it difficult dealing with the men. There was too much of an intellectual and class difference between him and them. He believed they could never understand him on his level, so he had to get down on their level and speak to them in their own language. The problem was that the words always sounded stilted when they came out of his mouth. I'm probably not a very good infantry officer, he thought. For that matter, I wasn't a good aviator either—that's for sure. And I quit the ambulance corps because it wasn't enough of a challenge.

He sighed, wondering what in hell he was good at. He felt as if he'd been floundering ever since getting out of college. The best he could say of his marriage to Patricia was that it had produced two beautiful children. His relationship with his wife, however, had early degenerated to one of tolerance at best, she pursuing the round of social events and he pursuing . . . something he hadn't yet found. Sometimes he envied Blake. Life seemed so easy for him, each challenge met and conquered with a self-confidence that neared bravado. Duncan, on the other hand, seemed to move from situation to situation, never quite succeeding, never quite finding what he wanted, never really coming into his own.

Outside the building, Private Sam Bell lit a cigarette. What a hard-ass that Lieutenant Hunter was, he thought. I just got here and already the son-of-a-bitch is talking about court-martials. That's no way to greet a new man.

Bell walked through the dark streets of Soulaucourt toward the outskirts of town. He passed a few soldiers and civilians, but no women—at least not any young ones. He'd thought that France would be crawling with women, but he hadn't seen anything except old bags so far. Maybe they'll let me go to Paris someday, he thought. I bet there's lots of women in Paris.

He came to the barn where his squad was billeted, and went inside. Men sat around an open fire, eating tinned beef. They looked up as Bell entered, then returned to their food and conversation. Bell rubbed the palms of his hands together and approached the fire.

"Well," he said, "anybody save any chow for me?"

Sergeant Tucker tossed him a can. "Here you go, Bell."

Bell caught it and nudged two men apart so he could sit between them. He snapped the key off the can, inserted it in the sliver of metal and peeled the top off the can. Then he took a fork out of his shirt pocket and began to eat the dry stringy meat that the men called canned willie. The faces of the men glowed in the light of the fire. Their rifles were stacked on the floor behind them.

"I don't understand," Corporal Canfield was saying, "how they could give us a goddamn gun that don't work. The son-of-a-bitchin' thing would be no good at all in a fight."

"Well," said Private Stewart, "it works sometimes."

"Yeah, but it's liable not to work just when you need it."

"What gun is that?" Bell asked, swallowing his canned willie. "The Chauchat," Canfield replied. "It's supposed to be a machine gun but it's a piece of shit as far as I'm concerned."

"Well," said Bell, "we din't have no machine guns in Mexico against old Pancho Villa. It was just rifles and cavalry sabres. General Black Jack said charge and we charged. Why, I remember the time—"

"You mean the time you deserted?" Private Murphy interrupted him.

Bell jerked his head around toward Murphy, eyeing the big burly man with a pug nose and dark hair cut close to his scalp. Somebody snickered, and Bell felt his face become warm.

"You say that?" Bell asked Murphy.

Murphy nodded. "Yeah, I said that."

"I ain't never been a deserter, and nobody's gonna call me one and get away with it."

Murphy shrugged. "I just did."

Bell looked him in the eye. "Then I guess you and me are gonna have to go back of the picket line and have this out."

"It don't make a damn to me either way."

Bell stood up and hooked his thumbs in his belt. Then Murphy rose, and to Bell he looked like a mountain. Murphy grinned and rolled his shoulders.

"I been wanting to put my fist in your big mouth ever since you got here, you little shit."

"Well, you're gonna get that chance right now, you fat slob," he said, trying not to betray his awe of Murphy's muscular bulk.

Sergeant Tucker continued eating his canned willie. "I don't know nothin' about this," he said. "I ain't heard nothin' and I ain't seen nothin'."

They put on their helmets and filed out of the barn, except for Sergeant Tucker and Corporal Canfield. The men walked into the fields, all of them accompanying Murphy. Bell was by himself, to their right, feeling fear right down to the pit of his stomach. It would be awfully difficult to beat a big guy like Murphy, and he was all alone, with no friends to offer encouragement and boost his morale.

It's always like this, he thought. Wherever he went he had trouble making friends. He didn't understand why. He always tried to be friendly. People said he talked too much, but he only said the things that came to his mind. Life would be different, he often thought, if he hadn't been so short. People always make fun of the little man. They look down on him in more ways than one.

The men walked over the crest of a little hill.

"This is as good a place as any," said Private White.

Bell took off his helmet and laid it on the ground, then peeled off his shirt and dropped it into his helmet. Murphy stood stripped to the waist, surrounded by his friends.

"Bust him up, Murph," one of them said.

"Kick his ass."

Murphy wiped his nose with the back of his hand. "I'll put the little loudmouth right in the hospital." He pushed through the crowd of his friends and placed his fists on his hips. "You ready—you damned deserter?"

"I'm ready," said Sam Bell.

Bell raised his fists and stalked toward Murphy. Bell had done some semi-professional boxing in Massachusetts before joining the cavalry, and was not altogether ignorant about what to do, but he'd never fought anybody as big as Murphy before. If Murphy hits me he'll kill me, he thought. I'll have to keep moving and jab, jab, jab.

Murphy held up his fists and stomped toward Bell, who got up on his toes and started dancing.

Private Giannini guffawed. "The little shit looks like a bantam rooster."

Bell danced from side to side in front of Murphy, feinting with his left hand, as Murphy lumbered after him, holding one fist over his chest and the other several inches forward.

"Kill him, Murph," said Private Skelton, a freckle-faced boy from Georgia.

Bell darted forward and threw his jab. It went over Murphy's guard and connected with his chin. Surprised, Murphy stepped backward, and Bell followed, jabbing twice more and landing an overhead right on Murphy's nose.

Bell danced backward to see if he'd done any damage, and to his surprise he saw blood dripping from Murphy's nose. Murphy touched the back of his hand to his nose, saw the blood, and became enraged. He charged Bell, swinging with both hands. Bell tried to block his punches, but he simply wasn't strong enough. Murphy battered through his defenses and slugged him again and again in the face. Bell tried to bob and weave and managed to dodge a lot of blows, but many of them got through. He heard the other soldiers cheering Murphy on. He tried to jab Murphy's face again, but Murphy was coming on too strong and Bell's blows flailed uselessly against Murphy's powerful arms. Bell rushed forward and tried to clinch Murphy to give himself a chance to clear his head, but Murphy pushed him off easily and landed a haymaker on Bell's right eye.

The next thing Bell knew he was lying stomach-down on the ground. He tried to get up, but couldn't get coordinated.

"Stomp him, Murph," somebody said.

Bell opened his eyes and saw Murphy's big boot a few inches from his face. Oh God, no, he thought. He saw the boot go up, and then felt a terrible crunching pain against the side of his face.

"What's going on there!" yelled a voice in the distance.

* * *

Duncan lay fully clothed on his bunk, reading von Clausewitz's *On War* by the light of a kerosene lamp. He knew that von Clausewitz was one of the guiding lights of the German army, and was curious to know what his enemy was like. Already three-quarters of the way through the book, he realized that much of the strategies and tactics were out of date, but some of the philosophy was useful even to an American infantry officer like himself. Von Clausewitz stressed bold action carefully planned in advance, and said that the most important quality of a good combat commander was the ability to remain calm and think clearly even in the face of defeat.

There was a commotion outside his door, and then a knock.

"Who is it?" he asked.

"Military police!" said the voice on the other side of the door.

"Just a minute!" Duncan slipped his feet into his shoes, walked to the door and opened it. Two military policemen were standing on either side of Private Murphy and Private Bell, the latter of whom had been in his office only two hours ago. Murphy had blood on his upper lip and Bell looked as though he had taken a terrific beating. His nose was mashed out of shape, his lip was split, and his eyes were blackened. Blood oozed from his nose, out of his mouth and from cuts on his face. He wiped the blood with the shirt he carried in his right hand.

"Sir," said one of the MPs, "we got them fighting back of the picket line."

"We wasn't fighting, sir!" Bell piped up. "We was just talking, and then I fell down."

Duncan frowned. It was such a blatant lie that he couldn't imagine how the man could bring himself to say it. He looked at the MPs. "You two can return to your rounds," he said. "I'll expect your report in the morning."

"Yes, sir," they replied, saluting and marching off.

Duncan looked at Murphy. "You go into my office," he said. Then he turned to Bell. "You wait out here until I call for you."

Duncan followed Murphy into his office. Murphy stood at attention in front of the desk, and Duncan sat heavily on the chair behind it.

"All right," Duncan said, "what happened?"

Murphy's eyes darted around frantically. "Nothing, sir."

"Don't tell me nothing," Duncan snapped. "The MPs didn't bring you here for nothing."

"We was just talking, sir . . . just walking and talking, and then we tripped over a log or something and fell down and hurt ourselves."

Duncan glowered at him. "Don't you lie to me, soldier!"

Murphy blanched and made no reply.

"How could you beat up a man so much smaller than you?" Duncan asked, contempt in his voice. "You ought to be ashamed of yourself. Get out of here and tell Bell to come in. Then return to your quarters and have Sergeant Tucker report to me immediately. Do you think you can remember all that?" he added sarcastically.

"Yes, sir."

"Get going."

Murphy saluted and walked out of the room, closing the door behind him. A few seconds later there was a knock on the door.

"Get in here, Bell!"

The door opened and Bell marched into Duncan's office as if on parade. He stopped abruptly in front of Duncan's desk and threw a sharp salute. "Private Bell reporting, sir!"

Duncan looked at his mangled, bloody features. "What went on out there, Bell?"

"Out where, sir?"

Duncan pounded his fist on his desk. "Don't act dumb with me!"

Bell jumped at the sound. "You mean where the MPs found us?"

"You know damn well that's where I mean!"

"Well, sir, you might have meant what went on while I was out there waiting in the hall."

Duncan narrowed his eyes at Bell. "You know very well I mean where the MPs found you."

"It was like I said, sir. I sort of fell down."

"You can't get hurt like that from falling down," Duncan said. "You and Private Murphy were fighting, isn't that so?"

"No, sir."

"You've been in this company less than a day, and already you're in trouble again. I ought to ship you right to the stockade."

Bell stood as still and erect as a tree. The blood was drying on his face. He'd taken a very severe beating, Duncan observed, and now he wasn't going to admit it. He wasn't going to point his finger at the man who'd beaten him up.

"Do you know where the dressing station is?" Duncan asked.

"No, sir."

"It's on the same street as battalion headquarters. Ask somebody there and they'll direct you to it. Get yourself looked at and then return to your quarters." He was going to tell Bell not to fight anymore, but knew that prohibition would be futile. They were all hot-headed, and would fight at the drop of a hat. "You're dismissed."

"May I ask a question, sir?"

"What is it?"

"Are you gonna punish me, sir?"

"I think you've been punished enough. Get going."

"Yes, sir."

Bell saluted and marched out of the office, leaving Duncan alone. Duncan stood and paced behind his chair, wondering how he could ever be a good officer when he disliked his men. They acted like a bunch of ignorant, drunken louts, only a cut or two above apes. They were always fighting, and you had to tell them something three times before they understood. In civilian life they had held the most menial jobs. They had been the faceless ones in the crowds on the city sidewalks, people he had ignored as he rode past. How could you win a war with such men? The German soldiers were surely of a higher quality, for they had centuries of culture behind them.

There was a knock on his door, and Sergeant Tucker entered the office, helmet in hand. "You wanted to see me, sir?"

"Have a seat, Sergeant."

Tucker sat opposite him at the desk. He was a Texan,

with lumpy, ruddy features, and had been in the army for fifteen years. Like most of the other veterans, he had served on the Mexican border for much of that time. Duncan didn't have a close working relationship with Tucker; he considered the sergeant as incompetent as all the others.

"I guess," Duncan began, "you know why I've called you here."

"Yes, sir."

"I want to know why you didn't stop Murphy and Bell from fighting—and *don't* tell me you didn't know they were fighting because you know everything that happens in your platoon."

Tucker smiled. "Do you mind if I have a smoke, sir?" he drawled. "I think better when I smoke."

"Go right ahead."

"Thank you, sir."

Tucker took out his dirty white bag of Bull Durham and a pack of cigarette paper. He rolled a cigarette, licked the paper with his big pink tongue, and stuck the soggy misshapen product of his handiwork into his mouth. Duncan waited impatiently while the man methodically replaced his makings in his shirt pocket, lit the cigarette and exhaled a cloud of smoke.

"I knew they were gonna fight," Tucker said at last, nodding slowly.

"Why didn't you stop them?"

Tucker narrowed his eyes against the acrid smoke of his cigarette. "What would've been the point of that, sir? If I stopped them they would've fought some other time when I wasn't around, and it might've been worse because they would've had to hold in their anger that much longer. I thought it was best to just get it over with."

Duncan leaned back in his chair. "I think you exercised very poor judgment, Sergeant. They might have hurt each other. Private Bell looks like he's hurt pretty badly as it is."

Tucker chuckled. "He ain't hurt that bad, sir. He stood up to Murphy, and now the men will respect him. I don't think there'll be any more trouble. Sometimes a man has to do a little fighting if he wants to be accepted into a new outfit. I guess you don't know that, sir, because you really ain't been in the army that long. You can't always go by the book, sir. These are a rough bunch of boys you got here. The army ain't no tea party."

"I know that," Duncan replied testily, "but I cannot condone fighting. The men are supposed to fight the Germans, not each other."

"They ain't no Germans around yet, sir, so they have to fight each other. They like to fight, sir. That's why they're soldiers. Fighting is what they're supposed to do."

Duncan felt he should say something to reassert his authority, but couldn't think of anything appropriate.

"All right, Tucker," he growled. "There'd better not be any more of this. You may return to your platoon."

Sergeant Tucker stubbed out his cigarette, stood, saluted, and left the office.

7

THANKS TO EVERETT DEWITT's letter of introduction, Blake Hunter now wore the uniform of a First Lieutenant in the American air service. He sat with his luggage outside the office of Major Carl Spaatz, commander of the flight training school at Issoudun. Blake was here to report for duty, but a loud argument was going on in the office, and Blake was getting impatient.

"What's going on in there?" Blake asked the clerk sitting behind the desk nearby.

"That's Captain Rickenbacker," the clerk said.

"What's the problem?"

"Oh, I imagine he wants a transfer again."

The door flew open and a tall, lean captain with large ears stormed out, his eyes flashing with rage. He slammed the door behind him and walked past Blake, turning left down the corridor.

Blake grinned. "He sure looks mad."

"He's always mad. I'll buzz the major."

The clerk pressed a button on his desk and spoke into the telephone. Then he returned the telephone to its cradle. "You can go in now, sir. You can leave your suitcase out here if you like."

Blake opened the door and entered the office. He saw a middle-aged officer sitting behind the desk, a frown on his face. Blake saluted him. "Lieutenant Hunter reporting for duty, sir."

"I hope you're not here to argue with me, Hunter."

"Oh no, sir."

"Good. Have a seat."

Blake sat and Spaatz opened the big brown envelope, pulling out the records. He lay them on his desk and looked them over, then suddenly snapped his eyes up and looked at Blake. "Oh, you're the Hunter who flew for the French."

"Yes, sir."

"I didn't realize that. I thought you'd just arrived from the States." He resumed his perusal of Blake's records. "A hundred and eighty-three sorties—eight confirmed kills. Well, this is quite a record you've got here, Hunter. You're just the sort of person we've been looking for to train our new pilots. Your experience will be valuable."

"I had hoped to be assigned to a pursuit squadron, sir."

"Maybe later. Right now we need you to train pilots. That fellow who was just in here wants to be in a pursuit squadron, too, but the service needs instructors right now. You can understand that, can't you, Hunter?"

Blake shrugged. "I suppose so, sir."

"Good. Well, that's all for now. Report to my office at 0800 hours in the morning and I'll have something for you to do." Spaatz stood behind his desk and held out his hand. "Welcome aboard, Hunter."

"Thank you, sir."

Blake left Spaatz's and carried his suitcase to the bachelor officers quarters, where he was assigned a private room, small but adequate. He was hungry, so he dropped his suitcases on the bed and immediately went downstairs to the officers club.

He finally located the room and walked inside. Paintings and photographs of airplanes were on the walls, and ribbons of brightly colored paper were hung underneath the ceiling. There was a bar and some tables, with flight officers sitting all around the room. Blake decided to have a good stiff drink before ordering his meal. He found a space at the bar, but the bartender was busy pouring drinks at the other end of the bar, where some officers were singing drunkenly.

"You look familiar," said a voice to his left.

Blake turned and saw the officer who'd stormed out of Major Spaatz's office. "Oh, hello there," he said with a smile.

"Where do I know you from?" the captain asked. "Are you one of my students?"

"No," Blake said. "You might have seen me outside Major Spaatz's office a little while ago. I was waiting to go in when you were coming out."

"Ah," said Rickenbacker. "So that's it. You've just arrived?"

"That's right."

"How are things in the States?"

"I wouldn't know. I haven't been there since 1914."

The captain knitted his eyebrows together. "Then where the hell were you?"

"Here in France. I was flying with the French *Aéronautique*, and just switched over."

The captain sat more erectly on his stool and looked Blake up and down. "What's your name?"

"Blake Hunter."

The captain smiled. "I've heard of you, Hunter. My name's Rickenbacker. Eddie Rickenbacker."

They shook hands.

"I hope you won't regret coming here," Rickenbacker said.

"Why would I?"

"You're going to be an instructor, aren't you?"

"Yes."

"Once you become an instructor at Issoudon, it's not easy to get out."

"I told Major Spaatz I wanted to be transferred to a pursuit squadron as soon as possible."

"I've been after him to transfer me for four months, and I'm still here."

The bartender leaned toward them. "May I help you, gentlemen?"

Blake ordered whisky for himself and for Rickenbacker.

"Why won't he transfer you?" Blake asked, reaching for his glass.

"He says he needs instructors."

Blake raised his glass and took a few gulps. "I won't mind instructing for a little while, but if he doesn't let me out of here by the end of the year, I'll get out some other way."

"You must have a friend someplace."

"I do. Maybe he can do something for you."

"I got a friend someplace, too," Rickenbacker said bitterly. "I used to be Pershing's chauffeur. He let me transfer to the air service, but now I can't get in to see him anymore. I might have to do something real crazy to get out of here."

Blake raised his glass to his lips and began to feel depressed. I hope I don't have to spend the rest of the war training other pilots to do what I want to do, he thought.

8

KAISER WILHELM II sat in his office in the Imperial
Palace in Berlin. The door opened and two el-
derly officers bedecked with medals entered. Side
by side, they walked to the desk and saluted. Wilhelm
returned their salute and asked them to be seated.

"I have important news," Wilhelm said gravely. "I
have just received word that the Bolsheviks have seized
power in Moscow."

Wilhelm paused to let the information sink in. Field
Marshal Paul Ludwig von Hindenburg, sitting in front
of Wilhelm, was resting his hands on the hilt of his
sword, as if it were a cane. He smiled faintly, for he
recognized the implications of the Kaiser's remark.
Colonel-General Erich Ludendorff, seated next to him,
showed no reaction whatever.

Wilhelm continued. "I anticipate that the Bolsheviks

will take Russia out of the war within the next few months. That means we'll be able to transfer the bulk of our troops on the eastern front to the West. Therefore, I am instructing you gentlemen to draw up plans for a major offensive in the West, to be launched as soon as possible after Russia is eliminated as an adversary in this war. We'll want to act quickly, before the Americans build up their forces in the West. The British and the French are just about finished, and the Americans hold the key to this war, as I'm sure you know. Therefore we must strike with unremitting violence, and win this war once and for all!".

"Yes, Your Excellency," said Hindenburg.

"To be sure," agreed Ludendorff. "Perhaps we can start withdrawing men from the East now. The Russians probably won't be much of a factor from now on."

Hindenburg turned to Ludendorff. "We shouldn't make any dangerous assumptions. The Russian bear may still have a lot of life in him."

"I doubt it, but perhaps you're right," Ludendorff replied. "At any rate, I'll direct the general staff to begin making plans, and I will supervise this offensive myself, of course. But with all due respect, Your Excellency, I doubt very much if the Americans will be as much of a factor as you think. From all I hear, they are just civilians in uniform. Once the bullets start flying over their heads, they'll just break and run. Why, I'm told that they're all in training in France, and that none of them have taken a position at the front yet. They still might not be on the line when we launch this offensive. I think that the Americans are the great myth of this war. Everybody thinks they're such an important factor, but I maintain my belief that they'll vanish like smoke once they get a taste of German bullets and bayonets."

"That may be so," the kaiser replied, "but at this point I don't think it would be wise to underestimate them. Americans are a rough and brawling people, and it may not take much to get them ready for war."

Hindenburg leaned forward, resting his hands on his sword. "We'll know soon enough," he said. "They won't be in training forever."

9

EVERETT DeWITT SAT with Danielle Giraud in a parterre box in the Théâtre de Châtelet, watching a performance of the Ballets Russes. On stage, dancers dressed as acrobats, horses and Chinamen cavorted about with a young American girl. Everett was flabbergasted; he'd never seen anything like it in his life. It bore no resemblance whatever to classical dance, with which he was somewhat familiar. And the music, costumes and sets were extremely bizarre. He didn't know whether he liked it or not. Opening his program, he looked to see who was responsible for the dance. Running his finger down the page, which he could barely read in the dim light, he found that the choreography was by Léonide Massine, the music by Erik Satie, and the scenery and costumes by Pablo Picasso. He hadn't heard of any of these people before, although he had seen something in the newspapers about the Ballets Russes' impressario, Serge Diaghilev.

"Stop rustling your program," Danielle whispered.

"Sorry."

Everett placed the program on his lap and continued to watch the dance. It was the last one of the evening, and then he would take Danielle home. He'd been seeing her for two months now, taking her to lunches, dinners and various entertainments. They had reached the point where she let him kiss her good night, but Everett was smitten by her and wanted very much to take her to bed. He wondered if this should be the night for him to make his main effort in that direction.

The ballet ended and the audience applauded thunderously. The curtain fell, the lights came up, and the curtain rose again, revealing the dancers standing in line to take their bows. Danielle got to her feet and clapped her hands. In the balcony, the audience was shouting, "Bravo!" Everett stood beside Danielle, smelling her apple blossom perfume, and applauding with the rest of the audience. There were three curtain calls, and bouquets of flowers rained upon the stage. Then the curtain fell for the last time and the audience began moving to the exits.

Everett and Danielle were swept along with the ocean of people to the lobby. The women were dressed to the nines, and many of the men wore military uniforms representing several countries, with France, England and the United States predominating. Civilian men wore tuxedos.

"Well," said Danielle as they moved outside with the crowd. "Did you like it?"

"I think I did," he said, "though it was rather . . . unconventional." He looked about at the throng lining the curb and jockeying for cabs. "Let's walk to the corner. It might be easier to get a cab there."

They walked sideways through the swarms of people underneath the marquee and finally broke loose from them. Danielle adjusted her mouton jacket on her shoulders and Everett tied the belt of his trenchcoat against the cold night air.

"Would you like to have a drink?" he asked.

"Where?"

"The Ritz?"

"I'm tired of the Ritz," she said. "Too much noise."

"We could go to a quiet little place—I know of several."

"I'm sure you do, but I really don't feel the need for liquid refreshment. Say, I know! Let's take a carriage through the Bois de Boulogne!"

"Marvelous idea," Everett said, thinking of cuddling with her in that most romantic setting.

He finally succeeded in hailing a cab, and told the driver to take them to the Bois du Boulogne. They rode through the city, passing famous buildings and darkened monuments. Even the Eiffel Tower was unlit, due to the fear of German bomb attacks. They reached the Bois du Boulogne and transferred from the taxicab to a horse-drawn carriage. It was open, with a chair of black leather, and they sat close to each other, their bodies touching, as the driver flicked his whip in the air. The horse clip-clopped on the winding road into the dark forest.

When the city streets were out of sight, Everett placed his arm around Danielle's shoulder and kissed her cheek. "I love you," he whispered.

"Be still and look at the trees."

"I can't."

He turned her face to him and kissed her lips. She touched her hand to his cheek, and he felt the warmth of her breath. They kissed again, and he gazed into her eyes.

"Whenever I tell you I love you, you change the subject," he whispered. "Why is that?"

"That's not the sort of question a gentleman asks."

"It most assuredly is. We're not exactly strangers anymore, you know."

"What are we, then?" she asked.

He kissed her cheek. "I'm not sure."

"Well, neither am I."

"Why can't you admit that you don't love me?"

"Why are you asking me all these questions?"

"You shouldn't answer a question with a question."

"Why not?"

"You just did it again."

She pushed him away. "I'll answer questions any way I like. If you were as smart as you think you are, you'd know that I truly am answering your questions."

He took out his cigarettes, offered her one and placed one between his lips. He lit both cigarettes and leaned back, looking at the huge old trees towering over the road.

"You're such a child sometimes," he said, annoyed.

She held her cigarette between two fingers and puffed elegantly. "You're just upset because I didn't give you the answer you want. But I did give you an answer."

"You gave me another question."

"It was my answer. You don't understand it for the same reason you don't understand the dancing of the Ballets Russes. It's too abstract for you."

"Obscure would be a better word. I don't understand why some people refuse to state their views clearly."

She looked at him haughtily. "Some views are subtle, and everyone knows that subtleties are beyond the intellectual range of many people."

If she were anyone else he would have deposited her at home immediately and never seen her again. He glanced at her, seeing the moonlight glinting on her golden hair. She looked regal and utterly magnificent. He was afraid of the power she had over him.

"Let's not argue," he said.

"You're the one who's arguing."

He kissed her cheek. "I love you," he said, his lips brushing her ear. "Can't you see that?"

"Yes," she said distractedly.

He hesitated, then said softly, "Come home with me."

"What!"

"Come home with me."

"What in heaven's name for?"

"You know very well what for."

"Don't be ridiculous!" she said, pushing him away. "The very idea!"

He looked at her morosely. "So you don't love me."

"I never said that."

"But that's how you feel."

"That's your opinion."

"What's your opinion?" he asked.

"I'm a Roman Catholic," she replied. "I may not be very religious, but I will never sleep with any man to whom I am not married. You probably don't realize it—you are, after all, an American—but your squalid proposition is an insult."

He looked at her, amazed. "Are you serious?"

She turned her head and looked him directly in the eye. "In the world I live in, when a man is in love with a woman he tells her by asking her to marry him. And *not* by asking her to come to his ridiculous little room."

"It's not that ridiculous," he said, trying to keep his tone light, to conceal his hurt.

"No? Then you're not what I thought you were. You have become just another soldier trying to have sex with a girl, and willing to say anything to get it."

He frowned. "You know that's not true, Danielle."

"How do I know that's not true?" She handed him her cigarette butt. "Put this out for me, please."

He stubbed it against the sole of his boot and tossed it over his shoulder. "I hadn't thought of marriage," he stammered. "Life is so uncertain these days. I only knew that I loved you and wanted to be with you."

"I quite understand," she replied. "It's not unusual for people to be selfish. You thought you'd have some fun with me and then go on to the next girl."

"It wasn't like that at all, and you know it."

"I know no such thing."

He smiled and stroked her cheek. "What must I do to change your mind? Ask you to marry me right now?"

Her eyes flashed with anger. "You don't have to do anything you don't want to do, Lieutenant DeWitt. No—I take that back. I would like you to take me home immediately!"

"But Danielle—"

"I said immediately."

Everett hesitated, then leaned forward, telling the driver to take them back to the Avenue Victor Hugo where they could get a cab.

"So soon?" asked the driver.

"Yes."

The driver turned around in the middle of the street and headed back. Everett looked sideways at Danielle, at her magnificent profile. She was sitting stiff as a statue and staring straight ahead. He wondered what to do. Had she been waiting for him to propose to her all along? He realized now that he should not have asked her to come to his room. She was a beautiful young woman from a good family, and his question had evidently been a breach of manners. You couldn't even do things like that with American girls from good families, but the atmosphere of Paris and the behavior of his fellow officers were having a bad influence on him and warping his judgment.

"I'm sorry," he said. "I can see that I've made a terrible blunder."

She didn't reply.

He offered her another cigarette, but she ignored him. He lit one for himself and inhaled deeply, then blew the smoke at the trees. "I guess I'm just not sure about whether or not I want to get married."

"Don't worry about it," she said coldly. "I'm sure there are many women in Paris who'll go to your room with you, or who'll take you to theirs. You may have to pay them a few francs, but I don't think you'll mind that."

"That's a cruel thing to say."

"It's nothing compared to what you have said to me."

He sighed. "Regardless of what you think, I really do love you, Danielle."

"Who needs your kind of love?" she replied.

"I don't think you're being fair. You've put the worst

possible interpretation on my intentions, but I apologize anyway. I'm afraid I can't do more than that."

"You don't have to do more than that," she said. "In fact, you don't have to do anything at all, Everett, because we're not going to see each other anymore."

10

IN NOVEMBER, the Twenty-third Regiment of the Second Division was moved up to a quiet section of the
line in the Lorraine area to get some experience of
actual conditions at the front. The French Fifty-eighth
Regiment, whom they relieved, were resentful of the
Americans' arrival; the sector was considered by the
French to be a rest area, and to leave it meant going to
a more active area. Grumbling and fearful, they left
their elaborate network of trenches, and the doughboys piled in.

It was a cold, cloudy day, and Lieutenant Duncan
Hunter stood on the edge of a trench, watching his
men running back and forth inside it, inspecting the
fortifications and poking their heads inside the dugouts
and pillboxes. They were in high spirits and eager to
start fighting the Germans. They positioned their

Springfield rifles on the parapets and aimed at the German lines, which were around five hundred yards away across no-man's-land.

"I think I can see the hun bastards!" said Private Gianinni.

"Where?" asked Private Hughes.

Gianinni pointed. "Over there."

"Well, if you can see them, they can see you. We'd better keep our heads down."

Duncan jumped into the trench and walked through it, his helmet slanted over his eyes and his forty-five dangling in its holster from his waist. He wore boots, leggings and his Sam Browne belt. His jacket had become loose on him because he'd lost weight during the past few months, but his lean body had lost none of its strength.

The trench was wickered and sandbagged, constructed with turns every several yards to limit the damage a direct hit from an artillery shell would make. It smelled of earth and urine, and was muddy at the bottom. It was the forward trench, and behind it were secondary and reserve trenches, so that the doughboys could fall back to shelter in the event of a strong German attack.

A group of men in front of him began to jump and shout.

"It's a rat!" yelled Private Skelton.

"Kill the son-of-a-bitch!" shouted Private White.

Private Stewart swung his rifle at the ground, and Duncan saw a furry gray rat scramble up the side of the trench and run into no-man's-land.

"That's it!" said Skelton. "Go bite the goddamn huns!"

Duncan approached the group of men. "Stewart!" he said.

Stewart came to attention. "Yes, sir?"

Duncan walked up to him. "Do you think your rifle is a baseball bat, Stewart?"

"No, sir."

"Then why are you using it as a baseball bat?"

"I don't know, sir."

"What if you'd broken the stock?" Duncan asked. "What would you use to fight with then?"

"The stock's made of awful strong wood, sir. It'd take more than that to break it."

Duncan could see the man was nervous, just as all of them were whenever he criticized them. Stewart had a pimply face and a nose like a carrot. He couldn't be much more than eighteen years old. Duncan leaned closer toward him and made his voice hard.

"I don't ever want to see you using your weapon for anything other than what it was intended. Is that clear, Stewart?"

"Yes, sir."

"Carry on."

"Yes, sir."

Duncan walked past him and the others, who stood silently and looked at him with a respect born of fear. He knew they didn't like him, but he didn't care. He spotted Sergeant Tucker.

"May I have a few words with you, Sergeant?"

"Yes, sir." Tucker sighed, knowing what was coming.

They walked several paces away from the other men. Duncan eyed Tucker, who looked back unflinchingly. Duncan knew that Tucker was the only man in the platoon who wasn't afraid of him, and he often wondered whether that was good or bad.

"Did you see what Private Stewart was just doing with his rifle, Sergeant?"

"Yes, sir."

"Why didn't you stop him?"

"You stopped him before I had a chance to, sir."

"It seems to me that the men should know better than that by now. We're at the front and we should all behave in a soldierly manner."

"Well," Tucker said with a smile, "they're a playful bunch, sir."

"They're going to have to grow up, Sergeant. We can't tolerate any foolishness here at the front. I expect you to make sure there are no repetitions of that sorry spectacle. Is that clear?"

"I'll do my best, sir."

"Come with me. I want to show you where you'll deploy the machine guns."

"Yes, sir."

A shot rang out. Duncan and Sergeant Tucker spun around.

"I got him!" shouted the unmistakable voice of Private Sam Bell.

"That fool," Duncan muttered.

Duncan and Tucker charged through the trench toward Bell's voice. Other men followed them. They turned a corner and saw Bell surrounded by three other soldiers. Bell held his rifle in the air and danced around in the trench.

"I got him—I got him!" he yelled.

Duncan charged toward him. "What the hell do you think you're doing, Bell!"

Bell snapped to attention. "Me, sir?"

"Did you just fire your weapon?"

"Yes, sir!" Bell replied proudly, puffing out his chest. "And I hit the son-of-a-bitch, too."

Duncan planted his fists on his hips and leaned toward Bell. "Who told you to fire your rifle?"

"Nobody, sir."

"Then why in the hell did you fire it?"

"Because I saw a German, sir, and I shot the son-of-a-bitch."

Duncan's face turned red with rage. "You don't fire any goddamn thing unless you get permission. Do you hear me?"

"Yes, sir!" Bell replied, glancing uncertainly at Tucker.

"You probably didn't hit a damn thing anyway!" Duncan growled.

"But I saw him fall, sir!"

Corporal Canfield, standing nearby, shuffled his feet. "I saw him go down too, sir."

Duncan blinked, feeling the tide turning against him. "You saw who go down?"

"The German, sir. I spotted him too and was looking at him when Private Bell fired. The German's whole head and part of his shoulders were showing. As soon as Private Bell fired, the German dropped out of sight."

There were footsteps and a commotion on the other side of the trench. Captain Harrington, the company commander, appeared with his executive officer, Lieutenant Dufford.

"What the hell's going on here?" demanded Harrington, a craggy-faced officer who'd risen from the ranks.

Duncan snapped to attention. "This man fired his rifle without permission, sir," he said, indicating Private Bell.

"I killed the son-of-a-bitch," Bell said weakly.

Harrington raised his bushy eyebrows. "You killed what son-of-a-bitch?"

"The German son-of-a-bitch, sir." Bell pointed toward the German lines. "I saw him over there and I shot him."

"How do you know you shot him?"

"I saw him go down."

Corporal Canfield cleared his throat. "I saw him go down too, sir."

"He might've ducked," Captain Harrington said, "but good work anyway." He patted Bell on the shoulder. "Shows you were keeping your eyes open. All men on duty should keep their eyes open at all times. This may be a quiet sector, but it might get hot—you never know."

Duncan felt all his men looking at him. "But sir," he said, "I thought the men weren't to fire their weapons unless ordered to do so."

"That's right, Lieutenant Hunter, but the situation is a little different now that we're at the front. I didn't think the men would have anything to shoot at in this particular sector, but evidently targets can present themselves, and the men should take advantage of them." He turned to the men standing nearby. "But I don't want anybody shooting just for the hell of it, understand?"

They all nodded.

"Carry on. Lieutenant Hunter—I'd like to speak with you alone for a moment."

"Yes, sir."

Duncan followed Captain Harrington and Lieutenant Dufford back to the other side of the trench, where Harrington stopped and examined Duncan's face.

"I take it that you chewed that man out?"

"I did, sir."

"I don't think you should have, but I suppose it was my fault, since my orders weren't explicit. Still, you shouldn't discourage your men from being aggressive, and you shouldn't make a mountain out of a molehill."

"Sir," said Duncan, "I thought your orders were very explicit. You said that the men weren't supposed to fire their weapons unless ordered to do so. What could be clearer than that?"

Harrington scowled. "You're not very flexible, Lieutenant. I don't know how you can learn to be flexible, but you've got to learn somehow. I hope you'll try."

"I'll do my best, sir," Duncan replied, "but I've always felt that in order to make my platoon an efficient combat unit, it should function as smoothly and unequivocally as a machine."

"Men aren't machines, Lieutenant Hunter," Harrington said gravely. "And that includes you and me. That is all. Carry on."

"Yes, sir."

Captain Harrington turned and walked away, followed by Lieutenant Dufford. Duncan watched them go, taking off his helmet and wiping his forehead with the back of his sleeve. I'm getting off to a bad start at the front, he thought. The men think I made a fool of myself and I probably did. Somehow I'll have to try to turn this situation around.

"Sergeant Tucker!" he shouted.

"Yes, sir!"

"Let's go check those machine guns!"

On the other side of no-man's-land, the German soldiers huddled over the body of their comrade.

"Right between the eyes," said Corporal Schneid-huber, shaking his head.

"I told him to keep his head down, but he wouldn't listen," said Private Bosch. "He always wanted to see what was going on."

"Let that be a lesson to all of you rookies," said Schneidhuber. "Keep your damned heads down."

They heard the rapid approach of footsteps and looked up. A private with a thin black mustache and burning eyes was moving swiftly through the trench. He carried a leather dispatch pouch and wore a soft pancake-styled cap.

The private slowed down and looked at the fallen soldier. "What happened to him?" he asked.

"Couldn't keep his head down," replied Schneid-huber. "He got it right between the eyes."

The private frowned. "Then he got what he deserved." He quickened his pace and passed them by, continuing through the trench and turning right at the corner.

"Cold-blooded one, isn't he?" asked Private Hau-shofer, kneeling over the body.

Schneidhuber nodded. "He's been around for a long time. He's one of the original regimental runners." He stood up and stretched. "Bosch, get a medical orderly."

"Yes, Corporal Schneidhuber."

In the trench perpendicular to the one in which the dead soldier lay, the private with the dispatches dodged around other soldiers as he made his way to the headquarters of the Third Company. He'd enlisted in the army on the day Germany declared war, and had participated in many of the biggest battles, so dead soldiers no longer affected him. He had been awarded the Iron Cross Second Class for his bravery under fire.

He reached the dugout that served as the Third *Sturm* Company's headquarters, and went inside. A corporal was sitting behind a makeshift desk.

"I have an important dispatch for the captain," the private said.

"Go right in."

The private walked around the desk and pushed aside the curtain to the captain's office. Walking inside, he marched to the captain's desk and saluted.

"Private Adolf Hitler, reporting with a dispatch from Colonel Englehardt, sir."

Captain Karl Ritter von Beck held out his hand. "Give it here. Were you ordered to wait for a reply?"

"No, sir." Private Hitler took the envelope from his dispatch case and handed it to Captain Beck.

"Wait anyway. I may have something to send back. You may stand at ease."

"Thank you, sir."

Hitler placed his arms behind his back and relaxed as Captain Beck read the message. It stated that a German spy had reported seeing an American military unit move into the line opposite the *List* Regiment, of which the Third *Sturm* Company was a part. The Third *Sturm* Company was to attack the Americans opposite them that night to find out what kind of soldiers they were, and take as many prisoners as possible. Captain Beck was to report to regimental headquarters at 1300 hours to receive his orders. He was to make certain his men would be especially quiet, so as not to alert the Americans that the attack was imminent. Beck took a piece of paper and wrote that he would be at regimental headquarters at the appointed time, along with his adjutant.

"Take this back with you," he said, handing the note to Hitler.

"Yes, sir. Anything else, sir?"

"That will be all."

"Yes, sir." Hitler saluted, turned, and walked quickly out of the orderly room.

By ten o'clock in the morning, Lieutenant Duncan Hunter had his platoon deployed with textbook precision. His two machine guns were in bunkers and had overlapping fields of fire. His two trench mortars were set up in the secondary trench and had all available targets zeroed in. Half the platoon was manning the trenches, and the rest was improving fortifications or performing other types of work on the position. The men from the Signal Corps had put in wires and telephones. An order had come down from battalion headquarters directing all companies to reinforce their positions with additional barbed wire, and Duncan planned to lead his men out to perform that task at night. All in all, things were going pretty well. He hoped it would stay quiet until he and his men learned the ropes.

He had selected a centrally located bunker for his platoon command post, and it had wooden cots built into its walls by the French. Now, seated at his desk, he heard the clink of shovel against earth nearby. He'd inspected everything in his platoon area several times already, and there was no point in going out again. Opening his knapsack, he took out some paper and an envelope to write his mother a letter. He wanted to tell her he was all right because he knew that she worried, but he wouldn't mention that he'd moved to the front. There was always the danger that the Germans might capture the letter and use it to help determine troop dispositions behind the Allied lines.

Outside, proud as a peacock, Private Bell was walking to the latrine while singing:

> Won't you pick up your dress
>   for a soldier,
> For a poor old soldier boooyyy . . .

Bell felt marvelous. He was the first man in the company, and maybe in the whole regiment, to kill a German, and that had made him the center of attraction, which he loved to be. Soldiers waved to him and said hello. They were already calling him Eagle Eye. He'd been accepted into the platoon rather well ever since his fight with Murphy, but now he was the most popular man. He'd even gained additional status because Lieutenant Hunter had been made to look foolish because of him. The lieutenant wasn't very popular in the platoon.

He walked into the latrine, which was a smelly cavern with a roof of dirt and stones. There was a big hole with a pole stretched over it, and you pulled down your pants and sat on the pole with your rear end hanging over it.

> Won't you pick up your dress
>   for a soldier,
> For a poor old soldier boy.

Along the far wall were urinals consisting of funnels with the kaiser's face painted on them. Bell took out a cigarette and lit up while emptying his bowels. The room stank horribly but Bell had been using outside latrines for so long he was used to them.

When finished, he buttoned up his pants and left the latrine. Looking around, he felt great to be alive, even though it was a cold, gloomy day. He loved the rough and ready life of soldiering and the camaraderie of the front lines. He also liked the country he was in, the rolling hills and fields with their patches of forests and small villages with red-tiled roofs. The scuttlebutt said there was a whorehouse in one of the towns nearby, and Bell was trying to figure a way to get there with a few of the guys.

He jumped back into the main trench and made his way back to his position, passing soldiers lined up, smoking cigarettes and joking around. They were all in high spirits and happy to be up on the line at last.

Bell reached his position in the second platoon, between Private Bailey and Private White.

"Everything come out all right?" asked White, a cigarette dangling from the corner of his mouth.

Bell laughed. "See any Fritzies?"

"Nope. They've been real quiet over there."

"Figgers," Bell said. "This is supposed to be a rest area—for us *and* them."

Private Bailey spat into the mud. "Maybe they'll let us do one of them attacks that we've been practicing so much."

Bell shook his head. "Not yet they won't. They don't think we're ready."

"We're ready."

"I know we're ready, but they don't think so. Shit, when we go after them Fritzies, they won't know what hit 'em."

White held up his rifle. "I'm gonna stick this right up the kaiser's ass."

"He'd probably like it," Bell said. "I heard he's a fairy."

"Here comes the padre."

Bell saw Father Donahue turn the corner and walk into the trench. He was a roly-poly man with a red nose and was always smiling.

"How're we doing, boys?" he asked with a wave of his hand. He was dressed like any other officer, except he had crosses on his lapels and wore no pistol.

"Just fine, Father," White replied.

Father Donahue looked at the sky. "Looks like rain."

"Sure does."

"Keep dry, boys."

"Hey, Father," said White. "You hear the news?"

Father Donahue stopped. "What news?"

"Bell here killed a German."

Father Donahue's mouth opened, and he appeared confused for a few seconds. Then he held out his hand to Bell. "Congratulations, soldier."

"Thank you, sir."

"Keep up the good work, boys." Father Donahue waved at them and proceeded to the next trench.

Bell shook his head. "That guy always gets me."

White chuckled. "I knew it'd shake his tree when I told him you shot a German. He didn't know whether to shit or go blind for awhile there."

"Sometimes I feel sorry for him," Bailey said. "He don't belong here."

The men had canned beans for lunch and then began their first afternoon at the front. At three o'clock it began to rain, and the men congregated in the bunkers, where they smoked cigarettes, played cards and swapped stories, then had another dinner of canned willie. As dusk was falling, trucks arrived with the barbed wire that was supposed to be laid in no-man's-land that night. The men unloaded the stiff coils of wire and stacked them behind the trenches. Many fingers were cut and uniforms torn. When the work was finished the men returned to their dugouts. At eight o'clock guards were posted and the men not on duty were permitted to go to sleep.

Sam Bell was one of the guards, and he stood alone in a section of the trench, shivering miserably as rain dropped on his helmet. His rifle with bayonet attached leaned against the wall of the trench within grabbing distance. His teeth chattered and he moved his soaked feet around in the mud in an effort to keep them warm. Occasionally he raised his head and peered into no-man's-land. He couldn't see farther than ten yards in front of him, and it reminded him of the nights of guard duty in Mexico, where he'd had to worry about some *bandito* suddenly appearing out of the darkness and sticking a shiv in his gut.

If he hadn't pulled so much guard duty already in his military career, he would have been frightened. He figured that was why he'd been put on guard this first night: he was experienced. But despite his experience, he was never able to rid himself of the uncertainties of the night. Sometimes his eyes played tricks on him and he thought he saw German spiked helmets out there, although the Germans hadn't worn spiked helmets since 1915. He thought he heard footsteps and quickly brought his rifle to his shoulder, but no one appeared.

His helmet was heavy on his head and pressed against his brain. He didn't dare move his head quickly; the helmet would spin right off. Sometimes his neck muscles ached from wearing the damn thing. And it magnified the ping of raindrops falling onto it.

He ducked in the trench, took off the helmet and ran his fingers through his curly hair. He wondered if the helmet would really stop a bullet. He doubted it very much, but put it back on his head nonetheless. What would girls back in New Bedford think it they could see him at the front? They'd probably admire him, he thought, as they never had when he was a waiter in that old hash house down on the docks. Hell, they'd probably even let him into their beds. Looking over the top of the trench again, he parted his lips and sang softly:

> Won't you pick up your dress
> for a soldier,
> For a poor old soldier boy . . .

Lieutenant Hunter heard a sound and sat upright in bed. There were footsteps outside his bunker, but they were probably just the changing of the guard. He glanced at his watch to make sure, and it was midnight exactly. The guards changed every two hours, so that was who he heard. Nothing to worry about. Go back to sleep.

He lay back on the hard wood, resting his head on his pack and listening to the rain patter on the roof. In two and a half hours he'd have to get up and prepare to lead the men out into no-man's-land with the barbed wire. He was a little nervous about it; it would be the first time in his life that he had been exposed to danger.

He was apprehensive, not just for himself but also for his men. If an ordinary soldier became scared, that

was his own business. But if an officer was scared, it
undermined the efforts of all the men under him.
After Duncan had washed out of flight school, he'd
thought about becoming an ordinary foot soldier, but
his parents would never have stood for that, and his
friends would have considered him a freak, so he had
become an officer and felt like even more of a freak.
I might have made a decent soldier, he thought, but
I'm not such a good officer.

Nervous, he swung around and planted his feet on
the floor. He wished there was something he could do.
Now he understood why most of the men smoked.
Maybe he should start smoking. A drink might not be
so bad, either.

I've got to calm down, he told himself. The men
are relying on me. I can't let them down. He looked
at his watch and wondered what he would do with
himself until it was time to get to work.

Five hundred yards away in the German trenches,
the soldiers of *Sturm* Company Three were preparing
for their foray into the American trenches. They sat
in their bunkers and dugouts, which were nearly
identical to those in which the Americans were sleeping, and sharpened their trench knives with pocket
whetstones. Some blew sand from the wires that activated their potato-masher grenades. The officers oiled
their Lugers and the armorer passed out ammunition.
It would be a quick attack in which they would surprise the Americans, kill as many as possible, capture
a dozen for questioning, destroy everything in sight,
and then speed back to their trenches.

Outside in the open trenches, the mortar squads
huddled around their weapons, which looked like nar-

row stovepipes on legs. Beside them were stacked boxes of mortar rounds which they would pour into the American position when the signal was given. Farther back were the howitzers and artillery pieces, which would also help launch the attack. The soldiers waiting in the trenches were so anxious to inflict a defeat upon the Americans that the minutes seemed to crawl by.

In his bunker, Captain Beck strapped on his Luger. His eyes glittered underneath the brim of his helmet and he smiled faintly, for he was confident of the outcome of the raid into the American position.

Lieutenant Strauss, his adjutant, stood in the corner. "I wish I could go with you."

"Don't be a fool," Beck replied.

Beck left the office and entered the room occupied by his orderly, Corporal Weber, who sat behind a desk. Private Hitler, the regimental orderly, sat on a chair nearby, his soft cap in his lap. He was to report the results of the raid to regimental headquarters. The light of a kerosene lamp shone on his gaunt features, and he gazed at Captain Beck with undisguised admiration.

Beck nodded to him and went outside to the trench. It was deserted except for a lone guard, who stood on a boulder and stared out through glassy eyes at no-man's-land. Beck passed him. The rain was moderately heavy now, but Beck wore no trenchcoat because it would slow him down. Speed was of the essence on an operation like this.

He entered the dugout on the other side of the trench and saw a group of men huddled around a kerosene lamp, their hair matted and dirty and faces unshaven, preparing their equipment for the raid.

"Sergeant Feldheimer?" asked Beck.

The lanky sergeant stood up. "Yes, sir?"

"Have the men fall out into the trench."

Beck turned and walked back to the middle of the trench, followed by the men who'd been in the dugout. They lined up against the parapets, carrying their rifles and bayonets, and some lugged Bangalore torpedoes. Beck could feel their tension and anxiety. Or maybe it was his own; he wasn't sure. No matter how easy the raid, a few men were always lost. Would he, after numerous major and minor battles spanning nearly four years, meet his own end tonight in the muddy fields of France?

The trench filled with men, and from nearby trenches he could hear the stomp of boots and clatter of equipment. He looked at his watch. It was nearly one o'clock in the morning.

"Just a few more minutes, boys," he said.

His men looked at one another. Most were battle-seasoned veterans like himself, and had fought on the Marne, at Ypres and on the Somme. They were confident that they were members of the finest army in the world. Tonight they would have the honor of bloodying the Americans for the first time.

Private Hitler came out of the bunker and looked at them, his heart swelling with pride in his fatherland. They were such fine men, so noble and magnificent. He wished he could go with them, but he'd volunteered for battle duty many times and had been told he was too valuable as a runner.

Suddenly the air was rent with the booming sound of artillery explosions. The bombardment was beginning, and they could hear the shells whistling over their heads on their way to the American lines. This was the prelude to the raid. Hitler ran to the parapet and peered over it.

He saw the shells rain down in orange and red explosions on the American positions.

Duncan Hunter was lacing on his boots when the first shell landed a few hundred yards away. Surprised, he raised his head. Then a shell landed near his bunker, the explosion nearly bursting his eardrums. The wall and ceiling caved in and he fell to the floor, the air filled with smoke and dirt. He blacked out for a few seconds, and when consciousness returned he lay in a tiny space with dirt covering his legs and timbers slanting in all directions. He looked up and saw a huge jagged hole in the roof. The door flew open and Sergeant Tucker charged in.

"Are you all right, sir?"

"I think so . . ."

"Let me help you up, sir."

Sergeant Tucker grabbed Duncan under the arm and pulled him to his feet. Duncan moved his limbs and took a few steps.

"I'm all right," he said, still slightly dazed.

"You're bleeding from your ears, sir."

Duncan touched his fingers to his ears and they came back smeared with blood. Tucker picked up Duncan's helmet and handed it to him. Duncan put the helmet on and picked up the telephone off the floor, touching it to his ear.

"It's dead," he muttered.

The earth shook with the violence of the explosions. Duncan felt for his pistol to make certain he still had it. He heard men shouting outside in the trenches. Placing his foot on a pile of debris, he resumed tying his laces.

"I don't know whether this is just a bombardment or they're going to attack us," he said to Tucker. "Tell the men to stay in their dugouts until I tell them to come out. They'll be safer there, and the Germans will stop shelling us before they attack."

"Yes, sir."

Tucker pushed aside the door and went out into the trench. Duncan found his binoculars and hung them around his neck, then dug his map case out of the debris and draped it over his shoulders. He felt as though he had everything under control. Then another shell slammed to earth near the bunker. A terrible roaring sound filled his ears and the ground shook like an earthquake. He lost his balance and toppled to the ground, and the strap on his helmet felt like it would tear his head off. The sound died away, to be replaced by shellbursts nearby. Duncan was terrified at the sudden thought of being crushed by earth and timbers. Scrambling to his feet, he ran to the door, pushed it open, and dashed into the trench outside.

There was a huge hole in the middle of the trench, and he threw himself inside it. At the bottom was the torso of a man lying facedown, his arms and legs gone. Duncan, his lips trembling, stared at this gruesome apparition in the flashes of explosions. Fascination overcame fear, and he reached to the mangled body to see who it was. He pushed it over and then dropped back, pressing his spine against the wall of the trench.

His eyes bulged in horror as he gazed at the distorted features of Private Giannini.

*   *   *

Captain Beck stood with his men in the German trenches. He looked at his watch—one o'clock, time to move forward. He took his Luger out of its holster, raised it high in the air and gestured toward the American lines.

"Forward!"

He scrambled up the side of the trench and advanced into no-man's-land, his men following him. Private Hitler watched them go and called out: "Good luck!" His body tingled with excitement at the thought of the mission they were on. He'd give anything to go with them, but orders were orders and he had to wait where he was until they came back.

Duncan crawled out of the hole and stood up. Explosions were thundering everywhere. He looked around and could only liken what he saw to being in the middle of hell. Sheets of flame rose into the sky and shock waves from shellbursts blew gales of dirt and debris in all directions. He looked down into the hole and again saw Private Giannini, who had been alive only a few minutes before.

The men are depending on me for leadership, Duncan thought. I can't let them down. Holding his hand against the trench for support, he made his way to the bunker at the end. He pushed the door open and stepped inside. The men, huddled around their kerosene lamp, glanced up at him, and he saw from the expressions on their faces that he must look a mess, with blood running out his ears and his uniform covered with dirt. I have to be calm and in control of the situation, he told himself. This is their first shelling and they mustn't think they're going through it without a leader.

"Anybody got a cigarette?" he asked.

Every one of the men in the bunker reached into his shirt and came up with a pack. Private Murphy was closest and Duncan picked a cigarette out of his pack.

Sergeant Tucker stepped forward with a lighter. "I didn't know you smoked, sir."

"I don't," Duncan said with a grin, "but I think it's time I started."

The men chuckled and Duncan sucked on the cigarette as Tucker held the match under it. He inhaled, and suddenly his lungs were on fire. Coughing, he fanned the air and looked at the cigarette.

"How do you fellows smoke these things?" he asked.

"They're real good once you get used to them, sir," Murphy said helpfully.

Duncan puffed again, and the tobacco actually didn't taste so bad. "I'll have to stay with you men for awhile," he said. "My bunker's just about finished off."

The men looked at one another, and he could see that they were uneasy, that they didn't feel comfortable around him. A good officer, he realized should have better rapport with his men.

A mortar round landed nearby, and clumps of dirt fell onto them from the ceiling. They ducked their heads and held their helmets as the light in the kerosene lamp wavered.

Duncan sat on the floor with the men and inhaled the cigarette again. It burned, but not as much as before. "Sounds like those Fritzies over there are mad at us."

"Well," said Private Bell, "if they don't stop this damned shelling, I'm gonna get mad at *them!*"

"It won't go on forever," Duncan told them, "and when it stops they might attack. So we'd better be ready to pour out into those trenches and fight the bastards. If it gets to that, remember your training, do as Sergeant Tucker and I tell you, and don't give up an inch of ground unless ordered to do so. Any questions?"

"Anybody see old Giannini?" asked Private Bailey.

Duncan didn't know how to say it, but Sergeant Tucker saved him the trouble.

"He's dead," Tucker grunted. "Shell landed on him out there. School days are over, kiddies. You're in a real war now."

Captain Beck led his men across the shellholes and barbed wire of no-man's-land. The area had been fought over fiercely two years ago and now resembled drawings he'd seen of the moon's surface. A few dead trees were still standing, stripped of bark and denuded of leaves. He looked to his left and right and saw his men following him in a straight skirmish line, their faces determined and hands carrying weapons high.

Turning ahead, he saw shells falling on the American positions. It was a classic box barrage: nothing could get through to the American trenches and nothing could get out. At exactly quarter to two the barrage would suddenly end, and then *Sturm* Company Three would go in and massacre the surviving Americans. The poor rookies wouldn't know what hit them.

The Germans continued moving forward, hunched over and watching their box barrage. The first coils of American barbed wire loomed up ahead. Beck held out both his arms and his men stopped. He motioned with his hands to the ground, and they all flopped onto their stomachs. Dropping to one knee, he pointed with his left hand toward the barbed wire.

Six men carrying Bangalore torpedoes leapt to their feet and ran toward the barbed wire, led by Sergeant Franck. He gave them the signal, a motion with his right hand. They activated the fuses and then ran back to where the others were, getting down on their stomachs again.

Captain Beck lay on his stomach, too. He gazed at his watch, the seconds ticking away. Then the Bangalore torpedoes exploded in brilliant yellow flashes. The men ducked their heads, and when they looked up they saw six huge holes blasted in the barbed wire.

Beck looked through the hole directly in front of him and saw shells still falling on the American trenches. The barrage had only a few minutes more to go.

Duncan and his men huddled together on the floor of their bunker as bone-shattering devastation ruptured the earth all around them. Timbers dropped from the roof and clods of dirt fell upon them. One of the timbers landed on the kerosene lamp, mangling it beyond repair and snuffing out the light.

"This can't go on forever, men," Duncan said, trying to make his voice sound confident.

Somebody screamed and sobbed in a corner.

"Get a hold of yourself!" said the deep drawling voice of Sergeant Tucker.

The man continued to whine. Duncan made his way through the frightened doughboys. He wanted to calm the man down so that he wouldn't panic the others. Something told him the man was Private Bell, but when he drew close he saw it was Private Skelton, the kid from Georgia.

"Take it easy," Duncan said, putting his arm around the man's shoulder. "It'll end pretty soon."

Skelton trembled and sobbed, and Duncan thought that if he hadn't been in charge he might be tempted to fall apart, too. The continual explosions and the fear they generated would grind down anyone's courage. Each time a shell landed he could feel the impact in his teeth.

"Anybody got another cigarette?" he asked.

Private Kincaid held out a pack. Duncan took a cigarette and Private Bell lit it for him. Inhaling, Duncan thought the smoke calmed him down a little.

The door was flung open and Captain Harrington walked into the bunker, followed by his runner, Private Shumsky. Harrington planted his fists on his hips and looked down at his men. He looked like a bulldog wearing a Second Division helmet.

"What the hell's going on in here!" he roared.

Sergeant Tucker turned toward him. "We're just having a little party, sir."

Duncan let go of Skelton and got to his feet. He didn't know whether to salute or not. Somehow it didn't seem the thing to do. He wished Captain Harrington would get down.

"Is that you, Hunter?" Harrington asked.

"Yes, sir."

"You-all look like a bunch of goddamn trench rats."

The men looked at one another, noticing for the first time that they were all covered with dirt. A few of them snickered.

"You-all ain't afraid in here, are you?"

"Hell, no!" said Private Bell.

"That's what I thought." Harrington looked at Duncan again. "Any casualties?"

"Only Private Giannini, sir."

"That's who's in the hole outside?"

"Yes, sir."

"We'll take care of him later. Our observers have reported seeing Germans out there in no-man's-land. We think they're gonna pay us a little visit, so you'd better fix bayonets as soon as the shelling stops, and go out there and give them a warm welcome."

Private Murphy took his bayonet out of its scabbard and prepared to hook it to his rifle.

Harrington held out his hand. "Not yet. You damn clowns are liable to stab each other going out the door. Do it when you get outside."

Sheepishly, Murphy returned the bayonet to his scabbard.

"Well," Harrington said, "pretty soon you're all gonna be doing what you've been training for these past few months. I know you'll give a good account of yourselves, because you're American soldiers. I've got to run along now, but I'll be with you in the trenches when the time comes. Carry on."

Harrington turned and walked out of the bunker, with Private Shumsky following him. Duncan sat on the floor again and thought of Harrington striding through the trenches with shells falling all around. That old son-of-a-bitch really has got guts, he admitted to himself. He was beginning to realize that there was more to being a front line officer than he'd thought.

Suddenly the shelling stopped.

Duncan drew his forty-five. "Everybody out!" he shouted.

Captain Beck jumped to his feet and pointed his Luger at the American lines. "Forward!" he screamed. He ran toward the American trenches, and his men leapt up and followed him. They raced through the holes in the barbed wire, holding their bayonets straight ahead. Jumping over shellholes, running around dead trees, they made their way toward the green American soldiers.

They came to another coil of barbed wire. Men with Bangalore torpedoes ran forward, pushed them under the barbed wire, set the detonators and ran back. The explosives blew the wire apart, and they all charged forward again through the holes in the barbed wire. Beck was out in front, holding the barrel of his Luger pointed in the air. He heard the crackle of rifle fire ahead of him; the Americans were getting into position.

"Faster! Follow me!"

In two straight skirmish lines, *Sturm* Company Three closed the distance between them and the first American trench. More Americans fired their rifles, and one German stumbled and fell to the ground, a bullet through his chest. Beck heard the *pop* of a Very pistol and saw a flare streak into the sky. It burst and suddenly no-man's-land became illuminated. Beck felt naked but he pointed his Luger straight ahead and bellowed: "Follow me!"

The American trenches came closer. The battle-hardened Germans lowered their bayonets and prepared to jump in.

"Here they come!" yelled Private Bell.

He took careful aim with his rifle and squeezed off a round. The German in his sights pitched forward onto his face.

"I got another one!"

A second flare was shot into the air, and the battle-field became brighter. Duncan stood in the trench with his men, holding his forty-five with both hands and aiming at a German, who was still a little too far away. In a few seconds he'd be closer, and Duncan would shoot the son-of-a-bitch. He pulled the trigger, his pistol blasted—but the German kept coming. Duncan and his doughboys fired a few quick volleys, but before they could do more the Germans were on top of them.

The Germans jumped into the trench, and hand-to-hand fighting began. Bell, gritting his teeth, lunged forward and rammed his bayonet into a German's stomach before the German's feet even hit the ground. Bell yanked his bayonet out, turned, and saw another German standing in front of him. The German shouted something and streaked his bayonet toward Bell's heart, but Bell was nimble and managed to dodge out of the way. He danced on the balls of his feet and feinted with his bayonet as the German followed him. The German lunged at Bell again, but Bell sidestepped, feinted, and then made his own lunge. The German was off balance and watched with horror as the bayonet sped toward his heart. It pierced his tunic and smashed through his ribs. Bell heaved backward yanking the bayonet out, and blood gushed after it.

Somebody fell against Bell, and he sagged against the side of the trench. As he tried to rise, he saw a German raise his rifle butt to bash him in the head. Bell leapt to the side. A shot rang out at the same time, and the German closed his eyes and fell forward, a bullet in his back. The trench was filled with grunting and cursing men, their rifles clashing against each other. Men fought shoulder to shoulder and sometimes the press became so great they could barely move their arms.

Duncan held his forty-five with two hands and shot Germans at point-blank range, while counting off the rounds in his mind. When he had only three left in the pistol he reached to his belt with his left hand and pulled out another clip as fighting raged all around him. He ejected the empty clip from the forty-five and slammed in the new one, but before he could load the chamber a German saw him and tried to attack him with his bayonet. Duncan raised his arm to protect himself and deflected the bayonet to the side, but it cut through his jacket and ripped open his arm. Nearly fainting from the sudden blazing pain, Duncan aimed wildly at the German and pulled the trigger. The forty-five kicked into the air and belched smoke, the big slug hitting the German in the shoulder, spinning him around. Duncan shot him again, and this time the slug hit the German in the back, smashing into his rib cavity and killing him. "Push them back!" Duncan yelled. "Kill them all!"

The doughboys fought in a wild fury. Although outnumbered by more experienced soldiers, they were rough men and they'd been eager to fight the Germans ever since they arrived in France. They parried bayonet thrusts with their rifles and slammed their butt plates against German skulls. Some swung their rifles like baseball bats, clobbering Germans on all sides, while others removed their bayonets from their rifles and fought close in.

In another section of the trench, Captain Beck was aiming his Luger at a doughboy when out of nowhere a rifle stock came down and whacked him on the wrist, knocking the Luger out of his hands. For a split second he didn't know whether to bend down and retrieve the Luger or attack the doughboy who'd swung at him.

He decided to attack realizing he wouldn't have time to pick up the Luger. The doughboy swung his rifle again, and Beck caught it in midair, kicking the doughboy in the groin. The doughboy's eyes rolled into his head and he sagged to his knees. Beck kicked him in the face, bent down, picked up his Luger, and shot the groaning doughboy in the stomach.

Beck looked around. He'd thought his *Sturm* soldiers would have overwhelmed the Americans by now, but the Americans were holding them off. An American charged with a bayonet and Beck shot him in the face. Another American took a step backward and fired his rifle from the waist at Beck. The muzzle of his rifle flashed, illuminating the long bayonet, and Beck felt as though a truck had crashed into his stomach. Dropping his Luger, he fell to the ground, trying to cover the wound with his hands.

Captain Harrington had taken a rifle and bayonet from a fallen doughboy and was slashing Germans with it. "We've got them, boys!" he yelled. "Press on!" A few yards away, a German fired his rifle at Harrington, blowing off one of his epaulettes. Harrington flinched and then pulled the trigger of the rifle he was carrying. The bullet hit the German in the chest, and he went down. Harrington jumped over the German's body and lunged at the German behind him, breaking through his guard and stabbing him in the belly. He yanked his bayonet downward, shouted victoriously, and smashed a German in the face with his rifle butt. The German fell backward and Harrington held the rifle in the slashing position and brought it down diagonally on the German. It caught the German in the neck and ripped across his torso to his waist. The

German screamed horribly and dropped to his knees. Harrington bashed him in the head and attacked the next German he saw, who charged with rifle and bayonet at the same moment. Their rifles clashed in midair and they pushed against each other, trying to knock each other off balance. Their faces were inches apart, and Harrington could see that his adversary was around twenty-five years old, unshaven, a look of determination on his face. He tried to kick Harrington in the groin, but Harrington sidestepped and heaved with all his strength at the German. The German cursed and gritted his teeth, straining against Captain Harrington. Suddenly, the German's eyes and mouth opened in surprise. He gasped and Harrington looked down to see the point of a bayonet sticking through the German's stomach. The German went limp and fell to the ground as a mountainous-looking doughboy behind him pulled out his bayonet and turned to find his next victim.

The brawny doughboy was Private Ambrose Murphy, the biggest soldier in the trench, who loved a good fight and was having the time of his life. He thrust his rifle and bayonet at a German who didn't have the strength to parry, and the bayonet broke through the German's ribs and sank to the hilt in his chest. Blood foamed out of the German's mouth and his legs sagged, but Murphy held him stuck in the air, looking at him for a few moments with morbid fascination and then pulling back suddenly and letting the German fall to the ground. "Get the bastards!" he yelled. He jumped in front of another German, feinted with his bayonet and bashed him in the face with his rifle stock. The blow broke the German's jaw and he went flying unconscious against the wall of the trench. Murphy saw a German pistol lying on the ground and picked it up with his left hand. In front of him was a German facing the opposite direction, and Murphy pulled the trigger, shooting him in the back and sending him pitching forward onto the doughboy he was fighting with. Murphy drew a bead on another German, shooting him in the rear. The German grabbed the seat of his pants and yelped pathetically while the doughboy in front of him thrust his bayonet through his innards.

Something zinged against Murphy's head, and his helmet flew off. Dropping to one knee, he blinked and saw a German pointing a rifle at him. Murphy dodged to the side as the mud beside him exploded with the impact of the German's bullet. Murphy threw his rifle at the German, and as the German ducked Murphy leapt at him, grabbing him by the throat. He squeezed with all his strength, and the German's eyes and tongue bulged out. Something went *snap* in Murphy's hands and the German went limp. Murphy let him fall, snatched the rifle and bayonet from his hands, and charged bareheaded through the trench, battering every German who got in his way.

The flares grew dimmer and it became difficult to see who was friend or foe in the trenches. Duncan, fighting with a rifle and bayonet he'd picked up, felt himself becoming weaker from loss of blood. A German attacked him, and Duncan tried to fend him off. He parried the German's first thrust but didn't have the strength to parry the next one. The German's rifle pushed Duncan's rifle to the side and the German's bayonet ripped into Duncan's face. He felt fierce pain and the sensation of a steel blade against his skull.

Everything went black as he fell into unconsciousness and dropped to the mud.

Someone shot up another flare, and night became day again. Corporal Schneidhuber of *Sturm* Company Three looked around and saw the trench filled with bodies. He was splattered with American blood, but as yet was unwounded himself. There were no Americans near him and he paused to catch his breath. Somebody moved a few feet away and he readied his rifle and bayonet to run him through if was an American. He jumped toward the writhing figure and was shocked to see Captain Beck moaning and trying to hold his guts in. It suddenly dawned on Schneidhuber that the raid had not gone as planned, and they'd better get out of there. He didn't know who was in charge now, but decided to take the responsibility on himself. "Retreat!" he screamed. "Fall back!"

He lifted Captain Beck, slung him over his shoulder, and picked Beck's Luger off the ground. "Fall back!" he bellowed again.

He was turning to climb the side of the trench when he heard footsteps running toward him. It was an American soldier. Schneidhuber took quick aim and pulled the trigger. The Luger fired but the shot missed. The American soldier kept coming, his helmet low over his eyes and his bayonet pointed at Schneidhuber, who took more careful aim and fired again. The American tripped and stumbled onto the other bodies lying in the trench.

"Back!" yelled Schneidhuber as he climbed the wall of the trench. "Retreat!"

Many of the Germans were too heavily engaged to break away, but some vaulted up the sides of the trenches and proceeded to run back to their lines. Private Hencke, dueling with a small American soldier and unable to fell him, saw Private Grunwald climbing the wall of the trench.

"Grunwald!" Hencke called out. "Help me take this one prisoner!"

Grunwald dropped to the bottom of the trench and crept up on the American soldier while Hencke kept his attention. At the last moment Private Bell heard somebody behind him and turned around to see who it was. Hencke shot the butt of his rifle forward and slammed Bell on the back of his head. Stunned, Bell dropped his rifle. Grunwald punched Bell in the face with the butt of his own rifle, and Bell flew backward to the bottom of the trench where he lay motionless.

Hencke scooped Bell up in his arms like a baby and looked at Grunwald. "Let's get the hell out of here!"

Hencke and Grunwald climbed up the side of the trench and ran into no-man's-land, heading toward their own lines. They saw small groups of other Germans out there, going in the same direction. Behind them they heard the crackle of rifle fire and shouts of victory from the American trench.

11

D UNCAN HEARD a low, rumbling sound and felt himself being bounced around. He didn't know who or where he was, and struggled to become fully conscious. He felt as though he were floating in space, surrounded by an infinity of darkness. He wondered if he were dead.

He was sick and nauseous, and his head was aflame. Groaning, he opened his eyes and made out dark, angular shapes. His mouth was dry and the pain in his head was almost too much to bear. He heard moans around him, and the sound of an engine. Something was making him rock from side to side. He took a deep breath and his ears pounded. He tried to raise his head and saw men stacked three high. Something was dripping onto his face, and he tried to wipe it away with his sleeve.

He realized he was in an ambulance moving along at high speed. Whenever it hit a bump he bounced in the air and hit the bottom of the canvas cot above him. The soldier up there was bleeding profusely, and his blood was dripping onto Duncan, but Duncan couldn't move out of the way. All he could do was brace himself with his legs, and remember how he used to drive an ambulance in the French army, with the back of the ambulance stacked with broken, bleeding men. Now he was a broken, bleeding man in the back of an ambulance, and somebody else was driving.

"Doctor . . ." moaned one of the men.

A woman's voice spoke from the front of the ambulance. "We'll be at the dressing station soon," she said. "Try to hang on."

She spoke with an English accent. Duncan knew that many English women drove ambulances for the Allied armies. He'd known some of them when he drove an ambulance.

"How far to the dressing station?" he asked weakly.

"A few more miles," the woman said.

Duncan smiled wryly. He'd driven many men back from the front, and when they asked how far they had to go he always told them *not much farther* even if the dressing station was ten miles off. He knew the woman in front was probably doing the same.

Blood continued to drop onto him, but he didn't have the strength to wipe it away. It splattered onto his face and the bandage wrapped around his head. His skull felt as though hot coals were heaped on top of it.

The man above him was delirious. "They just keep coming!" he muttered. "They just keep coming!"

Duncan closed his eyes and drifted into unconsciousness.

Private Adolf Hitler was in *Sturm* Company Three's
forward trench, waiting for the shock troops to return
so he could report the results of the mission to Colonel
Englehardt.

"What time is it now, sir?" Hitler asked Lieutenant
Strauss, Company Three's adjutant.

Strauss looked at his watch. "Two-thirty."

"Shouldn't they have been back by now?"

"Yes."

The rain fell lightly and Hitler shivered in the trench.
He hoped the shock troops from Company Three
would return soon so he could go back to his warm,
comfortable bunker at regimental headquarters. Being
out in the rain like this reminded him of his days in
Vienna, when he was destitute and often went without food, sometimes sleeping in parks and railroad
stations.

"I think they're coming," Lieutenant Strauss said,
peering over the top of the trench.

Hitler looked and saw small, dark shapes in no-
man's-land, dimly illuminated by flares. "Where are the
rest of them?" he muttered.

Strauss didn't reply. He counted the men as they
came closer. There were only forty-six, whereas ninety-
eight had gone on the raid. Some carried wounded
comrades and many had left their weapons behind.
Lieutenant Strauss felt a sinking sensation in his
stomach. He knew that the raid had failed.

Hitler came to the same realization. He felt dizzy
and his mind was unable to digest the conclusion he

was forced to draw. It's impossible, he thought. How could such a thing happen?

The soldiers tumbled into the trench, bleeding and carrying their wounded. Corporal Schneidhuber laid Captain Beck down in the mud and felt his pulse. "Still alive," he muttered.

Strauss saw Captain Beck and came rushing over, followed by Hitler. "What happened to him?" Strauss asked.

"Stomach wound," Schneidhuber replied. "He's still alive, though. Call the medics."

Strauss turned to Hitler. "Tell Sergeant Feldheimer to call the medics."

Hitler rushed off toward the Third Company command post bunker but paused momentarily when he saw a friend, Private Falkenstein, slide down the wall of the trench in front of him. "What happened over there, Falkenstein?"

Falkenstein looked exhausted. "They stopped us."

Hitler blinked. "How could they stop you?" he asked, amazed.

"I don't know . . ."

Hitler wanted to ask more questions, but he had to notify Sergeant Feldheimer about calling the medics. He sped through the bays and finally came to the command post bunker. Sergeant Feldheimer was sitting at the front desk, speaking on the field telephone. He cupped his hand over the mouthpiece and said, "What is it, Hitler?"

"The men are back, Sergeant, and some of them are badly wounded. Call the medics. Captain Beck was one of the casualties."

Feldheimer cut off the conversation he was having

and called the medics. Hitler left the bunker and returned outside, where he saw a group of soldiers standing around a short man wearing a strange uniform. The man was an American prisoner.

"He's awfully small," Hitler said.

"The others were much bigger than him," said Grunwald. "They were a tough bunch."

Hitler looked at the American soldier, who was standing defiantly with his hands tied behind his back. His uniform was torn and he was bleeding from a cut on his cheek. Hitler could sense the fighting spirit of the short soldier and was surprised. He'd thought that Americans would be cowards when they got into battle.

Lieutenant Strauss walked up to the group. "Come with me, Hitler," he said. "I'll give you the dispatch to take back to Colonel Englehardt."

Hitler followed Lieutenant Strauss back to the command post bunker, and tried to dispel the feelings of dread that curdled in his breast.

The ambulance stopped and the rear door opened.

"Take it easy with 'em, boys," somebody said.

Duncan opened his eyes. His face was covered with blood that was coagulating around his eyes.

Medics came into the ambulance and transferred the men to stretchers. "This one's dead," said one of the medics when he came to the man above Duncan.

"Leave him for last," said another voice. "Get the one beneath him."

The medics bent down and looked at Duncan, who tried to smile.

"I'm alive," Duncan said.

"I can see that, sir."

Two medics lifted him, laid him on a stretcher, and carried the stretcher to the door of an ambulance, where two more men took hold of it. Duncan emerged into the cool night. Something prompted him to glance to the side, and he saw a woman wearing a brown coat and beret standing there, hugging her arms under her breasts.

"Thanks for the lift," he said.

"Good luck, soldier," she replied.

Duncan was carried to a building and laid on the floor among other wounded men. The pain in his head was so fierce he felt like crying out. He gritted his teeth and tried to tolerate it, but when a soldier with a red cross on his sleeve walked by Duncan feebly held up his hand. "Can you give me something to stop the pain?" he asked.

The soldier stopped and looked down at him. "Only the doctors can give out medicine like that, sir."

"Can you get a doctor?"

"There'll be one here shortly, sir," the soldier said wearily, automatically, as he turned and walked off.

Duncan knew how the soldier felt; he had been in many dressing stations like this when he'd driven an ambulance. All the wounded men always wanted to be looked at right away, but there were never enough doctors. Sometimes men's lives could have been saved if they'd been able to see a doctor sooner, and he used to reflect on this, and on the capriciousness of fate; but now he was wounded himself and it didn't seem so abstract. He might die here while a doctor was treating someone in another part of the building. His mother would be devastated if he died, as would his sister, Allison, but his father would show no emotion.

His father would say something like: "Well, he did his duty." Duncan wondered how his brother Blake would take it. Probably it wouldn't bother him so much. Many of Blake's closest friends had died, and Blake had caused much death himself. No doubt he was immune to it by now. Blake, the younger brother . . . the stronger brother. . . .

He heard footsteps nearby and opened his eyes. He realized he must have been dreaming, and wondered how long he'd been asleep. His head hurt as though somebody had hit it with a hatchet. He looked out the corner of his eye to see a doctor and two nurses leaning over a man. Duncan wanted to ask the doctor for morphine to kill his pain, but knew he should wait his turn with the rest of them. He was terribly weak, and had difficulty thinking clearly. He kept seeing images of the fight in the trenches, the men grunting as they clashed with one another. Duncan was glad he'd stood his ground and fought like a soldier. He hadn't broken and run, as he'd feared he might. I don't have anything to be ashamed of, he thought. I did my duty as best I could.

"How do you feel, Lieutenant?" asked a voice above him.

Duncan opened his eyes and saw the doctor leaning over him, with two nurses standing in the background. "It hurts pretty bad, doctor. Could you give me some morphine?"

"Where does it hurt?"

"My head."

"What about your arm?"

"It's not nearly as bad as my head."

The doctor turned to a nurse. "Give him a shot."

"Yes, doctor."

Duncan closed his eyes. He felt something cold against his arm, and then the prick of the needle.

"You'll feel better in just a few moments," the nurse said.

Duncan felt them removing the bandage from his head. He opened his eyes and saw hands. Fingers touched his scalp. "He may have a concussion," the doctor said.

"The blood on my face isn't all mine," Duncan said, his voice no more than a whisper. "The soldier above me on the ambulance was bleeding on me."

"Don't try to talk," the doctor said.

Duncan closed his eyes and suddenly felt floaty. He took a deep breath and saw mists swirling against his eyelids. The pain in his head diminished. In the mists he saw the German soldier coming at him with the bayonet, and he raised his arm to deflect the blow.

"Take it easy, Lieutenant," the doctor said.

Duncan heard the nurse whisper: "He should be knocked out any moment now."

There was a roaring in Duncan's ears, and then the black night rose up and engulfed him.

Sam Bell stood with his hands tied behind him as the German officers looked him over. They were in a large office in a building about ten miles behind the German lines. A portrait of the kaiser hung behind the desk. Bell thought the German officers' uniforms were ridiculous, with all their medals and gold braid, but he was too scared to laugh. He stood erectly and jutted out his jaw as they chatted among themselves in German.

"He's rather small," said Colonel Englehardt, twirling his blond, kaiserlike mustache.

"They say most of them were much larger than this one," replied Major Holstein.

"Perhaps they're lying," Colonel Englehardt said. "Perhaps they're just saying that because they were beaten by the Americans and want to make excuses. But there can be no excuses for a defeat like this. Evidently *Sturm* Company Three is not the hard-fighting unit we thought they were."

"Or," said Captain Eulenburg, "the Americans are tougher than we thought they were."

Englehardt waved his hand. "Nonsense. What can they know of war?" He looked at Bell. "Ask him his name."

Eulenburg, an officer who was only in his early twenties, turned to Bell and said in English: "What is your name, soldier?"

"Bell."

"Ask him the name of his unit."

Eulenburg translated the question.

Bell stood ever straighter. "I ain't telling you the name of my unit."

The colonel smiled. "Tough little bird, isn't he?" He gazed at Bell, whose uniform was torn in several places. The American had evidently been in the thick of the fighting. "Ask him where he's from in America."

When Eulenburg repeated the question Bell wondered whether or not to answer. He realized that his answer would have no military significance whatever, but on the other hand, he and the other doughboys had been ordered to give only their names, ranks and serial numbers if captured.

"I ain't talking," Bell said.

The colonel looked annoyed as Eulenburg trans-

lated. "Take him away and see if you can get some
information out of him."

Eulenburg called the guards and ordered them to
escort Bell to his office. Eulenburg followed them into
the hall, passing Private Hitler, who sat beside the
door to make himself available in case Englehardt
wanted to send him on a mission.

Eulenburg entered his office and spoke to the guards
standing in front of his desk with Bell. "Untie him."

As the guards untied the ropes, Eulenburg walked
behind his desk and sat down. He opened his silver
cigarette case and took out a cigarette, lighting it with
a wooden match. When the guards were finished un-
tying Bell, Eulenburg told them to leave the room and
wait outside the door.

Alone now, Eulenburg smiled at Bell.

"Have a seat," he said. His English had a British
inflection, Bell noticed, in addition to his German
accent.

Bell knew he should remain standing, but he felt
tired and could use a rest, so he sat down, glancing
around quickly as he settled into the chair. There was
a window behind the German officer's desk and another
window to Bell's right. Bell had already calculated
that he was on the second floor of the building.

"Have a cigarette," said Eulenburg, holding out his
cigarette case.

Bell knew he should refuse the cigarette. He and the
other doughboys had received lectures about how the
Germans would try to soften them up if they were
captured; if they relaxed they were liable to give away
information that might get their buddies killed.

"Go ahead," said Eulenburg with a friendly smile.

"You never know when you might get a chance to smoke again."

Why not? Bell thought. If he had accepted the chair he might as well take a cigarette, too. He leaned forward and took one out of the case, and Eulenburg tossed him a wooden match. He inhaled, noticing that the cigarette tasted much different than American cigarettes.

"What unit did you say you were in?" asked Eulenburg.

"I ain't talking," Bell replied defiantly. "I'm gonna smoke the cigarette but I ain't gonna tell you nothing, so you might as well save your breath."

Eulenburg shrugged good-naturedly. "What harm would it do for you to tell me the name of your unit?"

"I don't know anything about anything."

"Where are you from?"

"Nowhere."

"I mean what city or town in the United States?"

"I ain't telling."

"I visited America once," Eulenburg said. "I was in New York, Boston and Washington, D.C. I liked it there very much. Are you from any of those three cities?"

"No."

"Are you from a city on the east coast of the United States?"

"I ain't talking."

Eulenburg smiled. "Come now," he said. "You mustn't be so stubborn. If you talk with me a little you'll be sent to a very nice prisoner camp. But if you don't, we'll have to put you someplace you won't like very much."

"I don't give a shit," Bell said.

"You will when you get into that little jail cell. You'll wish you'd been friendlier to me, and then it will be too late. I'd talk if I were you."

"You ain't me," Bell said, his eyes on the cigarette between his thumb and the nail of his forefinger.

"I'll give you one last chance," Eulenburg said, the evenness of his tone becoming forced now.

Bell raised his hand and flicked the cigarette into Eulenburg's face. Eulenburg shouted as sparks fell off his nose. Bell was already halfway across the room. He covered his face with his arms and leapt toward the window. His knees and elbows hit first and he went crashing through, sailing into the air along with shards of glass and pieces of wood from the window frame. He opened his eyes and saw the ground coming up fast. He braced himself, hit, and rolled immediately to cushion the shock. Glancing around quickly, he saw that he was in an alley behind the building. His left foot hurt but he ran quickly out of the alley. Behind him he could hear shouts and the shrill of whistles.

He came to the street behind the building. He didn't know which way to turn, but decided to bear right and keep going straight until he was out of town. He sped along in the cover of darkness. The streetlights were out in the town, to save fuel and make it difficult for Allied observers to spot it at night. The streets were deserted; it was only four in the morning. He knew that sooner or later he'd run into German soldiers but he'd worry about that when it happened.

He heard the sound of an automobile engine, and headlights flashed into the street behind him. Making a sharp right turn, Sam Bell ran toward the back yard of a house, where he dived under some bushes. He lay still for awhile, unable to see the street. He heard no unusual sounds and saw no German soldiers.

Peering about, he tried to get his bearings. The back of the house was in front of him, and nearby was a whitewashed shed. He decided that the shed might be a better hiding place. There might also be a tool in there that he could use for a weapon. Crawling out from underneath the bush, he tiptoed toward the shed and turned the handle of the door. It opened, and he quickly stepped inside.

It smelled like kerosene and dead leaves. In the dim light he saw that there were some tools lying upon the workbench. And on a hanger at the side of the work-bench were some clothes. Bell examined them; they were workpants, a jacket and a black beret. Hot dog, he thought, unbuttoning his tunic. I might get out of this mess after all.

12

LIEUTENANT EVERETT DEWITT walked quickly down the Avenue de la République, on his way from the French War Ministry to General Pershing's headquarters. It was eleven o'clock in the morning and he carried a briefcase bulging with papers. He turned a corner and nearly dropped the briefcase in surprise, for walking toward him, no more than ten feet away, was Danielle Giraud, whom he hadn't seen since their night at the ballet. He didn't know whether or not to say hello, considering the argument they'd had before parting.

Danielle smiled when she recognized him. "Well, hello," she said. Her manner, he noted, was not at all unfriendly.

"Hello, Danielle," he replied, tipping his hat and still unsure of himself.

"How have you been, Everett?" she asked. It was as if they'd never even had an argument.

"Rather well. And you?"

"Fine, thank you."

There were a few moments of awkward silence. He should hurry back to his office, but she looked lovely in her navy blue coat.

"I've missed you," he blurted.

She laughed gaily. "Don't be silly. I'm sure you have plenty of other girls to keep you occupied."

"I miss you, anyway," he said. "I'm very sorry about my behavior the last time we were together. It really was unpardonable. Do you . . . do you think we could see each other some time?"

She looked away. "I don't know," she said vaguely. "I suppose I really don't have any serious objection."

He glanced at his watch. "Are you doing anything for lunch?"

"It's rather early for lunch."

"We could have a glass of wine first."

"You appeared to be in a hurry, Everett. Weren't you going someplace?"

He frowned. "As a matter of fact I was. I must get back to my office."

"Then we can't very well have lunch, can we?"

"I guess not," he admitted.

"Everett!" shouted a male voice.

Everett turned in the direction of the voice, and saw Blake Hunter striding toward him out of the crowd of pedestrians. Blake held out his hand. "How are you, old man?"

Everett was surprised by the heartiness of Blake's greeting. They'd met only once, and Everett had received no reply after he'd sent Blake a written introduction to a friend in the American air service. Still, Blake had been Franklin DeWitt's friend. And Everett was no more immune to Blake's vitality and charm than was anyone else. Blake looked magnificent, he thought, like an officer on a recruiting poster. He wore an American uniform now. The result of Everett's introduction or of his own efforts?

"Hello, Blake," Everett said. "What brings you to Paris?"

Blake was nearly a head taller than Everett, with his visored cap worn low over his eyes. "My brother is in the hospital here. He was wounded at the front."

"Not seriously I hope."

"Fortunately not."

Everett turned to Danielle. "Danielle, this is a friend of mine, Blake Hunter. Blake, this is Danielle Giraud."

Danielle looked up at Blake and smiled. "How do you do."

He grinned, showing his dazzling white teeth. "Hi."

She saw his eyes scrutinize her face, then look her up and down. Her smile grew broader and she gave a light laugh.

Blake appeared amused. "Did I do something funny?"

"Never mind." She glanced away, but the smile still lit her face.

Everett could perceive that they liked each other, and felt a stab of jealousy. "What hospital is Duncan in?" he asked.

"The one on the Rue D'Orsay. I'm sure he'd enjoy a visit from time to time. He's taken up smoking and he'd probably appreciate cigarettes. I won't be able to attend to his personal needs very well, because I have to return to Issoudun tomorrow."

"How do you like it there?"

"Hate it. I'm trying to get a transfer to a pursuit squadron. You couldn't help me with something like that, could you?"

"I don't know anybody in the air service that well," Everett replied. Perhaps Blake had never received the introduction, he reflected. In any event, Blake Hunter seemed quite able to fend for himself.

Blake shrugged. "Then I guess I'll have to do what a friend of mine did. They wouldn't give him a transfer, so he took up his plane and terrorized some folks at a soccer game for about a half-hour, diving toward the grandstands and all. When he returned to base, the C.O. was so anxious to get rid of him that he was transferred out right away."

Everett wrinkled his brow. "That doesn't seem like the best way to go about it. They might throw you out of the service."

"Then I'll fly for the French again."

"You flew for France?" Danielle exclaimed.

"Yes," Blake admitted.

"You were in the Lafayette Escadrille?"

"Yes."

She gazed at him with new interest.

Everett looked at his watch. "I really must go back to my office. Can I put you in a cab, Danielle?"

"I can get along by myself, thank you."

"Where were you headed, Blake?"

"I was going to the Crillon for a drink."

"Wish I could join you." He turned to Danielle. "Well, good-bye."

"Good-bye," she replied.

He hesitated for a moment, wanting to say more, but

Danielle's earlier friendliness had vanished and her manner was not encouraging.

He looked at Blake and shook his hand. "Nice seeing you again."

"Likewise."

"I'll stop by to see your brother sometime."

"That would be kind of you."

"If you're ever in Paris and have nothing to do, give me a call."

"I'll do that."

Everett turned and walked away swiftly. He wanted to look back over his shoulder to see what Blake and Danielle were doing, but that would have been bad form. She'll probably fall in love with him, Everett thought. I imagine women find him irresistible.

They stood on the street corner, their eyes twinkling at each other. She knew she really should be going. It wouldn't do to have him think she was attracted to him, even if that happened to be the truth.

"Are you doing anything important right now?" he asked in his smooth baritone.

"No."

"Why don't you come to the Crillon with me and have a drink?"

"Isn't that the dreadful place where all the pilots go and get drunk?"

"As a matter of fact it is."

"I've always wanted to go there."

"Then let's go."

"Very well. But I don't like rowdiness, and if it gets that way I hope you won't mind if I leave."

"Of course not." He stepped toward the curb. "I'll get a cab."

"Why don't we walk? It's not far."

"Are you sure you won't mind walking?" he asked. "I've noticed that women generally don't like to walk very far. I think it has something to do with the strange shoes they wear."

She raised one of her tiny feet. "These shoes aren't strange, and moreover they're very comfortable. I could walk miles in them—and in fact I often have."

"You've convinced me," he said, linking his arm with hers.

They turned and walked toward the Crillon. It was a cool day and the wind whipped their coats and made their complexions rosy. They passed other pedestrians ambling by the gaily decorated windows of the Parisian shops.

He cleared his throat. "Do you know Everett very well?"

She glanced sideways at him. "What do you mean by well?"

"Are you lovers or something like that?"

"Don't be ridiculous!"

"Why am I being ridiculous? You two look very well together."

She wanted to say that she thought she looked much better with Blake. But instead she told him, "Everett is a very nice person, but we're not lovers by any means. However," she quickly added, "we have been out together on several dates in the past."

"I got the impression, while we all were standing together back there, that he liked you a lot."

"I believe that's so," she replied.

"I also had the impression that you didn't like him a lot. Is that so, too?"

She looked at him reproachfully. "Don't you think that's rather a personal question?"

"I suppose it is, but so what?"

"I don't like personal questions. They spoil everything. Are you and Everett close friends?"

"I hardly know him at all," Blake said. "Our families have had dealings with each other over the years, and I was sort of friendly with his brother Franklin, who was killed in action not long ago. He was in the escadrille also."

"Everett mentioned him to me. He thought quite a lot of Franklin. Evidently Franklin's death was quite a blow to Everett and his whole family. There was a wife too, I understand."

Blake stared at her for a moment, startled. Then he shrugged. "It happens all the time. The same thing will probably happen to me. What can one do?"

"Nothing. My brother was killed in the war also. He was an infantry officer."

"Like my brother."

"Yes. I hope your brother isn't hurt badly."

"He's not, but he's got a scar on his face that he'll probably wear for the rest of his life."

"Not necessarily," she said. "I understand that some skilled doctors can do wonders in erasing scars. Oh— look at that!"

He followed her eyes and saw a store window that displayed women's clothes. She walked to the window and looked inside like a greedy child. "What a beautiful dress!"

He stood beside her and looked at the clothes. "Which one?"

"The silk one with the pretty colors and black shoulder straps. Do you like it?"

"It's all right, I suppose."

"You don't like it," she pouted.

He shrugged. "I don't like it and I don't dislike it. As far as I'm concerned, fashion is the ultimate pettiness."

She looked at him sharply. "Are you saying that I'm a petty person?"

"No, I didn't say that."

"But you implied it."

He smiled. "Perhaps I did."

She wanted to turn around and walk briskly away from him, but couldn't bring herself to do so. She thought him awfully good-looking, and she'd always wanted to see the pilots at the Crillon.

"I can't help it if I like pretty clothes," she said. "I'm no different from any other woman in that respect."

He laughed. "No, I don't suppose you are."

"Are you laughing at me?"

"I'm laughing at the world."

"Now you're being dishonest. You are too laughing at me."

"Okay, so I'm laughing at you. You're a child, but you're an awfully pretty child." He gazed at her face. "Too pretty for your own good, I suppose."

She pursed her lips and gave him a sidelong look. "Nobody can be too pretty for her own good."

"Yes they can, because they can be spoiled."

"Then you must be spoiled, too, because you're a handsome man. Of your type."

"Of my *type*?" he asked. "I had no idea that I was a type. What type am I?"

She placed her forefinger against her chin and considered him. "The heartless, vicious type."

He laughed.

"It's not funny," she said.

"That's because you don't have a sense of humor."
He glanced at his watch. "We'd better get going." He
took her arm and began walking.

"Do you have an appointment?"

"No."

"Why the hurry?"

"Because I want to start drinking."

"Are you a drunkard?"

"Probably."

"I've heard that all you pilots are drunkards."

"We are."

"Why?"

"How should I know? For the same reason you like
pretty clothes, I imagine."

"I fail to see the connection."

"It may be too subtle for you."

She wrinkled her nose. That was the same argument
she had given Everett on the night of the ballet. She
realized now that it was an aggravating thing for someone to say. But if Blake was aggravating her, why did
she like him? She looked at him again. He seemed
strong and sure of himself, and he really was an
exceptionally good-looking man. The fact that he was
a pilot added to his glamour. Something told her she
ought to leave him and go home, but she was like a fish
that has been hooked and was now being reeled in.

They continued to quibble during their walk
through the streets of Paris. When they arrived at the
Crillon Hotel, they found the lobby filled with pilots
and women. Everybody seemed to know Blake, who
shook hands, slapped shoulders and exchanged wise-
cracks, introducing Danielle to all of them as they
made their way to the lounge. At the hatcheck room

just outside the entrance to the lounge, Danielle removed her navy blue coat, revealing a white sweater and a gray skirt underneath. Blake eyed her as he took off his hat and coat, noting that the simplicity of her expensive-looking clothes was more than compensated for by their flawless cut. They set off her small, neat figure and let her beauty speak for itself. And he had no doubt that it was a calculated effect.

He took Danielle's arm and led her into the lounge. It was a noisy and smoky place, and at first Danielle was repelled by it. A gigantic propellor was suspended above the bar mirror and paintings of airplanes hung on the walls. The bar and tables were crowded with pilots and women, everybody laughing and talking, singing songs, calling out to people on the other side of the room. Blake was recognized immediately, and the scene in the lobby was repeated, with men rising to shake his hand and ask how he was. Danielle saw pilots passed out cold with their faces lying on the tables as other people talked over their heads. She thought the women were dressed too flashily and their behavior seemed cheap. Some kissed men shamelessly. So this is the Crillon, Danielle thought. It looks like a pigsty to me.

"We might as well sit here," Blake said, pulling back a chair at a large table where a party was already in progress.

"Where'd you find the pretty little bird?" asked a drunken pilot at the table.

"I picked her up on the street," Blake replied, dropping into a chair. "Danielle, this is Raoul Lufberry."

Danielle smiled and nodded at the man, blushing because of what Blake had said.

"He really didn't pick me up on the street," she said softly.

Lufberry laughed uproariously.

"And this," said Blake, "is one of my illustrious countrymen, the irrepressible Lieutenant Elliott Springs."

Springs winked at her. "Nice to meet you."

"Hello," she said.

"Introduce yourself to the women," Blake said. "I don't remember their names." He raised his hand in the air. "*Garçon!*"

While Blake spoke with the waiter, Danielle introduced herself to the two women sitting at the table. One was a Briton named Peggy, and the other a Frenchwoman named Marie. Both were older than Danielle, who thought they wore too much make-up. They also appeared half-drunk.

Lufberry raised a glass of whisky to his lips. "How do you like the American air force?" he asked Blake.

"They won't let me fly," Blake replied.

"Why not?"

"They need me as an instructor, but I'll break away from that duty pretty soon." He looked at Springs. "How are you doing these days?"

"Not too well. We don't have any good planes."

"No Spads yet?"

"No. Sometimes I think I should have stayed with the British air force."

Danielle was confused. "You were with the British air force?"

"Yes," Springs replied. "I flew with the British just the way Blake flew with the French. What did you say your name was?"

"Danielle."

"Danielle what?"

"Daniele Giraud."

Lufberry leaned forward drunkenly. "You wouldn't be related to General Giraud, would you?"

"He's my father," Danielle replied.

Blake looked at Danielle in surprise. "You didn't tell me your father was a general."

"You didn't ask."

The band started to play a fast tune, and Lufberry and Springs took their girls to the dance floor. The waiter came with a bottle of champagne and two glasses and began to open the bottle, but Blake snatched it out of his hands and popped the cork himself. The cork hit the ceiling and people at surrounding tables cheered. Blake filled Danielle's glass as the waiter receded into the smoke and noise. Then he filled his own glass and raised it in the air.

"To your very substantial beauty," he said.

She raised her glass to her lips and sipped. The noise in the lounge was incredible. She looked about the smoke-filled room, feeling slightly out of place among the tipsy crowd of revelers.

"You don't like the champagne?" Blake asked, refilling his glass.

"No, it's fine," she replied.

"Then why do you look so unhappy?"

"I'm not unhappy."

"Sure you are. You don't like it here. I didn't think you would. I'll get you a cab if you like."

"I'll stay," she replied, "unless you really want me to leave . . ."

He shook his head. "No, I don't want you to leave. Whatever gave you that idea?"

"I'm afraid I might be spoiling your fun. I'm not accustomed to this sort of thing, you know."

"You're not spoiling my fun. I like to look at you. You make me realize that the world can be a very nice place, despite everything."

Her eyes softened. "That's a very sweet thing to say, Blake."

He appeared embarrassed for a few seconds, then he brightened again. "You want to dance?"

"All right."

They stood and threaded their way through the tables. Blake walked behind her, admiring the curves of her body. But she's just a child, he thought. Maybe I shouldn't have brought her here.

They sidestepped onto the crowded dance floor, and he placed his arm around her waist and took her hand. They could only take small steps, and the other dancers kept bumping into them.

"I don't dance very well," he said, "but I wanted to touch you anyway."

She looked into his eyes and felt a chill go through her.

"I don't know why I brought you," he confessed. "You really don't belong here."

"Well," she replied, looking around, "I always was curious about the Crillon. I'd heard so much about it. It certainly lives up to its reputation."

"Pilots are a little wild," Blake agreed. "Gee, you smell good."

He held her closer and she let him because she liked the way he felt. There was something gallant and fine about him, and also a bit of the naughty little boy.

"The daughter of a general," he whispered. "I should have known."

"Why should you have known?"

"Please don't get mad at me for saying so, but you're somewhat arrogant, my dear."

"Perhaps you confuse self-respect with arrogance."

"Perhaps. Do you do anything besides being pretty?"

"I study dancing."

"Ballet?"

"Exactly."

"I'd love to see you in your tights."

She didn't know how to respond to his remark, and he noticed her consternation.

"I shouldn't have said that," he told her. "I'd better put you in a cab before I say something worse."

Again she didn't know what to say, but she didn't want to leave. She thought she'd make a joke of it. "I'm the daughter of a soldier," she said gaily. "You couldn't say anything that could shock me."

"Oh yes I could. Come on."

He pulled her off the crowded dance floor and toward the crowded tables.

"Where are we going?" she asked.

"You're going home."

"But I don't want to go home!"

"You're going home anyway!"

"Let me go, Blake!"

"No."

"You're hurting me!"

He spun around suddenly and let her hand go. Stepping toward her, he grabbed her shoulders and brought his face close to hers.

"Please go before I behave badly," he said earnestly. "You're a sweet kid and I don't want to behave badly with you."

"Then why must you?" she asked above the chatter and laughter around her.

"I can't explain it."

She looked down at the wings on his jacket. "You want to go to bed with me, don't you?"

He nodded. "Yes."

"That's all you soldiers want to do."

He smiled sadly. "Yes."

"I guess maybe I'd better leave. Then you can find somebody to go to bed with."

"I'm sorry," he said. "I shouldn't have invited you here."

"You keep saying that."

"It's the truth. I don't want you on my conscience. Come on."

She followed him out of the noisy room, and the hatcheck girl got her coat. Blake helped her on with it and walked her out of the lobby to the sidewalk in front of the hotel. The wind was blowing, and she held the collar of her coat closed. As Blake raised his hand in the air, she remembered something her father had told her about the high death rate among pilots. He was handsome and vigorous, and yet she had the sudden conviction that he was going to die.

"Gee," he said, "you look like you're going to cry. Don't take it so hard, kid. I'm doing this for your own good."

"I know," she replied. "I'll be all right."

"It isn't because I don't like you or anything. The problem is that I do like you, and . . . well . . . you deserve somebody better." He laughed and shook his head. "Listen to me! I don't think too many people would believe I just said that."

She smiled sadly. "I don't think there is anybody better than you, Blake."

A taxicab stopped at the curb. They stood staring at each other for a few moments. Then his eyes flashed and he reached for her, clasping her in his arms. She raised her face and he kissed her lips passionately. She opened her mouth and tasted his tongue, feeling the stubble of his beard against her cheek, and smelling his fragrace, so like a meadow in the sun.

He moved away from her suddenly, his eyes wild. He opened the door of the taxicab.

"Go," he said, pushing her toward the cab.

She lowered her head and stepped inside and he closed the door behind her. As the driver steered the cab into the street, she turned around, looking out of the rear window to see Blake rushing up the steps of the Crillon Hotel.

13

THE FRENCH SOLDIER's name was Raoul Fleury and he'd been on guard in the trench for a half hour. It was night and he peered over the top of the parapet into no-man's-land looking for signs of a raid. A heavy cloud layer obscured the moon and it was pitch-black out there. He wouldn't be able to see the Germans until they were ten yards away.

"Don't shoot!" shouted a voice in English.

Fleury didn't speak English and was shocked by the voice. It was coming from no-man's-land, but he couldn't see anybody. "Who goes there!" he yelled in French.

"*Américain!*" replied the voice. "*Américain!*"

Fleury saw a white handkerchief being waved at him. If this was a German trick, he'd better get help.

"Sergeant of the guard!" he shouted. "Sergeant of the guard!"

A man in civilian clothes stood up, still waving the handkerchief, and walked forward in a crouch. Fleury took aim at him, eyes darting around to make sure the man was alone, but there didn't seem to be anyone with him.

"*Américain!*" the man said again. He approached the side of the trench, holding both his hands in the air. He smiled and slid down just as footsteps could be heard running inside the trench. The sergeant of the guard arrived with two privates. They looked suspiciously at the man and pointed their rifles at him.

The man smiled. "No speak French," he said.

The sergeant of the guard scowled and looked at Fleury. "What did he say?"

"I don't know," said Fleury.

"*Américain,*" the man said, smiling but evidently worried.

"I think," said Private Fleury, "that he's saying he's an American. Maybe we should get Lieutenant Langlois. He speaks English."

The sergeant of the guard nodded. "You men stay here and make sure nobody else is out there. I'll take this one to Langlois." He pointed the bayonet of his rifle in the direction of Lieutenant Langlois's dugout. "Start moving, you."

"*Américain,*" the man said weakly as he held his hands high and walked toward the dugout.

Inside the dugout, Lieutenant Langlois looked up from the letter he was writing to his wife. He had a long, sad face and close-cropped blond hair. "What the hell is this supposed to be?" he asked as the contingent descended upon him. He looked at the man in civilian clothes. "Who's he?"

"He just showed up from no-man's-land, sir," said the sergeant of the guard. "He says he's an American but we can't get much out of him because he doesn't speak French. That's why we brought him to you, sir."

"He was alone?"

"Yes, sir."

"Are you sure?"

"We didn't see anyone else out there, sir. Would you like me to take a patrol into no-man's-land to see if there's anyone else out there?"

"Maybe you'd better, just to be on the safe side."

"Yes, sir." The sergeant of the guard saluted and left the dugout.

Langlois looked at the little man in the civilian clothes. "You are American?" he asked in heavily accented English.

"Yes, sir," said the man, obviously relieved that he'd found someone who spoke English. "The Germans took me prisoner, but I broke away."

Langlois picked up a pencil calmly, as though American prisoners were commonplace in his trenches. "Your name?"

"Private Samuel William Bell, sir. Company B, Twenty-third Infantry Regiment, Second Division. Could I possibly get something to eat, sir? I ain't et nothing for two days."

Langlois looked at one of the soldiers guarding Bell. "Has he been searched yet?"

"Don't know, sir."

Langlois pointed to Bell and spoke to him in accented English again. "Take off all your clothes."

Bell grimaced. "But it's cold in here!"

"Do it next to the stove."

Grumbling, Bel stood next to the small, pot-bellied stove and unbuttoned his jacket. Langlois looked down at the letter he'd been writing his wife, smiled, and put pen to paper again. *You'll never believe what just happened. My guards brought in a man dressed in civilian clothes who claims to be an American soldier escaped from the Germans. He's a nasty little fellow, and he smells to high heaven, although all of us do down here, I suppose. If he is who he says he is, he'll be back in his unit by tomorrow. We never know what'll happen next in this war.*

Danielle Giraud stepped out of her bathtub into the huge, fluffy white towel held in the air by Georgette, her maid. She wrapped herself in the towel as Georgette rubbed her hair. She could see her reflection even through the foggy condensation that covered the mirror, and she smiled at her rosy complexion and the twisted strands of blonde hair that lay on her forehead.

She put on her slippers and walked out of the bathroom, leaving Georgette to drain the tub and tidy up the room. Danielle seated herself at her make-up table and looked at herself in the large mirror. She realized it was difficult to be objective about oneself, but she knew she was beautiful, and that knowledge gave her great pleasure. It would have given her more pleasure if she'd done something to achieve the beauty, but it had been a gift from God, and she accepted it as gracefully as her years would allow.

There were dangers connected to her beauty, and she was aware of many of them. One of the foremost was narcissism, of which she was quite unaware. Looking over her shoulder, she saw that the bathroom door was closed and heard Georgette working away. Danielle stood in front of the mirror and let the towel fall from her shoulders, uncovering her body.

She was always amazed at how perfect she was. Not too heavy nor too light. Nothing out of proportion. Skin like strawberries and cream. Her father was a rather unattractive man, though she loved him dearly, and her mother was quite plain also. Therefore she saw herself as a kind of miracle.

The bathroom door was flung open and Georgette marched out on her little matchstick legs. "Shall I help you with your clothes, *mademoiselle*?"

Danielle returned to her seat, drawing the towel closed around her shoulders. "I can manage."

"If *mademoiselle* should need me for anything, I'll be right down the hall."

Georgette left the room and closed the door behind her. Danielle picked up her hairbrush and began to pull it through her shoulder-length golden hair, and as she did so the towel dropped off her shoulders, uncovering the tops of her breasts. The effect was very fetching, she thought, but she could never wear a gown that fit like that. It would be too vulgar, and if there was anything in the world that she thoroughly detested it was vulgarity.

Human beings could not control their destinies, she thought, but they could at least control their vulgarity. She simply refused to behave like the other women her age, who went from one squalid love affair to another, with an endless procession of buffoons. And although she wasn't especially happy, she knew they weren't, either. At least she had her dignity, and if she ever met a man to whom she could give herself, he would not get a body that had been kissed by every pair of drunken lips in Paris.

Daniele had begun to think she'd never find a man who could meet her high standards—but then she had met Blake Hunter. Until him, the men she'd known had been either awkward and silly, like Everett De-Witt, or loud and obnoxious, like the older men who wanted to appear knowledgeable about everything but who were really no different from the younger men.

Blake had been different from any man she'd ever known. She'd met war heroes before, but they'd all seemed rather shy and embarrassed about what they'd done. Blake was so normal and natural, and yet there truly was a heroic quality about him. She'd only been with him a few short hours, but she considered herself a good judge of people. She could almost see him as one of the great knights of the Crusades, like Stephen de Blois or Raymond de Toulouse. Blake wasn't ashamed of what he was, and he wasn't excessively proud, either. And he suffered just like all the great knights did—she was sure of it. Danielle knew, just as certainly as she knew the address of her house, that Blake was lonely, that he needed her, and that only he, or a man like him, would be worthy of her.

Danielle sighed with exasperation, realizing that sometimes she was a little absurd. Yet, as she brushed her hair, she couldn't help thinking that on the deepest levels of life everything was exactly as she imagined it. Blake certainly wasn't, and could never hope to be, Stephen de Blois. But on the other hand, wasn't he the twentieth century equivalent of that great knight, riding an airplane instead of a horse, wielding machine guns instead of a sword?

Danielle wanted to write Blake a letter to invite him to tea with her when he next came to Paris, but she believed one shouldn't throw oneself at men. If they want you badly enough, they'll come for you, and if they don't, they shouldn't have you anyway.

I can wait forever, she thought as she stood and threw the towel onto her bed. Then she walked naked to the dresser, opened a drawer and selected the silk underthings that she intended to wear that evening.

Duncan spotted her at the officers' mess in the hospital in Paris. It was a large, poorly-lit room with high ceilings and paint peeling everywhere, and she sat alone at a table alongside a wall, sipping a cup of tea. She had on her brown wool coat and matching beret.

He thought he'd say hello to her and thank her for driving him to the dressing station in the ambulance, realizing all the while that he was being a hypocrite; if he hadn't found her attractive, he probably wouldn't make the effort.

He lifted his cup and saucer with his good arm and carried them toward her table. His face was still bandaged, and the pain from the bullet that had been removed from his leg made him limp. He knew he must look a mess, but he felt himself attracted to this young woman. And after fighting for his life in that trench, walking up to a woman and talking with her didn't seem quite as hazardous as it had before.

"Hello there," he said, stopping at her table.

She looked up and smiled sleepily. "Hello."

"I don't suppose you recognize me in this get-up." He pointed to the bandage on his face.

"Have we met?"

"Yes, but we haven't been introduced. You took me for a ride a few weeks ago in your lovely ambulance. I'm Duncan Hunter."

"I'm Catherine Hawkins," she replied. "Well, it's nice to see you up and around. Care to sit down?"

"Love to."

He sat opposite her and gazed at her face, thinking she was even prettier close up. There was something about her that he thought marvelously exciting, something besides the shining auburn hair, the eyes that were so dark against the pale skin of her face, the firm fullness of her figure.

"Where did I pick you up?" she asked.

"In Lorraine. Night of November 15."

"I recall that an American unit was raided around then, and we brought back quite a few loads. I imagine it must have been pretty terrible."

"Strangely enough," he replied, "it really wasn't. Everything was happening so quickly that I didn't have time to think about it. I suppose it's more terrible now, in my memory, than it was when it was happening."

"I never thought of it that way," she said, "but of course it would have to be like that, wouldn't it?"

Duncan nodded. "I suppose . . . How long have you been driving an ambulance?" he asked.

"Seven months."

"I drove an ambulance for the French, too. I was thinking of that the night you drove me to the dressing station—how I'd been the driver so many times, and suddenly I was back with the wounded."

She looked at him searchingly, and he noticed that her eyes were vaguely oriental. "I don't remember," she said. "Perhaps another driver brought you back. A number of us were in that sector then."

"I'm sure it was you."

She shrugged and pushed her teacup aside. "Anything is possible," she said. "You say you drove an ambulance for the French?"

"Yes."

"Which unit?"

"289th."

"Was the 289th in the Somme?"

"We sure were."

She looked down at the table, where she was toying with the handle of the teacup. "My husband died on the Somme," she said. "He was with the Thirty-sixth Ulster." She raised her eyes. "Do you remember driving back any men from the Thirty-sixth Ulster?"

He shook his head. "No, I don't."

She reached into the pocket of her coat. "I have a picture of him here. Would you take a look at it—just on the chance?"

"Sure."

She took out a leather wallet, extracting a photograph which she handed to him. He held it up to the light and saw a hale and jolly-looking fellow. That was exactly the kind of man she should have married, he thought. They'd have had a grand old time eating fabulous meals and raising children, but instead he had fallen in the mud of the battle on the Somme River, and she was driving ambulances in Lorraine.

"No," he said, handing the photo back. "I don't remember him."

She tried to smile. "Just thought I'd try."

"It's hard to keep track of the faces. I'm sure you know that."

"Yes—it was silly of me." She tucked the photograph into the wallet and laid the wallet beside the ashtray. "I see that you're married," she said, glancing down at his wedding ring.

"That I am," Duncan sighed.

"It's decent of you to wear your ring," she said. "Many men come to France and put their rings in their pockets because they don't want the French girls to know they're married."

"I don't blame them," Duncan told her. "The war has turned everything upside down. When people are facing death and destruction at every turn, they shouldn't be rebuked for taking whatever little pleasure comes their way."

She shrugged. "I don't know what to think about that. The war is beastly and everybody is beastly. I don't hate the Germans and I'm sure the Germans don't hate me. Sometimes I think that this war is the beginning of the end of the world." She touched her hand to her cheek, aware that she'd become more emotional than she liked to be with people whom she barely knew. "I think it's time I left," she said.

"Can I see you again?" Duncan asked.

"What for?" she asked, surprised.

"To talk like this, have a drink or two, perhaps go to the theatre."

She hesitated. "I don't really know how you'd get in touch with me. My unit moves around a lot. We're the 349th Ambulance. Right now we're in Saint-Étienne, but who knows where we'll be next week?"

"I'll find you."

She smiled. "I wonder what you'll look like without all those bandages?"

"Probably worse than you can imagine."

"I doubt that. Well . . . I hope you get well quickly. And if I don't see you again, good luck."

He stood as she did. "I'll see you again," he said.

She smoothed the front of her coat and adjusted the hat on her head. "Good-bye, Duncan. Godspeed."

"Same to you, Catherine."

She turned and walked away, her head half covered by the fur collar of her coat. He sat at the table again, looking at her cigarete butt in the ashtray. He glanced up and watched as she left the dining room. And then there were just the heads of the officers and nurses, the buzz of their voices, and the long, gray afternoon.

14

Captain Joseph Harrington sat behind the desk in his command post bunker, smoking a cigar his wife had sent him from Milwaukee, and reading a directive from headquarters about the dangers of venereal disease. Harrington didn't understand why venereal disease was such a big problem, considering there weren't any women around. He wished headquarters would spend their time figuring out a way to do something about the cooties, which were driving him crazy.

He reached down and scratched his groin, when suddenly he heard a great hullabaloo in the trench outside. Putting on his helmet and drawing his forty-five, he went out into the trench and saw half the company cheering and jumping up and down.

"What the hell's going on here!" he boomed.

They all stopped and looked at him, suddenly self-conscious. Parting ranks, they let a short soldier pass between them. Harrington's eyes lit up when he saw who it was.

"It's Sam Bell!" Harrington said. "Sam Bell is back!"

Bell stopped in front of him and saluted smartly. They'd given him a new uniform at division headquarters and he looked ready to go on parade.

"Private Sam Bell reporting back for regular duty, sir."

Harrington returned his salute. "Well, good for you, Bell! Glad to have you back! Come on into my office for a bit, and then you can get back to your platoon."

"Yes, sir."

Harrington entered first, and Bell followed him.

"Have a seat, Bell."

Bell sat on the rickety wood chair in front of the desk and Harrington lowered himself into his own chair.

"What the hell happened to you, anyway?"

"They took me prisoner, sir," Bell replied, grinning.

"How'd they do that?"

"Don't ask me. One minute I was here, and the next thing I was over there with the Fritzies. Boy, what a bunch of silly bastards they turned out to be. They put me in a room all alone with an officer, and I just jumped out the window and never stopped running until I crossed into the French lines day before yesterday. I spent all day yesterday telling the fellers up at division about it and they're gonna put it in a little book of some kind. So you can read all about it if you want to—I don't think I could go through the whole rigmarole again so soon."

"There's just one thing I wanna know," Harrington said. "How'd you make it across no-man's-land?"

Bell waved his hand in the air. "Twern't difficult at all. First of all, I went over at night when visibility was piss-poor. Second of all, I was coming from a direction where the Germans weren't looking. Third, they weren't expecting anything, so they didn't see anything." He paused and smiled. "Sir, you gotta get up pretty early in the morning to catch Sam Bell."

Harrington scratched his craggy nose. "Bell, I think I'm gonna make you a private, first class."

Bell beamed. "That's real kind of you, sir."

"I'll have the orders cut in the morning. You'd better have the stripes on your sleeves by 1200 hours tomorrow, or else. Glad to have you back. You may report to your platoon."

"Yes, sir."

Bell stood, saluted, left the bunker, and was greeted by his pals in the trench outside.

"I'm gonna be a Pfc," Bell said, elated. "Anybody got any whisky?"

Murphy draped his arm over Bell's shoulder. "We got a new man name of Stearns, and he's making some."

"Out of what?"

"Potato peels and other shit."

Bell spat. "Yuk."

"Well, what you think whisky is? It's only garbage juice that's been fermented and distilled."

"I guess so," Bell said. "I suppose the first thing I should do is report in to Lieutenant Hunter."

Private White piped up, "Oh—he ain't here."

"Where's he at?"

"In a hospital someplace. He got cut up in the raid. We lost about a third of the company."

"Did Tucker make it?"

"Shit," said Private Conroy, "you can't kill Tucker. That son-of-a-bitch is too mean to die. I saw him a-fightin' and a-pitchin' in that trench—I tell you it was a sight that would strike fear into the heart of the devil himself."

"Where's he at?" Bell asked.

Murphy chuckled. "With Private Stearns—where else?"

The Spad engine purred smoothly and Blake Hunter looked over the side at the Third Aviation Instruction Center at Issoudun, France. It was early in the morning and he'd just taken the plane up. He'd told them he just wanted to get a little practice above the field— and boy, were they going to be in for a surprise.

He'd eaten nothing for breakfast, preferring to sip only some water. He'd planned this flight for days, adding and rejecting new elements, and now he had it memorized completely and was ready to go. If Eddie Rickenbacker could get a transfer for buzzing a French soccer game, Blake thought he should get one even faster for buzzing the Aviation Instruction Center itself.

Well, here goes, Blake thought, pushing the stick forward. The engine howled and the Spad began its dive. He pulled out the throttle all the way and balanced the wings. The cold December wind took an end of his white silk scarf out of his leather jacket and made it trail a few feet behind him. He felt the wings strain against the struts and wires that held them in place. Directly below him was the headquarters build-

ing, where the staff members were sitting down to
begin their morning's work. He saw a few people come
out of buildings and look up into the sky, pointing at
him, no doubt wondering what in the hell he thought
he was doing.

The headquarters building came closer, and he
pulled the stick back at the last moment, certain that
if he'd waited two more seconds he would have put
one of his wheels through the roof. The Hispano-Suiza
engine whined as the Spad climbed into the sky, and
Blake looked behind him, seeing people pouring out
of the headquarters building and the other buildings
nearby. He continued to rise, performed a slow back
flip, and then pushed the stick forward again, diving
down at the building for his second pass.

The people in front of the building crowded around
and looked up at him, and in the final moments of the
dive he saw panic on their faces as they scattered in all
directions. He nearly touched the ground in front of
the building, then pulled back the stick and climbed
out again, his wing struts screaming and the Hispano-
Suiza engine snarling like an angry lion. Upward he
soared, chuckling to himself at the memory of the
men's faces.

Looking down at the road, he saw a truck convoy.
That hadn't been part of his plan, but he thought he'd
take advantage of it anyway. Easing the stick forward,
he dived down at the convoy, thinking how easy it
would be to strafe it if it had been an enemy convoy.

On the road, the driver of the first truck blew his
horn, but Blake kept diving. "Blow it out your ass,"
Blake muttered. The first truck drove off the road into
a ditch, the second truck followed it, and the third
truck stopped cold. Blake pulled out of the dive, skim-

ming the tops of the other trucks, and then banking to the side, dipping dangerously low over the gas tanks where the aviation fuel was stored. He zoomed toward the racks where new planes were stored, their noses down and tails high in the air.

He zipped over the tops of the stacked planes and then buzzed the operational planes lined up in ranks on the ground. Pilots and mechanics ducked underneath them, shaking their fists and cursing. Blake laughed as he pulled back his stick and took the Spad into the sky once more. This would be his last pass, the one for good measure. Then he'd land and report to Major Spaatz, telling him there was something wrong with the plane he'd taken up. He was sure Spaatz would take the hint.

Banking to the side, he dropped out of the sky. He looked sideways and it was as though the Spad were on a swing, looping down out of the clouds, heading for the headquarters building. The grounds and runway were filled with men running in all directions, probably unsure whether they would be safer in the buildings or out in the open. "You're safe no matter where you go," Blake said. "I won't hit you."

He swung over the building, the men flattening themselves on the ground again, and pointed the nose of the plane in the direction of headquarters, pulling back the stick and roaring toward the blue sky again. At five thousand feet he leveled off, circled a few times, and then began his descent. The wind was steady and he brought the Spad down with textbook precision. His left wheel touched down, and a split second later his right wheel also hit the ground. Pushing down his flaps, he coasted along the runway—and felt marvelous. The Spad had done just what he'd wanted it to do, and he hadn't made one mistake. Sometimes he even impressed himself with his flying skill.

The Spad came to a stop. He switched off the engine and unbuckled himself from the seat. Crowds of men from all parts of the aviation center ran toward him. He climbed out of the Spad and jumped to the ground.

The mechanics arrived first and looked at him as though he were crazy, but they didn't say anything because he was an officer and they were enlisted men. Lieutenant Donald Hudson, a young ace who was skinny as a sparrow, was the first officer to arrive.

"What happened up there?" he asked, greatly agitated.

"Something wrong with the Spad," Blake said. "Nearly killed myself. Lost complete control for awhile. Scary as hell."

Hudson climbed into the cockpit as the others crowded around with their questions. Blake told them the same story, that he'd had trouble with the Spad.

Hudson popped his head out of the cockpit. "I can't find anything wrong in here."

A corporal from the orderly room pushed his way through the crowd. "Major Spaatz wants to see you right away, sir!" he told Blake.

"That's where I'm heading."

The pilots and students followed Blake across the runway, chattering about how the Spad had nearly taken the roof off a building, or how they'd almost been crowned by one of the wheels.

"The plane's in bad shape," Blake said to them.

Blake entered the orderly room, and the sergeant pointed to Major Spaatz's office. When Blake opened the door Spaatz was sitting behind his desk, writing furiously. Spaatz stopped when he saw Blake and held up his hand. "Don't say a word!" he commanded.

"But, sir, I—"

"I said don't say a word!"

"Yes, sir."

Blake stood at attention. Spaatz continued to write, looking down at his desk. "I'm going to give you the transfer you've been asking for," Spaatz said. "You can pick it up at Sergeant Murray's desk at 1200 hours today. By 1230 hours I want you to be off this aviation center, lock, stock, and barrel. If you're still here after that time, I'm going to have you arrested. That is all. Get out of here and don't ever let me see your face again."

"Yes, sir."

Blake did an about-face and marched out of the office, his expression sober. But outside on the runway, he threw his long-eared flying hat into the air and laughed in triumph.

At five o'clock that evening Blake was in the lounge of the Crillon Hotel in Paris, moderately drunk. He was talking to a girl named Peggy who evidently knew everybody who'd ever left the ground, and gradually he began to feel maudlin, realizing that throughout his brief adulthood he'd spent most of his days risking his life for no reasonable purpose, and most of his nights trying to lure tarts like Peggy into bed.

"What's wrong with you, Blake?" she asked, grabbing his shoulder and shaking it, nearly tearing off his lieutenant bar. "I've never seen you like this. If you don't get happy I'm going to leave."

He shrugged. "Go ahead and leave. Who gives a shit?"

"Well!" she said, widening her eyes. "I never!" She stood, picked up her drink, and staggered to the next table, where she collapsed on a young captain's lap. "Hello there," she said. "I don't believe I know your name."

He pinched her behind. "If you can't remember my name, Peggy dear, then I suppose I should be greatly insulted."

She squinted at him and looked puzzled. "First of all, stop pinching me, and second, have you ever worn a mustache?"

"Never."

"Are you sure we know each other that well?"

"If I mentioned the Trafalgar Hotel in London, would that help?"

She touched her finger to her nose. "The Trafalgar Hotel in London?" Then her jaw dropped. "Oh my goodness!"

He smiled. "I knew that would jog your memory."

"Oh my word!"

"Would you like a drink?"

"I think I'd better have one, yes, thank you. Do you mind if I sit on a chair?"

"No, of course not."

She slid off his lap and wheezed as she dropped onto a nearby chair. By now she had forgotten all about Blake, who sat only a few feet away, drinking a glass of dark rum and feeling sorry for himself.

He was in one of those moods where he thought nobody cared about him. These moods overtook him at the most unlikely times, such as today when he'd

finally obtained the transfer he'd wanted for months.
Normally he was confident that he was liked and
admired, but when the black clouds gathered over
his soul he felt isolated and miserable. He wasn't even
sure of Duncan's loyalty; he'd seduced one of Duncan's
girlfriends a long time ago. And his "best friend,"
Franklin DeWitt? Not only was Franklin dead, but
their friendship had ended badly. It was a memory he
rarely allowed into his consciousness, but now he was
too drunk and depressed to close it out. He had vied
with Franklin for Brooke Madigan, although he hadn't
really been in love with her. No, it was more a matter
of not being able to believe that someone like Franklin, who was a writer, hardly a dashing figure—or
that anyone, for that matter—could successfully woo
a girl away from him. But Franklin had not only been
successful with Brooke but had also turned out to be
a damned good pilot, which had earned him a share
of the limelight that Blake had always enjoyed solo.

Then, when Blake's sister Allison had turned up
pregnant, probably, although not necessarily, by
Franklin, Blake had gone crazy. Oh, it had been Allison's fault as much as Franklin's. Allison was one of
the most decent-hearted people Blake knew, but she
wasn't exactly a prude and had initiated an affair with
Franklin at a time when Blake had been keeping
Franklin and Brooke at odds with each other. But
Blake had really lost his head about it, demanding
that Franklin divorce Brooke and marry his sister. He
had even goaded Franklin into an airfight, one-on-one,
which had ended tragically when the Germans had
spotted them and zoomed in for the kill. Both Franklin and Bulldog Teeter, who had tried to stop the
fight between the two friends, had been shot down.

Blake had written to Brooke to tell her of Franklin's heroic death at the hands of the Germans. He had by then realized that his friendship with Franklin meant more than his own ego. But it had been too late. After sending the letter off to Brooke, he hadn't once bothered to contact her. He had been too . . . ashamed? No, he told himself, he wasn't to blame for Franklin's death. But it was a touchy subject and he couldn't bring himself to face Brooke. He hadn't even been in touch with Allison, who had gone back to the States to have her baby. Allison knew him too well. And she had known of his enmity for Franklin. . . .

I'm not a good person, Blake thought. I'm selfish and crazy. The only one I ever think about is myself. Deep down I'm either a stupid killer or a bloody fool. Life is a bottomless pit of misery, and we have no hope of climbing out.

Suddenly the image of Danielle Giraud entered his mind, and the bottomless pit became invested with a golden glow. She's a special person, Blake thought, not like the sluts and tramps who hang around here. She's like the morning of a summer day, and these women here are like winter nights in the Arctic.

He wondered what she was doing right then. He looked at his watch, and it was around six thirty. She's probably at home, preparing to have dinner. Should I call her . . . ?

Now the great internal wrestling match began. One part of him said to call her; the worst thing she could do was hang up on him, which would be regrettable but not fatal. And the other part of him said to stop, that she was too fine for him, that he shouldn't meddle with such a person.

As always, his selfishness won out. Rising from the

table, he smoothed the front of his jacket and adjusted his Sam Browne belt, then walked unsteadily toward the lobby, where he would make the call.

Danielle sat in her room, looking through an illustrated society magazine, when Georgette knocked lightly on the door and entered.

"Telephone call for you, *mademoiselle*. A Lieutenant Hunter."

Danielle put down her magazine. "Lieutenant Hunter you say?"

"Yes, *mademoiselle*."

"I'll take the call in here."

Georgette closed the door, but Danielle sat for a moment, looking at the telephone on the table nearby. So he's finally calling, she thought. She'd known that sooner or later he would. She picked up the phone. "Blake?"

"Danielle?" he said. "Hello."

"Hello."

"I'm drunk."

"I think I can discern that."

"How are you?"

"All right. What about you, other than the fact that you're drunk?"

There was a long pause. "I shouldn't have called."

"Why not?"

The phone went dead in her ear. She tapped the bar and got the operator, who said she had no idea what had happened to the call or where it had originated. Danielle hung up the phone and in two seconds figured out where he must have called from: the Crillon. Then she reasoned that he had called her for help, but had passed out or been cut off.

I'll go to the Crillon, she thought, standing and heading toward her closet. Blake needs me.

Blake staggered back to the lounge, feeling worse than ever. He knew now that he shouldn't have called. He was a drunken lout, a known womanizer, and he should leave Danielle alone. She was special. Besides, she was the daughter of a French general, and French generals had notoriously bad tempers. It was a major miscalculation. He shouldn't have made the telephone call, especially not when he was drunk. He should just go to bed and sleep it off.

He crossed the lounge, bumping into some friends on their way out. Officers shook his hand and girls kissed his cheek. The band was playing a lively tune and a bunch of drunks were trying to dance to it. He spotted a vacant table for two in a corner and collapsed onto one of the chairs.

"It's all really too ridiculous," he mumbled as he looked around him. He was sinking lower every moment. Reaching into his jacket pocket, he took out a cigarette and lit it up.

"What's wrong, Blake?" The voice was that of a drinking pal who noticed Blake's long face as he passed by.

"It's all too ridiculous," Blake replied.

"You take life too seriously, Blake. It's just whisky and whores and the dawn patrol—not too bad a party, if you ask me."

The officer slapped him on the back and staggered off. Blake knew he was right, but sometimes it was difficult not to take life seriously. When you call a girl like Danielle Giraud and act like a drunken fool . . . Blake hated doing anything that would make him look

bad. He wanted to be splendid and perfect and gallant, like the young men in the cigarette ads. The
young men in the cigarette ads didn't get drunk and
call society girls for the hell of it.

Blake saw a waiter and flagged him down to order
a glass of rum. He should have visited his brother
today, he told himself as he waited for his drink. But
he'd felt a greater need for the gang at the Crillon,
these rowdy, drunken men and giddy, promiscuous
ladies. This war has ruined me, he thought. I was a
decent young man before I came to France, wasn't I?
But he knew deep down that he hadn't been.

The waiter brought his drink, and he gulped half
of it down. He felt very tired. He stubbed out his
cigarette and was tempted to loosen his tie . . . but no,
that wouldn't look very nice, so he just cradled his
head in his arms and closed his eyes.

She entered the noisy lounge and couldn't see him
anywhere. She was advancing farther into the room to
scan the tables when someone grabbed her arm.

"Siddown and have a drink, sweetheart!"

"Take your hand off me, please."

"Sorry about that, sweetheart."

She shook loose and then spotted him, passed out
at a table in a dark corner. She nearly burst into tears
at the sight of him, sprawled over the table, a war
hero like that, all alone. Well, he wouldn't be alone anymore. She pushed determinedly through the crowds
and sat on the chair opposite him, placing her hand
over his.

He cocked open an eye. Then, seeing her, he raised
his head. "Danielle!"

"How do you feel?" she asked.

"Um . . ." He rubbed his face and smoothed down his hair. "I'm not sure. What are you doing here?"

"I was worried about you, so I came to see you."

"I don't think that was such a great idea . . ."

"I think it's a good thing I did come. Have you any idea what time it is?"

"Sometime in the afternoon, I imagine."

"That's correct," she said, "and in case you've forgotten, it's a beautiful day. All the stores have their Christmas decorations up and the sky is blue. I think you need some fresh air. Besides, I can't stand this place."

He groaned. "Actually I don't think I can stand this place much more, either."

"I have a marvelous idea," she said. "Let's take a carriage through the Bois de Boulogne."

"Isn't it too cold?"

"Nonsense! It'll clear out your head, which I'm sure is just what you need."

He stared at her. "Have you really come here just to see me?"

"Of course," she said. "Listen, Blake, we both know that our meeting a few weeks ago was no random occurrence. We also know that one day you would have called and I would have come to you. We are not ordinary people, Blake, and that is why we are together."

Blake pondered that as he rose unsteadily to his feet. She took his arm, and together they walked toward the door.

2

15

IT was the first of March, 1918. The bootsteps of Field Marshal Hindenberg and General Ludendorff echoed along the marbled corridors of the Imperial Palace in Berlin. The two old warlords were in perfect step, as though on parade. They said nothing and looked straight ahead as they moved along. Guards lining the corridors gazed with admiration and wonder at the two foremost commanders in the German army.

Hindenberg and Ludendorff halted in front of Kaiser Wilhelm's door. Ludendorff bowed slightly from the waist, indicating that Hindenberg, the senior officer, should go first. Hindenberg opened the door and entered the office. Ludendorff followed and took his place at Hindenburg's side again. Together they marched toward the desk and saluted.

The kaiser returned their salute and told them to

sit down. He looked gravely at them, his chest shining with medals and decorations. "Gentlemen," he said, "our hour is at hand." He paused as if for dramatic effect, while Ludendorff and Hindenberg looked significantly at each other. "Gentlemen," the kaiser continued, "the Bolshevik government of Russia and my government have finally, after much negotiation, reached agreement over an armistice. It will be formally signed during the next two or three days. This means that the time we've been waiting for has at last arrived. Now we can transfer troops from east to west and smash the Allies into the sea. It has been a long, cold winter, gentlemen. We and the enemy have been at a stalemate. These have been difficult months for soldiers such as ourselves. But now God is smiling on us. Within two weeks I want you to launch our major offensive in the West. The three of us have labored over the details of this operation throughout the winter, and as far as I'm concerned, there is nothing further to discuss. Put the plan in motion, and win the war for Germany. That is all. You may go."

It was night at the AEF Headquarters at Chaumont. General Pershing sat behind his antique wooden desk, his glasses low over his nose, plowing through his paperwork, when there was a knock on the door.

"Come in?"

The door opened and First Lieutenant Everett De-Witt entered. "You wished to see me, sir?"

Pershing took off his glasses and rubbed his eyes. "Have a seat, Everett."

"Yes, sir."

Pershing pushed his glasses back up his nose and set his paperwork aside. His office was large and sparsely furnished; a six-foot map of Europe tacked to one of the walls seemed to dominate the room. One electric light bulb illuminated the map, another lit the top of Pershing's desk.

"I'm having another one of those little problems that you're so good with," Pershing said. "This time it's a legal problem. I know you were studying to be a lawyer when we declared war. That's why I wanted to talk to you. Here's the problem. Some of our soldiers are getting into trouble with the French civilian authorities, and nobody in the Judge Advocate's Corps can say for sure who has jurisdiction, us or the French. I guess you probably realize that our people in the Judge Advocate's Corps aren't up to this kind of thing. It's way the hell over their heads, the legal precedents and all, and I think we should get some professional civilian help. Do you think you can find somebody?"

"Sure," said Everett. "My uncle is a partner in a Wall Street law firm. I'm sure he can recommend somebody. He might even come himself."

"I'll make him a colonel if he does," Pershing said smilingly.

There was a knock on the door.

"Come in."

The door opened and Major Redford entered the office. "Something just came up, sir, and I thought I'd better tell you right away." He glanced at Everett. "Am I interrupting anything important?"

"Not at all," said Pershing. "Pull up a chair and have a seat."

Redford, a tall rangy man who was an intelligence officer, sat beside Everett. "Sir," he said, leaning forward, "the Germans have just changed all their codes."

"When did you find this out?"

"Shortly after midnight, sir."

Pershing frowned and looked at his watch. It was nearly half past midnight. "I wonder what they're up to . . ."

"If we piece this together with information we've received about troop movements behind their lines, and the fact that the British have seen an unusual number of German officers observing the troop movements . . . well, it would seem that the Germans are planning an offensive, probably in the British sector."

"The French sector," said Everett, "is weaker. I think that when they come, it'll be through the French sector."

"My guess," said Pershing, "is that they'll try to split the French and British apart and drive through to the channel ports. I have a feeling we'll know for sure soon enough. Well, Everett, I think I'm finished with what I had for you. Ralph, would you stay for a few minutes, please?"

Redford remained in his chair and Everett rose, gathered up his papers and walked out of the office. He didn't bother to salute because he was in and out of there so much it didn't make sense anymore.

16

First Lieutenant Duncan Hunter sat in the first class compartment of a train and looked out the window as it pulled into the Gare de l'Est. He had wrangled a few days leave in Paris and was overjoyed to have a respite from the trenches. He intended to spend his time taking it easy and trying to find the ambulance driver, Catherine Hawkins.

He hadn't had much chance to look for her since he was discharged from the hospital, and although women ambulance drivers sometimes showed up near the trenches, she was never among them and none of the ones he talked with knew her. Sometimes he figured she'd returned to England.

He looked out the window at the people rushing about alongside the train, and noticed that at least half of them were in uniform. Everybody's a soldier now, he thought, and had to admit to himself that he couldn't imagine the world being any other way anymore.

The train stopped. He took his little cloth satchel from the overhead webbing and waited until two old gentlemen left the compartment. Then he followed them out, made his way down the aisle and debarked from the train.

The station was noisy and filled with people hurrying about. He walked swiftly away from the platform and into the main station, looking forward to seeing Blake, who was supposed to be getting a short leave around this time, too. Everyone was trying to get some time off; they all knew that something big was in the air, and once it got underway no one would be going anywhere for a long time.

Suddenly he thought he saw her. Freezing in his tracks, he stared at the woman in the dark brown coat across the vast floor. Duncan blinked and his heart began to race. Was that her, or was he imagining things? A path cleared in the crowd and he was able to see her again. He was astounded—the woman looked just like Catherine Hawkins.

"Catherine!" he shouted, waving his satchel in the air.

But many people were shouting and waving things, and the woman didn't turn around. Duncan moved toward her, weaving his way through the crowd. I hope that's her, he thought. What an extraordinary thing it would be if it was.

Duncan didn't know it, but the Germans had launched their huge attack that morning, pouring sixty-two divisions into the British sector on a forty-three-mile front between Arras and La Fere. The attack had been preceded by the most extensive artillery barrage in the history of the world, and the fog and mist were so terrible that the British couldn't see the Germans until the Germans were right on top of them.

The German offensive was making brilliant progress, and the kaiser had every right to be elated as he stepped from his Mercedes-Benz in a wooded area near the town of Laon. In front of him, wreathed with camouflage netting, was the famous Krupp seige cannon. It was monstrously long, with an effective range of eighty miles. The kaiser had come to Laon today to watch the gun fire a few shells at Paris.

Everything was in readiness for the kaiser's visit. The major in charge of the gun saluted and bowed. The Krupp factory officials shook his hand. The kaiser, followed by his entourage, inspected the gun and its crew, asking numerous technical questions. It seemed unbelievable that an artillery piece could fire a shell at Paris from Laon with any reasonable degree of accuracy. When the kaiser's curiosity was satisfied, he told the major to open fire.

The kaiser was escorted to a bunker a few hundred yards away, in case the gun blew up. The gun was a new invention, temperamental, and no one was completely sure of what it might do. Moreover, its muzzle blast was earsplitting. The kaiser and his entourage huddled in the bunker, looking through narrow slits at the gun.

The crew loaded a gigantic shell and closed the breech. The major held the string in his hand and closed his eyes. The gun had been scientifically aimed by him and his men throughout the morning. He pulled the string and the shell exploded thunderously, wreathing the gun in clouds of smoke.

The shell rose twenty-five miles in the sky, and then began to drop toward Paris.

Inside the Gare de l'Est, Duncan pushed through the crowd toward the woman he thought to be Catherine Hawkins. She was struggling toward an exit, carrying two suitcases, and the closer he came the more certain he was that she was Catherine.

Only around twenty yards away now, he called out her name again. He saw her stop and look around. Now that he could see her full-face, he knew it was she. "Catherine!" he shouted.

Her eyes suddenly shone with recognition. He saw the beginning of a smile on her face as she took a step toward him. Elated, he surged toward her through the crowd.

At that moment the German artillery shell crashed into the Gare de l'Est and exploded. Huge columns came crashing to the floor and segments of the roof followed them down. Duncan saw Catherine's smiling face become a mask of terror. He pushed through the shrieking throngs and jumped on top of her as the debris began to hit the floor. Shielding her body with his, he buried his face in her hair and covered his head with his hands. People screamed hysterically and the floor trembled as immense chunks of concrete and marble slammed into it. Duncan and Catherine shivered against each other for a few moments, and then Duncan realized that there were no more explosions and no more debris falling. He opened his eyes and looked around.

All the electric lights were out and a thick fog of dust was everywhere. Broken columns and walls leaned in all directions, and people staggered in a daze among them. The only light came in long shafts through the holes in the roof. People wailed and screamed in every corner of the station.

"I think we're safe now," he said, getting off her.

She rolled over onto her back, raising her knees. "What happened?" she asked, slowly sitting up and looking at the devastation around them.

"German bomb of some kind."

"My God! We've got to help these people. . . ."

A Supreme Allied War Council was scheduled to be held in the town of Beauvais, about forty-five miles north of Paris, and General Pershing arrived early in the morning, accompanied by his staff. He was early for the meeting, so he visited the local cathedral, a fine specimen of thirteenth century Gothic architecture, and then went to the nearby Hôtel de Ville, where the meeting would take place. Marshal Haig, General Foch, General Pétain and Sir Henry Wilson were already there. They had to wait an hour before the arrival of Georges Clemenceau, who was the new premier of France, and Lloyd George, the prime minister of England.

A platform made from banquet tables was set up in the middle of the room, and on it were spread the appropriate maps. The meeting got underway with a discussion of the latest military situation. From all indications, it appeared that the German army was making great gains against the British.

After the British generals finished explaining their

situation, Clemenceau, the famed Lion of France, placed one hand on the map table and the other on his lapel.

"Gentlemen," he said, "I fear that we face the gravest days of this war, and that all the blood we have spilled will be for nothing if we fail to deal forthrightly with our problems. We're gathered here today to settle one very simple problem regarding the appointment of an overall commander for our military forces in Europe. It has been suggested that General Foch be given this appointment, providing we can all reach an understanding as to the nature of his authority and its legal basis. I believe it is crucial that we appoint an overall commander today, so that we can begin fighting as a unified force. Gentlemen, I needn't remind you that the duty of the foot soldier is to fight for his country, and the duty of his country's leaders is to make difficult decisions wisely and expeditiously. Does anyone care to comment on this matter?"

Lloyd George stepped forward. "We have had more than three years of this war," he said, "and we have not had unity of action during any of that time. During this last year we've had two kinds of strategy, one by Haig and another by Pétain, both different, and nothing was gained. Now recent events have stirred up the British people very much. The Germans must be stopped. History hangs in the balance here—make no mistake about it. It's late for us, but not too late to reap the benefits of unified action under one supreme commander. I should like to hear General Pershing's views on this matter."

All eyes turned to old Black Jack as he stood and faced them. Placing both his hands behind his back and squaring his shoulders, he said: "The principle of unity of command is undoubtedly the correct one for the Allies to follow. I do not believe it is possible to have unity of action without a supreme commander. I think the necessary action should be taken by this council at once. I am in favor of conferring the supreme command upon General Foch."

Everyone appeared to be in agreement over this matter, so the necessary resolution was drawn up. The leaders of each nation signed it, and as of that hour General Foch became Field Marshal Foch and commander in chief of Allied forces in Europe.

The next topic of discussion was the deployment of American troops in the present crisis. This time General Pershing made no objections, because he was aware that the situation was reaching critical proportions. He agreed to make himself and his men available to Foch, but with the proviso that American divisions be permitted to serve intact.

The meeting adjourned and the men returned to their respective military units or governments.

Meanwhile, in Paris, the first exodus of citizens began. People were beginning to believe that nothing could stop the Germans from capturing their city.

In a hotel room on the Rue Devosge, Duncan and Catherine lay in each other's arms. In the distance they could hear the faint sound of artillery barrages. He held Catherine tightly against him, relishing the firm curvaceous warmth of her body.

"You know," she said, "you remind me of my husband. He was built very much like you."

He sighed and rolled off her. Reaching to the night table, he picked up his pack of cigarettes.

"Did I just make you mad?" she asked.

He shrugged. "What's the point of talking about your husband now?"

"Because I'm thinking of him now. I'm not supposed to think about him when you're around?"

"If you must," he replied, lighting a cigarette and then passing the cigarettes and matches to her.

"I get so sick of men," she said wearily.

"You talk as though you know so many of them.'"

"No, but I'm sick of them anyway. You're all fine when you're being people, but when you're being men you're disgusting."

"Men aren't people?"

"Men are men. They're childish, selfish, and they grab you."

"You don't like to be grabbed?" he said, grinning.

"I don't like to be told that I shouldn't talk about my husband. I'll talk about him whenever I like. And if you don't like it, leave."

She took a cigarette, lit it, and handed the pack and matches back to him. He lay back and stared up at the dark ceiling, wondering what his platoon was doing. He should cut his leave short and get back to them.

"I wish this war would go away," he said, blowing smoke at the ceiling. "It's getting to be so grim."

"Yes," she replied. "It's strange how much the world has changed. When the war started everybody was so happy. It was all glory and parades. Now it's horror and funeral processions. Everybody feels so hopeless. If I didn't feel so hopeless myself, I'd never have gone to bed with you, Duncan. But I can't say no anymore. I don't care about anything."

Duncan was stung by the remark but reminded himself that Catherine was every bit a lady—one of the things he liked in her—and that under other circumstances she indeed would not have gone to bed with him on such short acquaintance.

"You must care about something if you keep driving for the French," he said.

"I just do it—I really don't think about it that much. But you still care about things, Duncan. I like that about you. You're actually optimistic. Of course, your country hasn't been through what my country has in this war. When America starts losing a half million men in a few days of fighting, I don't think any of you will be so optimistic, not even you."

Duncan shook his head in the darkness. "We're aware of the mistakes that the other countries have already made in this war, and we're not going to repeat them. All the other countries are tired and demoralized. Even the Germans, although they're making good progress now, are tired and demoralized. But the doughboys are raring to go. You should see my men, Catherine. They can't wait to get out there. And they're tough boys, crack shots with their rifles. They'd rather fight than eat. They follow orders to the letter and have a strong sense of camaraderie. God help the Germans when they run up against those crazy doughboys."

Catherine smiled. "You really like your men, don't you?"

"Yes, they're a helluva bunch. I didn't like them so much at first, but they're starting to grow on me."

"Edward used to like his men very much, too. He always wrote about them in his letters to me. Do you write about your men to your wife?"

"I don't write to her that often."

"Why?"

"We really don't have much of a marriage," he said. "We married when we were too young to realize what we were doing, and our parents really pushed us into it. It was a very advantageous marriage from our families' viewpoint. I have two little children, so the family name will live on."

"Tell me what she's like, Duncan. Does she look like me?"

"No."

"That's strange. I thought she might look like me, since you look so much like Edward. Sometimes, while you were making love to me there, I thought you *were* Edward. It was so strange."

"I have a theory," Duncan said, "and maybe it's derived from something I read once—that people really aren't the distinct entities they think they are, and that once you look beneath their superficial characteristics, their personalities all melt together into one fundamental being."

"God?" she asked.

"I'm not religious," Duncan replied. "I don't think much about God."

"Look, Duncan—it's getting light."

He too had noticed that the room had lightened while they'd been talking. "We'll have to leave pretty soon," he said, stubbing out his cigarette in the ashtray.

She rolled toward him, touched her body to his, and put out her own cigarette. "I'm going to miss you," she said, kissing his neck.

He wrapped his arms around her. "I'll miss you, too."

They kissed, squirming against each other. He was amazed at how magnificent her body felt. She was firm and strong. Her stomach was flat and her bottom all muscle. He rolled her onto her back, and they made love wistfully, knowing that soon they'd be parted.

17

IN A WOODED AREA not far from the front, General Ludendorff stood over his map table, trying to figure out what to do next. He looked like a little walrus, with his spiked helmet and droopy mustache, but he was considered the greatest military mind of the war, and it was widely known among the upper strata of German society that he was the power behind the throne, behind the *Reichstag,* and behind the army.

Although Hindenberg was nominally commander in chief of the army, in reality its commander was Ludendorff. Hindenberg was the mere figurehead. Ludendorff signed Hindenberg's name to orders without even bothering to ask permission.

Now Ludendorff had to figure out how to maintain the force of his offensive, which was clearly running out of steam. The British were falling back, but they weren't broken yet by any means. His strategic objectives in the offensive were to separate the British army from the French army, and then destroy the British. He'd accomplished neither objective and was forced to admit that thus far his great offensive was a failure, despite the impressive gains on the map.

And there were other problems. His infantry couldn't advance very rapidly through the destruction in front of them, and his artillery was even slower than the infantry. His transport was having great difficulty re-supplying the front over nonexistent roads.

Ludendorff gazed thoughtfully at the map. His aides looked at him respectfully, careful not to make any noise that might distract his great strategic mind. Among the aides was Major Karl Ritter von Beck who'd recently joined Ludendorff's staff after being released from the hospital. Beck had lost half his intestines, but was otherwise recovered from his wounds. He often visited the front lines for Ludendorff, and was among the few who realized that the great offensive had failed to attain its strategic objectives.

On the map Ludendorff saw a move that he thought might win him a victory. If he turned his armies around and headed for Paris, he might be able to capture it in two or three days. Then the French would probably surrender; if they didn't, at least their army would be greatly demoralized. He would ride into Paris on a white horse, and historians would inscribe his name on the page with all the great conquerors of history. Then he could wheel his army north and deal with the British once and for all.

As for the Americans, he didn't think they'd amount to much in this war. They'd declared war almost a year ago, and had still been unable to field an army. They were a hoax.

Ludendorff studied the map to see how to move on Paris. His eyes fell on the names of many obscure and unheard-of villages. Soon those sleepy villages, which had managed to stay free from harm for so long, would be ripped apart by the German war machine.

One of those villages was nothing more than a whistle-stop on the Paris-Nancy railroad line. It was located near the banks of the Marne River, and was called Château-Thierry.

Blake sat in the cockpit of his new Spad as it droned through the sky. His goggles were tight around his eyes and his white scarf flowed into the air behind him. Holding his stick tightly, he glanced around at the seven other planes from his squadron. They were all out on the dawn patrol, and the Marne River was below them.

Eddie Rickenbacker, in a plane up ahead, pointed down to the ground. Blake looked down and saw dots moving on the landscape. The Germans were up to something down there. There was heavy traffic on the roads. Were the Germans preparing an attack through this region?

They continued to fly along in an northwesterly direction. Visibility was good and there were no clouds. They'd report those peculiar enemy movements as soon as they returned to base. The people in intelligence would know how to evaluate the information.

Blake felt tired and bored. He hoped they wouldn't run into any German planes; his attitude toward fighting had changed greatly since he'd fallen in love with

Danielle Giraud. He had a gold locket with her picture in it stuffed into his breast pocket. They were planning to get engaged. He saw that he could have a happy life with her, and didn't want to get killed before it began.

The sky disappeared as he thought of Danielle. She was so lovely, like a dream come true. And she loved him back. She had given him her virginity and sworn to stand by him forever. Never had love been so sweet to him. Never had he known that he, a rowdy and wastrel, could fall so deeply in love. But it had happened, as miracles sometimes do.

He became aware that the formation in front of him was changing. Arms waved out of cockpits and a faint roaring sound could be heard above. Duncan snapped to his senses and looked up toward the sun. Small dark forms were there and he knew they must be German planes. Aero Squadron Ninety-four was about to be attacked.

Blake pushed his stick to the side to begin evasion tactics. His Spad veered away from the formation and away from the attack configuration of the Germans. He wondered how many there were. They surprised us, he rebuked himself. Maybe if I'd had my eyes open I would have seen them sooner.

He did a barrel roll through the air, and then another. He straightened out the Spad and pulled back the stick, climbing into the morning sky. He heard the first bursts of machine-gun fire; the battle was being joined. Looking up, he saw German planes swarming all around him and the other Spads from the Ninety-fourth. Bullets whistled through the air and Blake positioned his flaps so that he spun as he climbed. A spray of bullets hit the engine cowling and he saw a white German Fokker bearing down at him from above.

A white Fokker, Blake thought. Who's that? He pulled back his stick and did a back flip in the sky, diving down to earth again, but the white Fokker followed him. As Blake tried to get away he remembered that a famous German aviator flew a white Fokker, but he couldn't recall his name.

Bullets slipped through the fabric of his fuselage as he tried to out-maneuver the white Fokker. Pulling back his stick, he sent the Spad climbing again, but the Fokker stayed on his tail. Glancing around quickly, Blake saw that he and the other doughboy pilots were outnumbered by two or three to one. They had fallen into a trap like a bunch of rookies. They might never make it back to their lines with information about the suspicious German movements; in fact, this big German patrol was probably in the air to prevent any Allied planes from seeing or reporting what was taking place down there.

Blake climbed and dived repeatedly in an ever-diminishing circle, but the white Fokker stayed on his tail, firing machine guns. Blake twisted and turned, trying every escape tactic he knew, but still the German stayed after him. The most he could do was prevent the German from getting a straight, clear shot at him, but he couldn't get away.

He's very good, whoever he is, Blake thought as he gritted his teeth and worked his controls frantically. Another Fokker dove directly in front of him and he gave him a burst from his machine guns, shooting away a section of the Fokker's tail.

There was wild confusion in the air, with planes

diving all around each other. Two of the Fokkers crashed into each other and exploded into an orange ball of fire. The debris dropped to earth, and then an American plane was shot out of the sky.

The white Fokker stayed after him. How relentless he is, Blake thought, climbing into the sky once more. He hasn't thought of anything except me since this fight began. He must have spotted me from above and noticed that I wasn't paying any attention. He thought I'd be easy prey.

Then he remembered who flew a white Fokker. It was the flamboyant Captain Hermann Goering, one of Germany's top aces and a winner of the *Pour le Mérite*, Germany's highest award for valor. Goering is after me, Blake thought, a chill passing through him. How can I ever get away from a pilot like that?

He realized he had only one chance: to lure Goering into the path of an American plane that might be able to shoot him down. Goering was paying so much attention to him that he might not notice. The ruse might work.

Blake performed another loop through the air, while trying to lure Goering into the path of another Spad, but everyone was heavily engaged. Another American plane disintegrated in midair, the victim of a Fokker attack from behind. They're going to get us all, Blake thought. If I had been paying attention we might have avoided this.

He glanced back and saw Goering still behind him, trying to swing into position. Blake's stomach ached with nervous cramps as he struggled to get away. He knew he didn't have much time. Once a few of those Fokkers ganged up on him it would be all over.

Then he heard a new sound. Glancing up into the

sky, he saw more planes. Oh my God, he thought. Now we're finished for sure. There were about a dozen of them in vee formation, and they peeled off one by one as they began to dive. Goering's Fokker suddenly snarled. Blake turned around and was astonished to see Goering breaking off the fight and climbing into the sky. Blake looked at the new group of attacking planes again, and realized they were Nieuports— French planes. The French were coming to the rescue!

The French pilots sped down out of the sky, and the Fokkers scattered in front of them. Goering was already heading back to Germany and the other Fokkers would try to follow him. Blake scanned the sky and saw no more Fokkers menacing him. Heaving a sigh of relief, he pulled back his stick and began to climb, resolving to stay awake in the future.

It was evening when the Second Division arrived in the vicinity of Château-Thierry. The word had been passed down that a German offensive was imminent, and they were ordered to construct a defensive position in the area, with the American Third Division on their left and a brigade of French soldiers on their right.

The doughboys had no trench mortars or hand grenades. There were also critical ammunition shortages. But Foch really hadn't expected the green Americans to do much fighting. He was confident that the French soldiers ahead would stop the German drive, and then the Americans could move up quickly to plug holes in the line. There was plenty of everything closer to the front where it was needed.

The doughboys had bacon sandwiches for dinner and slept on the ground without benefit of shelters. It was a pleasant spring night and fresh buds could be smelled. By this time tomorrow there'd be trenches and latrines all over the place, but tonight they slept in untouched meadows and woods, underneath a half moon, and it made the farm boys among them wish they were home.

They were awakened at three o'clock in the morning by a thunderous shell barrage in the distance. Sitting up on the ground, they saw the eastern horizon glow with light. Earth tremors could be felt in the seats of their pants, and they realized that only an incredibly massive bombardment could be felt at such a great distance. Unable to sleep anymore, they stood and watched the bombardment, glad it wasn't the Second Division that was receiving the shelling.

A half hour later the Twenty-third Regiment was ordered to saddle up and move out. They formed double columns and marched off into the night. Their new mission was to fortify a forest area near the Marne River called Belleau Wood.

At four o'clock in the morning, General Pershing and his staff were gathered in the AEF conference room at Chaumont. They surrounded the map table and looked down as Lieutenant Everett DeWitt read the communication from Field Marshal Foch. It said that the French army in the south had been subjected to a fierce enemy bombardment beginning at 0300 hours, followed by a ground attack that tore the French front apart. The French were falling back in disarray, and the Germans were in hot pursuit. The only organized military units left to stop the Germans were the American Second and Third Divisions and the French brigade. Foch ordered Pershing to hold the Germans until French reinforcements could be brought to bear against the Germans.

DeWitt finished reading the communiqué. All the officers stared down at the map. They could see the line of German advance and the marks that indicated the positions of the Second and Third Divisions.

"We won't give them an inch," General Pershing said, his jaw set angrily. "I want the word passed to all commands in the Château-Thierry sector that they are not to fall back no matter what. They're under orders to stop the Germans and throw them back. All other echelons throughout the AEF will focus on giving the men of the Second and Third everything they need in the way of ammunition and equipment. We're finally going into action as an army in this war, and we are not going to lose our first battle. That would be unthinkable."

As Pershing continued his impromptu speech, Everett looked down at the map. He tried to imagine how he'd react if a few thousand Germans came running directly at him. Would he be able to stand and fight, or would he be a coward? At times like this, Everett wondered what he was made of. Sometimes he thought he ought to transfer to the front, so he could find out one way or the other.

In the dawn light, the sound of pick and shovel working the ground could be heard in Belleau Wood. The men were in high spirits, stripped naked to the waist and their helmets hanging from branches, as they wielded their tools and sang one of their favorite songs.

The Second Division was digging a ditch,
  parlez-vous;
The Second Division was digging a ditch,
  parlez-vous;
The Second Division was digging a ditch
To bury the kaiser
That son-of-a-bitch,
Inky dinky parlez-vous.

Duncan thought his men were amazing. They'd been told that the Germans were coming soon in force, and they had cheered like a bunch of kids going to a baseball game. They couldn't wait to get their hands on the Germans and pay them back for that sneak attack in November.

Duncan checked his platoon perimeter, feeling pride in his unit and men. They worked hard and happily for their few pennies a day and the lousy food they were given to eat. All of them were crack shots and understood open warfare. If his men ever received an order to attack, the Germans were going to be surprised. These big farm boys and city hoodlums would be awfully hard to stop once they got rolling.

A field kitchen showed up at six o'clock in the morning, and the men paused for a breakfast of scrambled eggs, bread and coffee. Then they went back to work and continued to build fortifications. Duncan set up his four machine guns at the edge of the woods, facing the fields ahead. If the Germans attacked, those machine guns would mean everything. A British officer had once told him that two German machine guns had held up a British regiment for a day. British bodies were heaped six feet high all over the field, and the German machine guns were overwhelmed only when they ran out of ammunition.

After digging the machine guns into the ground, the men felled trees and sawed logs to make roofs for the dugouts. They covered the roofs with alternating layers of dirt and stone. When they finished, a long narrow opening was all that could be seen in front of the bunkers. If Germans entered the field, the machine guns would slice them down.

Captain Harrington came by to inspect the positions and pronounced them fine. He joked with the men and slapped them on the backs.

"Hey, Bell!" he thundered, looking into a freshly dug trench. "What the hell are you doing down there, Bell?"

Bell, naked to the waist and covered with dirt, was digging at the bottom of his trench. "I'm digging a hole for grenades, sir."

"But we don't have any grenades, Bell."

"I'm talking about German grenades, sir."

"You're gonna let a German get close enough to throw grenades at you, Bell?"

Bell straightened up and grinned. "No, sir!"

"Then what the hell you digging the hole for?"

"Well, sir, maybe somebody else might let a German get that close."

"What!" Harrington thundered. "Are you trying to tell me that another good Second Division man would let a German through?"

"No, sir!"

"Then what the hell are you talking about, Bell?"

Bell wiped the top of his head with his hand. "I don't know exactly *how* it's gonna happen, sir, but if a hand grenade ever happens to fall into this trench, I'm gonna kick it right down this goddamn hole, where it won't be able to hurt anybody."

"Hey, that isn't a bad idea, Bell."

"I thought you'd think so once you knew what it was for, sir."

There was some shouting on the other side of the line, and Harrington looked up. The men were pointing at a road in the distance that was filling with marching figures. Harrington raised his binoculars and focused on the road. He saw men wearing the blue uniforms of the French army. They were evidently in headlong retreat from the Germans, who were no doubt hot on their heels.

"Lieutenant Hunter!"

Duncan jumped over the trench and marched toward Harrington.

"You'd better tell your men to get a move on. The French soldiers are coming yonder, and the Germans won't be far behind them."

Duncan and his men watched as the battered French soldiers moved back through their position. The French were bleeding and tattered, with haunted looks in their eyes.

Bel, ever the comedian, pointed toward the German lines. "Hey—the Germans are that way!" he shouted.

The French soldiers couldn't speak English, but it wasn't hard for them to figure out what he was saying. One gnarled old French sergeant looked down into the trenches and said in his language, "We've waited so long for you Americans, and now you've got here too late!"

The French and Americans talked back and forth to

each other, although neither could speak the other's language. But Duncan could speak both languages, and he knew what was going on. The French were angry at the Americans for staying out of the fight for so long, and the Americans were criticizing the French for retreating.

The processions of French soldiers continued throughout the morning, as the Americans worked to improve their fortifications. Then, around noon, the last French soldiers passed by, and the fields ahead became still. It was ominously quiet in the distance. Everybody figured that the Germans must be moving their artillery closer so they could go to work on the new American positions.

A rolling kitchen arrived at the trenches and the men were served beef stew with thick slices of French bread for lunch. Many of the doughboys, sobered now, wondered if this would be their last meal. When they finished they put their messkits away and took their positions in the trenches.

They looked at the field ahead, watching and waiting for the Germans to come.

On the French front near Le-Mesnil-Saint-d'Esperey, Catherine Hawkins stood behind her ambulance and smoked a cigarette as the wounded were carried in. Shells were bursting close by and people kept telling her to get down, but she didn't think a bomb would dare to fall on an ambulance girl.

She was no military strategist, but she knew the French had been falling back steadily for three days. Men rushed about, carrying rifles and bayonets, in the fields all around her. The front trenches were about a thousand yards from when she was, but the front trenches kept moving backward.

The medical corpsmen handed her the roster and she put it in her pocket.

"I'll be back in about an hour," she said.

"We probably won't be here in another hour," the corpsman replied.

"I'll find you wherever you are. Good luck."

"You too," he replied. "We're all gonna need all the luck we can get today. From what I've heard, the Germans have torn the entire front apart from top to bottom. I've even heard that they're attacking the Americans down south."

"The Americans, you say?"

"That's what I heard. We're finally gonna find out what those big-mouth bastards are all about." Suddenly the corpsman became embarrassed. "Sorry," he said, "I forgot you were an American."

"I'm not an American—I'm British."

"Sorry anyway."

The corpsman walked away. Catherine got into her ambulance and started it up. "Hang on back there," she said. "The ride might be a little bumpy."

She shifted into gear and drove away, thinking about Duncan and his Second Division on the southern end of the line. Deep in her heart, Catherine didn't think the American soldiers could hold. They didn't have enough experience to stop the Germans. No one could stop the Germans now. Even Paris was being evacuated.

She feared that the war was coming to an end, and Imperial Germany would be the victor. But more than that, she was afraid that Duncan would be killed. Oh,

Lord, she thought, don't let him die. I don't think I could bear to lose another one.

"You okay, ma'am?" asked a voice from the rear of the ambulance.

"I'm fine," she replied above the roar of the engine, wiping her eye with her knuckle. "How are you feeling?"

"I'm not sure."

"Try to get some rest. We'll be at the dressing station in a little while."

Catherine held the wheel with both hands as she sped toward the French rear lines. Columns of marching soldiers moved to the side of the road to make way for her, their faces suddenly lit as a defective shell burst high in the sky. It looked like a gigantic red gladiolus for a few moments. Then it simply disappeared.

How like a human life, she thought.

18

DUNCAN WATCHED THE FIELD ahead for signs of the advancing Germans. It had been quiet too long, and the Germans were long overdue. It wasn't like them to dawdle. They attacked like a hurricane and didn't let up unless you kicked their teeth down their throats. His eyeballs stung and he lowered the binoculars.

"See anything, sir?" asked Sergeant Tucker.

"Nothing."

"Somebody ought to send a fucking patrol down there to find out where the Fritzies are."

"I imagine quite a few patrols are out already."

"How come they didn't send us out on patrol?"

"I don't know."

"We deserved the chance, didn't we?"

"Yes, but there'll be lots more patrols. As soon as

this platoon is called to furnish one, you'll be the first to go."

"That'd be real nice of you, sir."

Duncan smiled inwardly as he raised his binoculars to his eyes. The childish antics of his men used to distress him, but now they amused him. They were like a bunch of big, happy kids, with all the exuberance and decency of kids and none of the deviousness of adults. That's the way they were when they were sober, anyway. When they were drunk, they were quite another matter.

"Look, sir!" said Private Sinclair.

"What is it?"

"At the edge of the woods . . ."

Duncan scanned the edge of the woods with his binoculars and saw a few dozen Germans. They were about eight hundred yards away and were probably the vanguard of an attacking force. Duncan wondered how many of them would charge. Would they just come pouring across the field or would they try some tricky tactical maneuvers? More of them came out of the woods, and they began to form into long ranks. They'll try to rush us, Duncan decided. They think they can run right over us.

"Man your posts!" shouted Captain Harrington.

There was bustling and rushing as men who'd been working and shoveling in the trench grabbed their rifles and took their positions. The machine gunners positioned themselves behind their guns, and the crews prepared to feed in the ammunition. They all wore their steel helmets low over their eyes and they were all certain they could stop the Germans.

Duncan walked through the trench, adjusting the positions of his men, and crawled into one of the ma-

chine gun dugouts. It was commanded by Corporal
Davidson, who sat behind the gun, working it from
side to side on its transverse mechanism. His field of
fire enfiladed most of the area before him, and Davidson licked his lips in anticipation of the action. The
other men fidgeted with the belts of ammunition. One
of them wiped the breech with a cloth that had a few
drops of oil on it. Duncan checked the gun's field of
fire and worked the bolt a few times. The machine gun
was brand new and had never been fired in warfare.

"Make every shot count," Duncan said. "Kill 'em all."

"Yes, sir."

Duncan crawled out of the dugout. As he was raising himself to his full height, he heard Captain Harrington's voice shouting: "Open fire!"

Duncan dashed to the side of the trench and looked
over it. The Germans were advancing across the field
in long gray ranks, and the Americans opened fire with
all they had. The well-trained German troops, instead
of hesitating, began to double-time with their rifles and
bayonets held high. Their lines remained straight but
many of them were falling to the ground.

"Keep firing!" Duncan yelled. "Keep firing!"

Halfway down the trench, Bell stood behind his
Springfield rifle and slowly squeezed off rounds. He
held one German in his sights, shot him, sighted another German, and shot him, too. He was amazed at
how simple it was. How can they charge like this? he
wondered. I wouldn't do it.

The machine gun dugouts were filling with gun-
smoke as the guns were fired in rapid bursts. The
belts of ammo zipped through the breeches, and when
the last bullet fired off a new belt was fed in. The
gunners swung their weapons back and forth, not

bothering to aim because their transverse mechanisms had been set to the correct height.

And then suddenly the Germans ranks stopped. They picked up their wounded, turned, and ran back to the shelter of the woods. Soon they were gone, and the field looked exactly as it had when the sun had dawned upon it that morning.

The men from Company B looked at one another in surprise.

"Gee," said Corporal Murphy, "I didn't think it'd be that easy."

"It's not over yet," Duncan said.

They heard booming sounds in the distance. Moments later they heard the whistle of incoming shells. Huddling in the bottom of the trench, they knew what would happen next. The big German 155 shells began crashing to earth, smoke and debris blocking out the sun. The ground heaved and men held onto their helmets. A direct hit in one of the trenches blew half of the Fourth Platoon into the air. Captain Harrington's voice could be heard above the explosions, shouting orders. The men hadn't had time to build an extensive network of bunkers, so all they could do was crowd beneath their unfinished fortifications and hope a shell wouldn't fall down on them.

"Goddamned Heinie pigs!" Bell shouted. "I hope they'll try to come up here again. Oh boy, do I hope they'll just goddamn try it."

Like most of the doughboys, Bell was itching for a fight. They'd been in France so long and had trained so hard, but the only action they'd seen had been that cold night in November in Lorraine. Most of the doughboys hadn't even had that. It was getting to be embarrassing, as well as frustrating.

Duncan cautiously crawled up the side of the trench and peered through his binoculars over the top, but he couldn't see anything through the smoke and haze. An explosion nearby made him duck his head.

"See anything, sir?" asked Private White.

"Not a thing."

Duncan got down in the trench with the rest of them. He figured that the Germans had thought they could overrun the doughboys without the necessity of an artillery bombardment, but they'd found out they were wrong. Now they were pouring out the artillery and would follow with an attack. Duncan suddenly became aware that there was something peculiar in the sky.

"Gas!" he yelled.

"Gas!" somebody repeated.

They ripped open their little canvas bags and pulled out their gas masks. Draping them over their faces, they placed the big rubber clips over their nostrils and took the air tubes into their mouths. Their vision was restricted and the masks were awkward, but at least they could breathe without having the gas eat holes in their lungs.

The artillery shells continued to fall. One landed near the parapet of the Second Platoon trench and caved in part of the wall, burying three soldiers. The others came to their aid and dug them out, as the trenches became covered by a yellowish-green mist.

Duncan climbed to the top of the trench again and looked through his binoculars. He thought he saw movement in the field, but it was difficult to be certain because the lenses of his gas mask inhibited his vision. Then he heard a machine gun volley from his left, followed by some random rifle shots. Straining his eyes, he was certain now that the Germans were advancing through the field, trying to gain a favorable position for their attack when the shelling stopped.

"Let's go!" Duncan shouted. "They're coming! Open fire!"

The men raised their heads as German shells fell all around them. Some of them coughed from gas that had crept into their masks. They positioned their rifles and opened fire at targets they could see only indistinctly. Whenever a shell landed nearby they all ducked, their fire easing for a few seconds.

Suddenly the shelling stopped. The doughboys knew the attack was coming, and fired wildly into the smoke and haze ahead of them. The machine guns sprayed back and forth, and soon, far out in the mists, the dark shapes of moving bodies could be seen. The wind was blowing the gas away, allowing the doughboys to see the German shock troops racing toward them across the field.

It seemed strangely quiet. After the shelling they'd had, the rifle and machine gun fire didn't sound like very much. But in the field the Germans were being cut down. They had about three hundred yards to go now to reach the doughboy trenches, but they were faltering. The doughboys had been trained in marksmanship, and their shots were piling up the German dead. The machine guns chopped them down. Unholy screams erupted in the field, and then the German attack broke. But instead of retreating to the line of woods in back of them, they swooped toward the woods on their flank, woods that were supposed to be held by other units of the Second Division.

Within minutes the Germans had fled the field, but

this time they didn't have time to take their dead and wounded with them.

The gas had blown away, and Sergeant Tucker tore off his mask. "After the bastards!" he shouted, going over the top.

Duncan watched in horror as the men followed Tucker. He took off his mask and yelled: "Wait a minute!"

But the whole platoon climbed out of the trench and followed Sergeant Tucker toward the woods. Duncan decided he couldn't stop them now; they were too excited and hungry for German blood. All he could do was go with them and try to provide leadership. He scrambled up the side of the trench and ran after them.

Sergeant Tucker held his rifle high in the air. "Come on, you sons of bitches!" he shouted. "Do you want to live forever?"

The other platoons in the company saw what the Second Platoon was doing and came out of their trenches to run after them. Even the machine gun crews broke down their weapons and fell in behind the main charge.

"Come back here!" Captain Harrington screamed. "Where do you people think you're going?"

Everybody heard him but pretended they didn't. Duncan ran past most of his men and got in front of them with Tucker. Muzzle blasts flashed in the woods as the Germans fired back. The other companies in the battalion saw that B Company was charging Belleau Wood, and they came up out of their holes, too, to join the charge. Soon Sergeant Tucker and Lieutenant Hunter were leading the entire battalion in an attack that no commander had ordered.

They charged into the woods like wild animals. The Germans hadn't had time to dig holes and fortify themselves, and they soon had the doughboys right in their laps.

This was the moment the doughboys had been waiting for, and they ripped into the Germans with relish, stabbing and slashing with bayonets, banking their rifle butts into German faces.

The Germans didn't know what hit them and fell back immediately. The doughboys stayed close, cutting the Germans down. The Germans retreated into the deepest part of the forest, and the doughboys went after them. Rifle shots rang out and machine gun positions were set up. The forest became littered with bodies. The Germans tried to pull together and launch a counterattack, but the doughboys fought them off from behind trees and fallen logs. When it became clear that the German attack would not succeed, the doughboys went after them, routing them once again, chasing them into gullies and killing them behind huge boulders.

In the late afternoon, the Germans obtained reinforcements and pushed the doughboys back a hundred and fifty yards, but then the doughboys received a new support battalion and hammered the Germans into another retreat. As the sun sank in the sky, no one could say for sure how much of the woods had been taken by the Americans and how much by the Germans.

Tripping over rocks and bumping into trees, carrying a German rifle and bayonet that dripped blood, Duncan fired through the darkening woods at Germans crossing a river up ahead. Duncan believed that he ought to get his men across the river by nightfall;

otherwise the Germans would fortify it by morning and the doughboys might never get across.

"Follow me!" he yelled. "Across the river!"

He fired the German rifle from his waist as he plunged into the rushing water. The Germans were halfway across, swimming and dragging their wounded. They yelped as they were shot. Soldier after soldier fell wounded into the water, their bodies carried downstream by the current.

"Forward!"

Duncan went first and the Second Platoon followed him. Behind them came the rest of B Company. A shell dropped and a group of doughboys near the river's edge was blown into the air.

"Forward!"

The water came up to Duncan's chest as he pushed ahead, holding his German rifle high in the air. When the water got too high he swam. The Germans reached the other side and turned around, firing at the advancing doughboys.

"Forward!"

Bullets zipped into the water but Duncan kept swimming. His feet hit bottom on the other side and he ran to shore, firing his rifle from the waist. The Germans on the shore ran into the woods as the doughboys charged toward them.

Duncan was gasping for breath, and he badly needed a few moments' rest. But first he had to get his men dug in for counterattacks. They were haggard and covered with blood, their helmets slanted over eyes that glowed like hot coals in the night, but they could afford a rest no better than he could.

"Get those machine guns up here!" Duncan shouted.

He was telling the men how to deploy, pointing to

boulders, trees and natural depressions in the ground, when mortar shells suddenly began to fall upon them, with machine guns opening up to their front.

"Forward!" he yelled.

The Second Platoon began another charge, but a huge number of Germans came out of the woods and counterattacked. The doughboys held their ground for about two minutes, then retreated to the river.

Duncan went with them, seeing that his men were outnumbered. "Back to the other side," he screamed. "Hurry up—get the hell out of here!"

They moved as quickly as they could, but the German mortar squads adjusted their sights and the shells fell into the river, on top of the retreating doughboys. Duncan fired wildly behind him as he retreated. The doughboys were running like dogs with their tails between their legs, but they just wanted to get the hell out of there. Many were shot in the back, and would soon join their dead German enemies downstream. The living doughboys swam like demons, then paused to fire behind them as they came to shallow water. Finally they reached the far side of the river and hid behind the trees. They saw that the Germans had not come after them. The river was going to be the line of demarcation for the night.

Dripping water from head to foot, Duncan slogged up the bank and collapsed behind a boulder. He looked over it and saw the Germans retreating into the woods. They'd probably send a mortar barrage over in a little while, but that would probably be it for the rest of the night.

"All right—dig in right here!" he said. "Post guards and send back for chow!"

Then he reached into his shirt pocket and took out his cigarettes.

"Who gave the order to attack?" screamed Lieutenant Colonel Foster.

Before him in the command post tent, Captain Harrington and the other company commanders stood with pale, worried faces. Today had been the first major action of the AEF in the war, and there had been major insubordination.

"Well?" Foster demanded, his small frame rigid with anger. "What the hell happened out there?"

Harrington cleared his throat. "Well, sir, I think it might have begun in my company. When the Germans fell back, my boys just went after them. I tried to stop them, but they wouldn't stop."

"Did they have leaders?"

"I didn't see any, sir."

"Were any officers among them?"

Harrington remembered seeing Lieutenant Hunter, but said, "No."

Foster was pacing in front of the map table. "The heads are going to roll for this—let me tell you! We cannot have such gross instances of insubordination again. A soldier's first duty is to obey orders! If entire companies have to be put into the stockade, that's fine with me. If officers have to be relieved of command, that's okay too. I'm going to get this goddamn battalion into shape once and for all, or else I'm going to know why!"

"But, sir," Harrington protested, "the boys were just a little eager. They saw a chance to kill some Germans, so they went after them. They've been training for so long that they couldn't help themselves. Why not just let it ride this time, sir? I doubt it will happen again."

Foster stopped cold and narrowed his eyes. "You *doubt* it will happen again? Is that what you said? I can't run this battalion on what you doubt and what you don't. I have to run it on discipline, and by God I'll have the discipline I want in this battalion or know the reason why!"

There was a commotion outside the tent, and everybody turned to the flap. It was pushed aside, and somebody shouted, "Ten-hut!" The group of officers who entered the tent had General Staff written all over them. Foster blanched when his eyes fell on the wide-shouldered frame of the Iron Commander.

"What's going on in here?" asked Pershing.

Foster and his officers stood ramrod straight. "Sir," said Foster, "I was just dealing with a serious case of insubordination."

"Stand at ease, men," Pershing said, looking around. "Insubordination you say? What kind of insubordination?"

Colonel Foster explained the disgraceful situation. Captain Harrington stood with the other company commanders, fully expecting that in the next five minutes he'd be a private again. Pershing listened closely, his brow furrowed.

"Why didn't an officer step forward and try to stop them?" Pershing demanded after Foster was finished.

"Evidently, they tried but couldn't," Foster replied.

Pershing looked at Harrington and the others. "Are these the company commanders?"

"Yes, sir."

Pershing turned to them. "Why couldn't you stop your men?"

Harrington answered first. "They were too eager to get the enemy, sir. If the German army couldn't stop them I certainly couldn't. Actually, I don't think they even heard me. They just wanted to get their hands on the Germans, sir."

"Hmmm," said Pershing. He looked at the other company commanders. "Anybody have anything to add to that?"

"It was the same with my men, sir," said Captain Swenson of A Company.

The other captains nodded in agreement.

"I see," said Pershing.

He clasped his hands behind his back and paced in front of the map table, lost in thought. Finally he stopped and looked up at them. "It's highly undesirable," he said, "to check the fine fighting spirit of such troops. Experience will teach them caution soon enough, but gallantry can never be taught to them. That, thank God, they were born with. Colonel Foster?"

"Yes, sir."

"I suggest you let the matter drop quietly."

"That's just what I was thinking myself, sir."

"Good." Pershing turned to the map table. "Could you give me an idea of where your men are, please?"

The officers gathered around the map table as Foster attempted to explain what had become of his battalion.

It was night and Duncan lay in his shallow foxhole. "Help . . ."

No one stirred at the cry from across the river. They'd heard it all evening and knew it was Private White, but a rescue seemed near impossible.

Duncan smoked a cigarette and wondered what to do. Private White had been wounded and couldn't make it back. He was alive and delirious and the Germans were probably letting him carry on so that his plaintive voice would demoralize the doughboys.

"Help—Lieutenant Hunter! Help me, somebody, please!"

Duncan heard movement in the woods and a few seconds later Sergeant Tucker slid into the hole.

"How're we doing sir?" Tucker asked, pushing his helmet back on his head.

"I'm wondering what to do about White out there."

"That's what I came to talk to you about. A few of the boys from the platoon want to go and get him."

"No."

"But sir," Tucker said, "we just can't leave him like that."

"That's right," Duncan said, puffing his cigarette. "We can't, and that's why I'm going to get him."

"You!"

"Yes, me. I brought the poor bastard over there and I'm going to bring him back."

"But—"

Duncan held up his hand. "Pass the word along to the men in the platoon that I'm going alone, and they should cover me. You'll be in command of the platoon while I'm gone. If anything happens, use your judgment. Any questions?"

Tucker took off his helmet and scratched his matted black hair. "You're going alone?"

"I think it's best that way. There'll be less noise, less bother. I'll be in and out before the Germans know what's happened."

"The Germans might be waiting for somebody to come."

"If they are, one person can get away quicker than a bunch of guys who don't follow orders so well. Anything else?"

"Be careful, sir. We'd hate to lose you."

"You're not going to lose me. Tell the men to get ready, and tell them to be completely goddamn quiet. I'll be moving out in about five minutes."

"Yes, sir."

"Help me somebody . . ."

Duncan started unbuttoning his shirt. "Jesus, I wish he'd shut up," he muttered.

"He ain't gonna shut up until somebody shuts him up, or until you get him back over here."

Tucker crawled out of the trench, and Duncan stubbed out his cigarette as he undressed. When completely naked he rubbed his skin with dirt to make him blend in with the night. Then he removed his belt from his pants and strapped his forty-five to his head.

Private White was moaning on the other side of the river as Duncan crawled out of his foxhole. The breeze whistled by his body, chilling him as he made his way on hands and knees to the water. The stones and twigs hurt but he gritted his teeth and kept going. He reached the cold mud of the river and then came to the water itself. Pausing for a few moments, he peered through the mists on the other side. There was no moon, but his eyes had adjusted to the dark. Somewhere behind those mists was Private White, and Duncan was going to get him out of there.

Duncan slipped into the water and swam silently. It

was icy cold and nearly took his breath away at first, but he quickly grew used to it. He was reminded of how he and Blake used to go into the woods of Virginia at night, swimming streams like this, climbing trees, and stalking the animals. Sometimes they even slept all night in the woods. Their father approved of their Indian game and sometimes went with them to be their chief.

Duncan swam against the strong current, aiming for Private White's plaintive voice. It was a miracle the soldier hadn't bled to death by now. He must have one of those wounds that heals and then festers—and hurts like hell. As Duncan swam he scanned the shore for the Germans, but there was no sign of them. Still, the Germans might be hunkered down in their holes, just waiting for him.

His hand touched bottom. He stopped swimming and crawled along the riverbed to the shore, keeping only his eyes and nose out of the water. If anything moved back there he'd pull the forty-five off his head and start shooting. The Germans might get him, but he'd take a few of them with him first.

"Help . . . Help me . . ."

The cries came from a section of riverfront straight ahead. Duncan slowly emerged from the water and crawled up on the bank. He kept looking for signs of German soldiers but could see nothing yet. The voice kept calling to him and he crept silently toward it. Something moved in the woods behind the voice, and he stopped cold. He waited for a few minutes, but when the sound didn't repeat he crawled forward again. After a few more paces he saw Private White lying on his back near the trunk of a tree. White's helmet was gone and only his head moved as he whimpered and moaned.

Duncan crept up to him and crouched beside him. "Sssshhhh," Duncan said.

White turned toward him and went tense.

"It's only me," Duncan whispered. "I'm going to get you out of here."

White blinked his eyes. Dnucan checked him over and saw an ugly wound in the man's groin. It was just as he'd thought: a wound that had coagulated. Duncan doubted White would have much of a sex life from then on.

"Can you hear me, White?"

White nodded.

"Any Germans around here?"

"Don't know."

"Don't make a sound."

Duncan picked up White and draped him over his shoulders. Crouching low, he carried White to the river and stepped in slowly so as not to make any loud splashing sounds. The river went roaring past. Duncan expected a bullet in his back at any moment. He wondered if the Germans had pulled back farther than he'd thought. That must have been what happened. They were regrouping someplace farther east.

He slowly dropped into the river, laying White back so that the wounded man was floating. Then he hugged him across the chest and swam back with him. The night was silent except for the sounds of the river.

"Are you all right, White?"

"Yes, sir."

"We're almost there."

Duncan continued to swim across the river. It had

been much simpler than he'd thought, but now the whole thing made sense to him. The Germans must have pulled out earlier, while White was still unconscious. White regained consciousness after they left, and started calling for help. There had been no real danger at all. But Duncan could not have known that.

He touched bottom on the far side of the river. Soldiers came out of the darkness to help. They carried White back into the woods. Sergeant Tucker brought Duncan his clothes.

"You sure got guts, sir," Tucker said. "Never seen nothing like that one in my life."

Duncan spat as he put on his underwear. "There wasn't anything to it, Sergeant. The goddamned Heinies are gone. Get the men together and tell them to get across that river. If the Heinies come back in the morning, it'll be easier to fight them over there than over here."

"But the river is a great natural protection for us, sir."

"I'm not worried about protection for us, Sergeant, because we're going to be the ones who are attacking. I just don't want the Heinies to have the river for protection. Got it?"

"Yes, sir."

"Then move out."

19

GENERAL LUDENDORFF STOOD in front of the map table in a chateau he had commandeered ten miles behind his lines. He was alone in the room, which was lit by a single electric light bulb hanging over the map. Littered along the edges of the map table were communiqués from the front. It was three o'clock in the morning and Ludendorff was sick with worry for it was beginning to dawn on him that the battle was lost.

After so much intricate planning, after so many gains, and even though he had the best troops, the best officers and the best equipment, he realized that his great offensive had failed.

Others might not think so, but they didn't have the facts at hand that he had. He had lost three hundred thousand of his best assault troops and had attained none of his strategic objectives. He hadn't captured Paris, he hadn't split the French and British armies, and he hadn't broken through to the English Channel.

The drive he had put into effect was slowing down. In some places it had stopped. He'd never be able to mount such an offensive again. All he could do now was hold fast and try to wear the Allies down to the point where they'd sign an armistice. They were sick of the war, too. A deal would be made.

There was just one fly in the ointment: the Americans. His spies had informed him that new American divisions were arriving in France every week. They were fresh, eager troops and they weren't looking for an armistice. They wanted to win the war. Ludendorff wondered if he could hold back this swelling mass of soldiers. He hadn't thought they'd mean much in this war, but now he knew he'd been wrong. The Americans had fought well and defeated some of his best troops. Sooner or later they'd attack him. He wondered if he could hold them off.

Sighing, Ludendorff left the map room. He walked down the dark corridors of the chateau, passing guards every several paces, and went to his bedroom. As he stood in front of the mirror and unbuttoned his tunic, his hands trembled and his throat was dry. He wondered whether he'd be able to sleep tonight. After four years of war, he was beginning to feel as though he was falling apart. How much more of the strain could he manage? He knew he wasn't as sharp now as he'd been when the war began.

I've got to keep going somehow, he told himself. The Fatherland is depending on me. I dare not slack off now.

* * *

It was night in Belleau Wood. Private Bell was tired and cold and didn't feel like getting up to relieve himself, but there was no longer any waiting. He pushed himself onto his knees and looked around.

It was pitch-black in the woods. Bell could make out only the vaguest shapes of trees and boulders. It looked eerie and haunted and he felt alone although two divisions of men were in the woods with him.

No latrines had been dug, so he had to find a quiet little spot. Picking up his rifle, he walked away from the front lines and angled toward a bush he saw in the distance. He went behind the bush, pulled down his pants, and squatted. Then he picked up some leaves from the ground and wiped himself.

It was as if someone had touched him with burning acid. Bell swallowed his scream and grimaced, nearly falling into the mess he'd made. The pain, almost unbearable, made him feel faint. He closed his eyes and his head spun.

As the wooziness passed he took out his bayonet and cut away part of his sleeve, wiping himself with the fabric. That relieved the pain somewhat. Breathing heavily, he stood and pulled up his pants. He knew what had happened: there had been some mustard gas on the ground and he'd wiped himself with it. He'd have to see a doctor now. But where the hell would he find a doctor?

He limped back to the spot where he'd been sleeping. What irony, he thought. He'd been engaged in so much tough fighting and hadn't got a scratch yet, but now he had been laid low by that damned mustard gas. He wanted to wake up Sergeant Tucker and ask him what to do, but he didn't dare. On the other hand, he didn't dare leave to look for an aid station without asking permission.

He sat gingerly on the ground, but the pain worsened. He turned onto his side and closed his eyes. Despite the pain, he began to doze off. Suddenly there was an explosion not far away, followed by several more. German artillery shells began to rain down on the Second and Third Divisions. The shelling became gradually more intense until the woods were a mass of smoke, flame and fallen trees.

Bell huddled behind a boulder, and was soon joined by Corporal Murphy.

"Holy shit," Murphy said, as the woods resounded with the din. "I don't think the kitchens are gonna get through this."

"All you think about is food," Bell muttered.

"What else is there? What's the matter with you, anyway? You look like you just et something that didn't agree with you."

"I had a little accident."

"What kind of accident?"

"I took a shit this morning and wiped my ass with some leaves that had mustard gas on them. Boy, does it hurt."

Murphy began to laugh. "You goddamn fool!"

"How was I supposed to know there was mustard gas around?"

"You shoulda smelled it."

"Everything smells the same around here."

"You know what I'm gonna call you from now on?" Murphy asked. "I'm gonna call you the red-assed baboon."

"I think I'm gonna ask Sergeant Tucker if he'll let

me go back to the battalion aid station. He must be awake by now."

Murphy shrugged. "I don't suppose even Tucker could sleep through this."

Crouched over and carrying his rifle, Bell went to look for Sergeant Tucker. Shells fell throughout the company area, knocking down trees and sending debris flying through the air. Bell passed soldiers clustered in shellholes and hiding under fallen trees. They smoked cigarettes and chewed hardtack while awaiting further orders. Finally Bell found Tucker and Lieutenant Hunter lying in a shellhole.

"What do you want, Bell?" Tucker growled.

"I gotta go back to the aid station, sir."

"What's wrong with you?"

Bell told him the story, and Tucker laughed as hard as Murphy had.

"That's about the funniest goddamn thing I ever heard in my life," Tucker said. "Only a birdbrain like you would do a thing like that."

"Can I go back?"

"Do you know where the aid station is?"

"No, but I'll find it."

"Go ahead, then. Don't get lost. We'll expect you back by noon."

"Thanks, Sarge." Bell crept away, keeping his head down.

The ground heaved from the shock of artillery explosions. Duncan looked at his watch. It was five o'clock in the morning and dawn was glimmering slightly behind the trees.

"The Heinies are going to attack when all this is over," Duncan said. "I think you'd better find out how much ammunition we've got left."

"About a quarter of our usual allowance," Tucker replied. "I checked last night."

"We need more," Duncan said. "Send a runner back to battalion headquarters and tell him we need more."

The two German artillery observation balloons sat plumply above the woods, directing fire onto the American positions in Belleau Wood. Half the sun had risen on the horizon, making the balloons shine pink against the pale blue sky. The German officers studied the woods beneath them through binoculars, and relayed coordinates through their field telephones. Flying above them was a squadron of German airplanes, assigned to protect the balloons from the American air service. They knew the Americans would be along sooner or later to try and shoot down the balloons.

And they were not wrong. American soldiers all along the front had seen the balloons go up in the first light of dawn. They'd reported their sightings, and the air service had been ordered to shoot them down. As the sun became a fiery silver ball on the horizon, the Ninety-fourth Aero Squadron was streaking across the sky from their base at Villeneuve.

Lieutenant Blake Hunter was at the rear of one of the vee formations, wide awake and looking around to make sure no Fokkers were sneaking up on them. His face was thin and deeply lined, for he had been losing weight. Like many of his compatriots, he was worn out by the incessant round of combat missions.

The American aviators knew exactly where the balloons were, and should sight them soon. Blake hunched behind the wheel of his Spad, hearing the thunder of his engine and feeling a queasy fear in the pit of his stomach. The sensation of fear was fairly new to him. The way things were going, the old days with the escadrille seemed all stunts and heroics, but now too many of his friends had been killed, and he'd faced death too many times himself. He was beginning to realize that the odds were starting to run against him. He used to think he could never be killed, but now he couldn't imagine how he would get out of this war alive.

He saw specks in the distance ahead, and pointed. The other pilots were also pointing. The Fokkers were coming, but the Americans had tactics all worked out. One group would fight the Fokkers, and the other group would go in and shoot down the balloons. Blake was in the group that would go after the balloons.

One squadron rose into the air to fight the German planes, but Blake continued straight ahead. His orders were to avoid a fight with the Fokkers if possible. He should try to get away if it became necessary, but he was not to engage.

The balloons emerged out of the dawn like big eggs floating in the sky. Blake's group held their vee formation, heading directly at the balloons while the other Spads fought the Fokkers. Whenever one of the Fokkers tried to get away to stop the planes in Blake's group, a Spad would go after it and try to hound it back.

One Fokker broke through though, heading down on the Spads flying toward the balloons. When it opened fire from above, Blake decided he'd better ignore orders and try to stop it. Pulling out of formation, he climbed up to attack the Fokker from the blind spot underneath it. The Fokker kept diving and firing, and one of the Spads began to smoke. Blake opened fire on the Fokker and held it in his sights. The fuselage of the Fokker flew into the air, disintegrating into a thousand pieces. The Fokker fell from the sky, and Blake returned to his formation. The escort Spads were keeping the other Fokkers busy. The balloons were straight ahead, and in the baskets beneath them he could see that the observers were gesticulating wildly.

The Spads in Blake's group peeled off for their strafing run. The pilots pulled the triggers of their machine guns, and the tracer bullets ripped into the balloons. On the ground, the German crews tried to pull the balloons in but they were too late. Blake dove toward one of the balloons, firing his machine guns, and the balloon burst into flame. The observers in the basket looked up fearfully. The fire spread over the balloon and air began to hiss out of it. Blake kept firing and the balloon ripped apart. The gasses inside exploded and the fire crept down to the basket, which plummeted to earth. The observers jumped out of the flaming baskets to their deaths.

Blake pulled back his stick and climbed into the sky. Some of the Spads were already attacking the second balloon. Blake looked to the side and saw one of the Spads falling to earth, its tail on fire. Just then, a burst of bullets tore into Blake's wings.

Blake's plane bucked like a wild horse. He pushed his stick to the side to get away from whoever was attacking him. As he dropped he saw a Fokker following him down, and behind the Fokker was another Spad. The Fokker fired at Blake and the other Spad fired at the Fokker. Blake's Spad went out of control. He struggled with his stick, but couldn't pull the Spad out of the dive. The ground was coming up fast. He heard an explosion and glanced back to see the Fokker burst into flame.

Blake looked at the bottom of his stick and saw that the wires had broken loose. He grabbed them with his gloved hands and tried to manipulate them. He was sweating profusely, despite the wind that rushed at him. He pulled the wires and managed to level off the Spad, but knew he'd never make it back to the aerodrome. He was losing altitude steadily.

Many of the struts holding up his wings had been shot away. The Spad wobbled dangerously as it glided to earth. His engine sputtered because it had taken a burst of bullets in the intake manifold. Blake was headed toward American lines, but he didn't know if that's where he'd crash. He might wind up behind enemy lines, and he'd heard that German soldiers sometimes shot the Allied pilots they'd captured behind their lines.

Blake's Spad skirted the tops of trees. He pulled his throttle and tried to get some power, but his engine conked out. There was a terrible cracking sound and part of his wing fell away. His wheels touched the treetops and he yanked the cords desperately to keep himself in the air. The treetops dropped away and he saw a small pond dead ahead. That's my only chance, Blake thought. I've got to land in that pond.

The Spad sank lower, and the pond widened beneath him as he drew closer to it. He tried to raise the nose of his Spad so that it wouldn't topple over as soon as it hit the water. But he couldn't do it. His wheels hit the water and his speed made the Spad flip suddenly onto its back. Blake tried to leap from the cockpit but before he was clear he hit the water and something slammed down on his arm.

He was dazed as the Spad began to sink, dragging him down, but the icy water revived him and he managed to swim clear. He kicked his feet and his buoyancy vest raised him up. His head broke through the surface and he looked around. His plane could no longer be seen, and his right arm ached fiercely, too much so to use it for swimming. With one arm and both legs he swam toward shore. The pond was small and he soon reached its banks. He climbed up onto the grass, sat down and felt his right arm. The bone appeared to be broken just below his elbow. Otherwise he felt in reasonably good condition. Shot down, he thought. Well, what do you know about that?

He had no idea whether he was behind the German or Allied lines. He should have remembered to take his compass out of the cockpit, but things had been happening too quickly toward the end of his flight. Then he remembered the sun—you could always orient yourself by the sun. It was still early morning. All he had to do now was walk west, in the direction toward which the sun was moving.

He got up and began walking, holding his aching right arm with his left hand. He was soaking wet and his feet squished in his boots, but it was a fairly warm spring day and once he got moving he didn't feel so cold. He made his way through a beautiful forest where birds sang and there were no signs of war. This realization troubled him, because he knew that the Allied positions had been bombed thoroughly that morning. In fact, he could still hear shelling in the distance. Either he was very far behind his own lines, which was unlikely, or he was in German territory.

He hoped that a miracle had happened, that he was behind his own lines. His arm was broken and he was sure he could go to a hospital for awhile. That meant he could stay out of a plane for a couple of months and get away from the damned war. He'd have more time to spend with Danielle.

He walked for a long time and finally came to a narrow dirt road. He turned left, continuing to move in a westerly direction. Noticing blood on his sleeve, he realized that his broken bone had pierced his skin. He'd give anything for a nice rest in a hospital, and then a holiday in Paris with Danielle. He was amazed that she loved him so much. Sometimes he wondered how much she'd love him if she knew what he was really like.

"Halt!"

Blake froze in his tracks and his heart sank as he saw four German soldiers emerge from behind a bush. They approached cautiously, and one raised his rifle at Blake.

My God! thought Blake. He's going to shoot me!

Another German slapped down the rifle of the soldier who was going to shoot. Then all the Germans got into a heated argument, pointing at Blake and pushing each other around. They were getting so angry that Blake thought they might shoot each other. They were arguing about whether or not to shoot him, that much was clear. Whenever one soldier tried to assert his authority, the other soldiers shouted him down. Blake smiled and tried to look friendly, but he became frightened as he became more aware of the predicament he was in. One of those Germans might kill him at any moment.

He heard the sound of an automobile. Turning around, he saw a vehicle speeding toward him down the road. As it came closer he saw that it was a large convertible, its black finish highly polished. The German soldiers stopped fighting at the sound of its approach and turned to look.

The vehicle slowed and halted. The rear door opened and a tall and dapper-looking officer got out—a major, Blake saw. He wore the wings of a pilot and had a medal hanging from his throat. A captain who was similarly dressed got out behind him. The German soldiers snapped to attention and saluted. The major asked them some questions, and they replied nervously. Then the major turned to Blake and smiled.

"Do you speak French?" the major asked, his French accent sounding as harsh as if he were speaking his native German.

"Yes," Blake replied, "rather well."

"So do I." The major bowed slightly. "I am Major Rudolph Kessler of the German Imperial Air Corps. Who might you be?"

"Lieutenant Blake Hunter, American air service."

"May I introduce you to Captain Gerd Steinhardt."

"How do you do," the captain said.

"Not too well actually," Blake replied. "I believe I've broken my arm."

"We have a doctor at our chateau," Major Kessler said. He pointed to the rear seat of the car. "Won't you have a seat?"

"Thank you."

Blake got into the car and sat down. A driver sat stiffly behind the wheel, his pancake hat squarely on his head. Major Kessler spoke with the soldiers, then he and Captain Steinhardt returned to the car.

"You wouldn't be carrying a weapon with you by any chance, would you?" Kessler asked.

"I do have a pistol here."

"They really should have taken it from you."

"Why don't you take it? I'm having a problem with my arm."

Kessler reached around and took it, holding it up in his fingers. "Crude-looking thing," he said to Steinhardt. Then he turned to the driver. "Back to the chateau."

The driver shifted into gear and backed around in the road, then shifted again and drove off in the direction from which the limousine had come.

"Tomorrow," said Kessler to Blake, "you'll have to show us where your plane is."

"I landed in a pond," Blake said. "I doubt you'll be able to see it."

"A lieutenant named Hettel shot you down, but then he was killed himself. You were his third kill."

"I didn't see him," Blake said. It was odd, this excessive politeness in the German's tone, and it made Blake all the more wary. Best, however, to respond in the same manner.

"He showed great promise," Kessler went on. "It's too bad."

"I believe a number of American planes were shot down, too."

"I imagine that's very upsetting to you Americans, because you've just got into the war. We've been fighting for a long time, and we're more used to it than you are."

"On the contrary," Blake replied, "I'm very used to it. I flew for the French before my country declared war."

"Oh? You flew for one of the American escadrilles?"

"Yes. And I was with the French foreign legion before transferring over to the escadrille."

"What a coincidence. I've fought against them. Perhaps we've seen each other up in the sky."

"Very possible," Blake agreed wryly. "By the way, where are we going?"

"To our headquarters," Kessler replied, once again examining Blake's gun. "We'd like you to have dinner with us, but then I'm afraid we'll have to send you to a prisoner camp."

Blake shrugged. "If that's the way it has to be."

"We can't very well let you go."

"No, of course not."

The car sped past the trees, kicking up clouds of dust behind. Blake's sleeve was becoming soaked with blood.

Steinhardt leaned forward and looked at it. "Nasty wound you've got there. Perhaps you'd better have something to drink."

"Do you have anything?"

Steinhardt and Kessler laughed.

"Of course we have something," Steinhardt said. Reaching into his back pocket, he took out a silver flask and handed it to Blake.

"Can't unscrew the top," Blake told him.

"Of course, sorry." Steinhardt took back the flask, unscrewed it and handed it to Blake. He was blond and wore his hat at a cocky angle. Kessler had darker hair and wore a neatly trimmed mustache. His hat was low over his eyes. They are both rather spiffy, Blake thought . . . just as he had been before the war had begun to take its toll.

"Here you are," said Steinhardt.

Blake accepted the open flask and took a big swig. The fiery liquid burned all the way down. He took another big swig, then handed the flask back.

"Just what I needed," he said.

"How many kills do you have?" Kessler asked.

"Nine."

"That many!"

"Yes. All confirmed."

"Quite impressive."

"Not after nearly four years in the air. Say, I had a dogfight with one of your most famous flyers about a month ago. He flew a white Fokker and I believe he was Goering, isn't that so?"

"Yes—Goering flies a white Fokker. You fought Goering?"

"Evidently. Someone in a white Fokker almost shot me down, but the arrival of additional American planes chased him away."

"Isn't that interesting!" Kessler said. "I'll bet Goering would love to meet you."

"I wouldn't mind meeting him either," Blake replied, "as long as it's not in the sky. He certainly lived up to his reputation."

Kessler looked at Steinhardt. "Maybe we should invite him to dinner."

Steinhardt shrugged. "I've never known him to turn down a free meal."

"Perhaps we can have a little party." Kessler elbowed Blake gently. "You like parties, don't you?"

"Love them."

"Then it's settled. We'll have a party."

The driver turned a corner and the steep-roofed chateau came into view. Nearby was an airfield and a hangar. The limousine continued down the winding road and turned onto the circular drive in front of the chateau. A group of officers had come out of the huge castle as the limousine pulled up. Kessler got out and spoke to them in German before he and Steinhardt helped Blake out of the back seat and introduced him to the assembled men. Blake noticed that all of them seemed quite friendly, with the exception of one officer who scowled as he shook Blake's left hand.

Blake felt weak, but two of the officers held him up, following Kessler into the chateau and to the doctor's office. A nurse and two orderlies were there with the doctor.

"Well," Kessler said, "we'll be back for you in a little while."

The orderlies and nurse helped Blake to one of the beds and told him to lie down. They removed his jacket and shirt, remaining silent even as they saw the bone sticking through the skin of his arm.

The doctor held a hypodermic needle in the air and squirted a bit of serum out of it. "This won't hurt," he said.

He stabbed the needle into Blake's shoulder, and seconds later Blake began to feel dizzy. The room spun around and the doctor, nurse and orderlies gazed down at him and smiled. It occurred to Blake that the whole experience had been a dream and he'd awaken soon in his bed at Villeneueve, with all his old friends, and maybe they'd go out to shoot down some German balloons.

20

M Y DEAR, I'M VERY SORRY but it is just as you suspected. You are pregnant."

Danielle stared at him, unwilling to believe her ears. "But Doctor Saulnier, it can't be!"

The white-whiskered old man shook his head sadly. "It is."

She raised her hands to her cheeks. "What am I going to do?"

"It might be a good idea to have a talk with your mother."

"My mother!"

"Who else?"

Danielle dropped her hands into her lap. She looked around the doctor's office, from the degrees on the walls, to the immense bookcases, to the glass-doored cabinets that held the gleaming instruments, but she saw none of it. "I can't believe this," she said. "It can't be happening to me."

"Surely, my dear," he said gently, "surely you know that babies don't come out of thin air."

"Yes, but . . ." Danielle didn't know what to say. She had never believed such a thing—such a disgrace —could happen to her. "My mother will kill me," Danielle said.

"I doubt that," Saulnier said, repressing a smile.

"If she doesn't my father will."

"Extremely doubtful also."

"Doctor, will you do me a favor? Will . . . will you tell my mother for me?"

The doctor raised his white eyebrows. "Me? I'm sorry, Danielle, but that's a responsibility that falls on your shoulders, not mine. And I doubt that having me break the news would make any difference."

"But I can't face my mother!"

The doctor reached over and held her hand. "My dear, you're a woman now. You must take control of this situation. You must determine what to do, and not expect others to do it for you. This is not a catastrophe. These things happen all the time and everyone knows it. Now I suggest that you go home and tell your mother right now. The sooner she knows the sooner you can all start working together on the problem."

Danielle was so nervous that she was wringing her hands. "I may be able to reason with my mother, but my father may shoot somebody."

"In my experience," the doctor said, "and mind you I have two daughters of my own, fathers are notoriously weak with their daughters. They'll kill their sons at the drop of a hat, but they'll let their daughters get away with just about anything."

"He'll kill Blake!" Danielle said.

"Is that the father's name?"

"Yes."

"Then don't tell him Blake's name until you determine that it's wise to do so."

The doctor took Danielle's hand and led her out of his office. Georgette was sittting in the waiting room and got up as the door opened. Georgette could see that Danielle had been crying and she knew the verdict. But she'd known it all along, for she knew what morning sickness was.

The two young women walked through the corridor and down the front steps of the building. It was a bright summer day but so many people had left the city already for their vacations that the streets seemed relatively empty.

"Well," Georgette said, taking Danielle's arm, "are you going to have it?"

"What do you mean?" asked Danielle. "What other choice do I have?"

"Well," said Georgette, "I happen to know a doctor—"

Danielle stopped on the sidewalk and turned to Georgette. "Are you talking about an abortion, Georgette?"

Georgette looked Danielle in the eye. She wasn't afraid of her; she had known Danielle too long, for ten years, through all of her tempers and whims. "Yes," she said.

"Never!" Danielle replied.

"Never say never," Georgette advised her.

"I said never and I meant never," Danielle replied vehemently. "I'm going to have this child one way or the other."

"Whatever you say, ma'am," Georgette replied. "Shall I get a cab?"

"Please do," Danielle snapped.

Georgette raised her arm but there were no cabs on the street. They had to wait a long time before they finally found a cab to take them home.

Blake awoke in mid-afternoon and at first didn't know where he was. Then he saw his right arm in a cast on the bedspread and remembered everything. His pack of cigarettes had been placed on the table near his bed, and he lit one up. It was only a few minutes later that the nurse stopped by and asked how he was doing. He said he thought he was all right.

I might as well enjoy this while I can, he thought; tomorrow I'll be going to a prisoner camp, a grim prospect indeed. I might spend the rest of my life there. When he and Franklin DeWitt enlisted in the foreign legion in 1914, he'd never dreamed that he might spend five or ten years in a prisoner camp. But at least he was still alive. Franklin had not been as lucky. . . .

An aide brought him some soup to eat, and when he finished that, Captain Steinhardt arrived with Blake's uniform on a hanger. "We cleaned your uniform for you, Steinhardt said. "Captain Goering has indicated that he would come tonight, and I'm sure you'll want to look your best."

"Surely," Blake said, surprised and pleased.

"How are you feeling?"

"Quite well, actually."

"Nice here, isn't it?"

"Very nice."

"Belonged to a French count. He's gone of course,

with his family. Kept a magnificent wine cellar. We German pilots always get the best accommodations. I imagine it's the same with you?"

"Not always," Blake admitted.

Steinhardt returned to his duties, leaving Blake alone. Blake slept for a while, then woke in late afternoon and stood to look out the window. As he was doing so, a German ambulance drove onto the estate and made its way around the circular drive to the front of the chateau. It stopped, the attendants got out, and a crowd of pilots formed. The attendants opened the rear door of the ambulance and removed a stretcher bearing a man who was obviously dead. The man was carried into the chateau, and among those closest to the stretcher was the young officer who'd been so cold to Blake earlier in the day. Now Blake knew why. This man was a friend of the pilot whom he had killed. Well, he thought, we can all be killed at any time in this game, but the main thing is that we all remain gentlemen.

Marie Giraud sat in her living room, reading a newspaper. She was forty-five years old, still trim and petite, but her hair was graying and lines were becoming imprinted at the corners of her eyes and mouth. She had a large nose and had never been a particularly attractive woman, but she was deeply religious and considered almost saintly among her friends and family.

Danielle entered the living room. "Hello, mother," she said.

"Hello, dear. Where have you been all morning?"

Danielle leaned toward her mother and kissed her cheek. "At the doctor's."

Her mother looked up with an expression of concern. "Nothing serious, I hope."

"Yes and no . . ." Danielle sat on the chair opposite her mother. The fireplace was nearby and a huge oil painting of her father in uniform hung over it. "Mother," said Danielle, "you'd better prepare yourself, because I . . . I have some rather bad news."

"What is it?" her mother asked, sitting forward on her chair.

"I'm pregnant, mother . . ."

Marie Giraud paled. "Pregnant?" she asked, dazed.

"Yes, mother . . ."

Blake finished dressing and looked at himself in the mirror. His uniform fit loosely because he'd lost so much weight lately, but otherwise he looked fine. They'd mended his sleeve where the fabric had been torn. He'd taken a bath and shaved. Sitting on the bed, he lit a cigarette and looked out the window. The sun had set and darkness had fallen on the chateau.

There was a knock on the door.

"Come in."

Captain Steinhardt entered the room. "How are you feeling, Lieutenant?"

"Rather well, thank you."

"Dinner is being served soon. Would you care to come downstairs?"

"Sure. Is Captain Goering still going to join us?"

"Yes, he just arrived."

"I've been looking out the window. I haven't seen anybody new arrive."

"He flew here in his plane."

They descended the stairs to a dazzling hallway that was crowded with officers. All the chandeliers were on and the hall was brilliant. Major Kessler stood at the foot of the stairs, smoking a cigar. His breast was covered with decorations, and a large medal of some kind hung around his neck.

"Lieutenant Hunter—how are you?" he asked, holding out his hand.

"Much better, thank you."

Kessler again introduced Blake to the other officers, and he shook all their hands. One of them was Count Leo von Viebahn, the young officer whose friend Blake had shot down. This time he was polite, if somewhat reserved.

A hush suddenly fell over the room. Everyone looked toward the door, where a tall, lean man wearing a monocle was standing. Blake knew that this had to be Goering.

Kessler clicked his heels. "Captain Goering, may I present Lieutenant Blake Hunter."

Goering smiled as he approached Blake. Goering's posture was one of perfect military bearing. Confidence seemed to radiate from his being.

Goering gripped Blake's hand firmly and gave him an amicable smile. "So good to meet you," he said. And Blake could have sworn that he meant it, so sincere was the German's manner.

Just then a servant walked by carrying a tray of champagne glasses, and Goering lifted two glasses off the tray and handed one to Blake. When all the officers had glasses of champagne, Goering raised his glass. "To men of courage everywhere!" he said.

They heartily echoed his toast, then sipped their champagne and fell into conversation.

"I understand you flew with the French," Goering said to Blake.

"Yes, since the beginning of the war, practically."

"The French are good pilots, as are the British. But the Americans have yet to prove themselves."

"We will."

"No doubt."

They were stopped from further conversation when everyone started moving into the dining room. A long table was set up at its center, with light coming from clusters of candelabra set along its length. Goering sat at the head of the table, and invited Blake to sit beside him. Major Kessler sat at the other end of the table.

The servants poured more champagne, then returned to the kitchen and brought out tureens of chicken consomme. It was only then that Blake realized that Leo von Viebahn was sitting on his other side. Blake was uncomfortably wondering what to say to Viebahn when Goering interrupted his thoughts.

"Where are you stationed?" Goering asked.

"Villenueve," Blake replied, grateful to postpone conversation with the young German officer.

"I am at Metz. On what day did we meet?"

"It was about two weeks ago. You're the only German pilot who flies a white Fokker, aren't you?"

"Yes."

"Then it was you for sure. As I recall, it was early in the morning, on the dawn patrol. You and your pilots flew out of the sun and attacked us. I tried to get away, but you got on my tail. I did loops and turns—everything I could think of, but I couldn't shake you. I thought you had me, and indeed you would have if more of our planes hadn't arrived and chased you away."

"I remember!" he exclaimed. "We were returning

to Metz after observing the front. We saw you before
you saw us and I ordered my men to attack. I selected
you for my target—don't remember why now—but I
couldn't seem to get you. It's true—you did try every
trick in the book. I remember thinking what an ex-
cellent pilot you were. If you weren't, let me tell you
that you wouldn't be here right now."

Blake shrugged. "I was lucky then but not so lucky
today."

Goering's eyes glittered as he smiled. "Too bad we'll
never meet again to finish our little joust."

"Fate holds of sorts of possibilities," Blake replied.

"You're a prisoner. You won't fly again in this war."

"Captain Goering," Blake said, "I've been thinking
about something. Both sides capture enemy aviators
all the time. Why don't you trade me for one of the
captured German aviators? You must have a friend
or a close comrade you'd like to have back."

Goering looked at him appraisingly. "I have many,"
he finally said.

"Then surely something can be arranged."

Goering nodded. "It's not a bad idea. I suppose we
could give it a try."

"No!"

The cry came from next to Blake. Everyone looked
as Lieutenant Leo von Viebahn shot to his feet. His
face was pale and his lips trembled.

"I can't stand this nonsense anymore!" Viebahn
screamed. He pointed at Blake. "This enemy aviator
killed Franz today, and we're treating him like a
hero! Have you all gone mad? Have you forgotten
that we're at war? You're acting as if it's all a game,
but it is not! How dare anyone suggest that this aviator
be permitted to return to his side! He should be put

up against a wall and shot as an enemy of the kaiser!"

Goering stood to look at the young man. "Count von Viebahn, would you please be so good as to leave this room," he said calmly.

Viebahn looked from Blake to Goering, shaking with the effort to control himself. Finally he pushed his chair back, turned, and marched out of the room. There was awkward silence as Goering returned to his seat.

Goering leaned toward Blake. "I apologize for the bad manners of Count von Viebahn."

"I accept your apology," Blake said, "but it is unnecessary. I understand how the young man feels. I am responsible for the death of his friend, and indeed I imagine that many here in this room were friendly with the dead man."

Goering nodded. "Yes, but we are all volunteers. We know what may happen to us. And there is nothing personal in what you did. You are a soldier, and we are soldiers. You fight for your country, and we fight for ours." Goering sighed and shook his head. "I detest politics. I doubt I could even explain what this war is about. But I'll tell you one thing—I have no love for those of my countrymen who would betray their soldiers. We have an unfortunate situation in our country where cowards and slackers are blaming the soldiers for this war, when we only do our duty, as you do. It's disgusting. I imagine you have the same sort of thing happening in your country?"

"I don't know," Blake said. "I haven't been home for so long."

"You're lucky. You might not like what you see there." Goering smiled suddenly and raised his glass. "We're getting awfully gloomy, aren't we? Let's drink up and enjoy tonight's festivities for tomorrow will come soon enough. It isn't every day that two people like us have the opportunity to meet. After this war is over, you must come and visit me, Lieutenant Hunter. You have a standing invitation, as of now. We'll dine together again and remember when we were aviators for our countries during this great war."

"I'll look forward to that," Blake said, touching the rim of his glass to Hermann Goering's.

The dust-covered Citroen screeched to a halt in front of the building on the Rue St. Fauberg. The rear door opened and General Hercule Giraud got out. He was a short man with a bulldog face, and his eyes were ablaze with anger as he vaulted up the steps. He pounded on the door, which was opened by Georgette, and he entered his home.

"Where is she!" he demanded.

His wife came down the corridor. "Hercule!" she said. "What are you doing here?"

"What am I doing here?" he bellowed. "I'm here to get to the bottom of this disgraceful matter. Where is my daughter?"

"In her room, but please calm down, dear. There's no reason for you to get upset. The child is pregnant. You wouldn't want her to have a miscarriage, would you?"

She led her husband into the living room and sat him on the sofa. Georgette went for coffee, and Marie Giraud sat beside her husband, taking his hand.

"I should have known you'd come," she said.

"Of course I'd come!" he replied. "How could I not come?"

"But you must have plenty to do at the front."

"Who is the young man?"

"He's an American aviator."

"Good grief! An American aviator? What kind of idiot have I raised?"

"These things happen, dear. I understand he's a very nice man."

General Giraud sat stiffly on the sofa. "He can't be very nice if he gets young girls pregnant. Well, is he going to do the right thing?"

"You mean marry Danielle?"

"What else would I mean?"

"We don't know," she said.

"You don't know! Why don't you know?"

"The young gentleman has been missing in action since last Thursday."

General Giraud stared at the wall, then buried his face in his hands. "Oh my God!" he muttered.

"Daddy?" said Danielle, entering the room.

Marie motioned for Danielle to go away, but it was too late. General Giraud spun around, shot to his feet, and glowered at his daughter. She saw immediately that he knew and wasn't happy about it. He pointed at her. "How could you do such a thing!" he demanded.

"I love him," she said simply.

"You love him?" the general cried. "What do you know of love—you silly little girl!"

"Daddy, calm down," she said.

He began to sputter, but when Marie gestured for him to be silent he grumbled and sat down again. Just then Georgette brought a pot of coffee and cups into the room. She stole anxious looks at their faces as she poured, but could see it was too early to know the outcome.

The room remained quiet for a few moments after

Georgette's departure. Then General Giraud looked angrily at his daughter. "You have dishonored me, young lady."

"Stop being so melodramatic," she replied. "You're only thinking about yourself. What about me? And what about Blake?"

"Is that his name?"

"Yes. He's missing in action, maybe even dead." A tear rolled down her cheek. "He's a wonderful man. I love him with all my heart. He was the man for me and I was the woman for him," she said, her voice beginning to quaver.

"Please stop," General Giraud growled. "I'm becoming nauseous. I can't believe you'd do a thing like this to me and your mother." He shook his head, eyeing her sternly. "There's a war on," he said. "My duty is to be a soldier, your mother's duty is to manage this household, and your duty is to remain chaste. You, young lady, have failed in your duty!"

Danielle began to cry. "I'm sorry, daddy. I didn't mean it."

General Giraud looked to his wife for support, but she was frowning at him. General Giraud cleared his throat and sipped some coffee. "Well," he said, "I suppose we'll all get through this somehow."

21

SECOND DIVISION HEADQUARTERS was set up in a tent deep in Belleau Wood. The officers were clustered around the map table, trying to keep track of the battle, when somebody shouted: "Attention!"

The officers snapped to as Major General Jean Degoutte of the French army entered the tent. He was commander in chief of all the American and French troops in that sector.

"At ease," he said. "Is General Bundy here?"

Preston Brown, the Second Division Chief of Staff, stepped forward. "No, sir, he's away inspecting the lines."

"I see," replied Degoutte, approaching the map. "Can anyone here tell me what is going on in front of this division?"

"What specifically do you want to know, sir?"

"Are you holding?"

"Yes," replied Brown. "We're holding."

"Good," said Degoutte. "It is very important that you hold. If the Germans break through anywhere on this front, there will be nothing to stop them from advancing all the way to Paris."

Preston Brown grinned and pointed in the direction of the front. "I wouldn't worry about that if I were you, sir," he said. "Those are American soldiers down there and they haven't been beat in one hundred fifty years."

Private Bell ran around a tree, jumped over a fallen log and dived into a shell crater. Bullets whizzed over his head and his chest heaved as he struggled to catch his breath. He was hungry and his canteen was nearly empty.

"Get those fucking machine guns!" shouted Sergeant Tucker.

Bell raised his head an inch and looked for the machine guns. They were somewhere in front, behind the bushes and trees. He raised his rifle to take a shot in the direction of the machine guns when suddenly he heard a shell whistling down on him. He hastily drew back down into the hole and pulled his helmet tight over his head. It sounded as though the shell was going to land right on him, and he swallowed hard with fear. He looked up and could see it, a gray blur hurtling down toward him. He gritted his teeth and waited.

The shell slammed into the ground only two feet away from the hole he was in. Dirt flew into the air— but the shell didn't explode. Bell cautiously raised himself to look at it. The shell was half in the ground and half out. "A dud," he muttered. "I'd better get out of here."

He jumped out of the hole and ran across the woods, while bullets zipped over his head and mortar shells exploded all around him. He saw a big boulder in front of him and jumped behind it.

Private Sullivan was there, firing his rifle.

"Sully," said Bell, "you'll never believe what just happened to me."

Sullivan wasn't listening. He was too busy firing his rifle. Bell took out his dirty handkerchief and wiped his filthy face with it. Uncapping his canteen, he took a swig but was careful not to finish it all.

"Move up on the machine gun!" Tucker shouted.

Sullivan ran out from behind the boulder. Bell followed him, and saw other men moving toward the German machine gun. They ran several steps, dropped to their stomachs, fired a few shots, and charged again. Somebody on the right screamed and went down with a machine gun bullet in his stomach. Bell jumped up and ran forward, wishing he had some hand grenades. When he thought he could see the machine gun, he dropped to his stomach again. Peering over the dead leaves, he saw bursts of blue smoke and the trembling of branches. When the machine gun fired, he saw more smoke and movement.

"It's over there!" he screamed, pointing with his rifle.

"Where?" It was Duncan Hunter's voice.

"Over there!"

Duncan jumped up and started running toward the machine gun. "Follow me!"

Bell and the other survivors of the platoon scrambled to their feet and rushed the machine gun. It was only twenty-five yards away, swinging back and forth and spreading death before it. Sullivan yelped and fell, writhing on the leaves. Bell jumped over him and followed Duncan toward the machine gun nest. Another soldier screamed and yelled as he tumbled to the ground. Duncan fired his pistol as he ran. Sergeant Tucker and a few other soldiers were firing steadily at the machine gun nest, trying to keep its occupants down. Duncan ran out of ammunition and dropped to one knee to load up again. Bell trotted around him and charged the machine gun nest. He could see the long, ugly snout of the barrel. Darting to the side, he put on one final burst of speed and jumped over the wall of the embankment, landing inside the machine gun nest.

The four Germans inside wore Red Cross armbands and were surprised to see an American soldier in the hole with them. Bell fired his rifle from the waist and shot one of the Germans through the throat. He ran another one through the chest as he was trying to get up. The third went for his pistol, but Bell slammed him in the face with the rifle butt. The fourth was on his feet now, but before he could shoot, Duncan jumped into the nest and fired his forty-five. The last German slumped to the ground.

Bell was outraged, pointing at the Red Cross armband on one of the German soldiers. "Look at these bastards, sir!" he said. "They're making believe they're in the Red Cross!"

Duncan took off his helmet and wiped his forehead with the back of his arm. "We'll have to report this to headquarters."

Sergeant Tucker and the others piled into the machine gun nest, stepping all over the dead Germans.

"Looka these bums," said Private Gomez. "Posing as

Red Cross men. These damn Heinies will do anything."

"Let's stay after them," Duncan said. "Form a skirmish line and let's go."

They jumped out of the hole and formed a line behind it. Duncan waved his arm forward and they moved out. An occasional shell fell to their rear, but only random bullets were fired at them now that the machine gun nest had been silenced. Bell looked to his left and saw only fourteen men left in a platoon that once had numbered forty.

Duncan motioned with his arms to the ground and they all dropped down. "Sergeant Tucker!" he called out.

Tucker crawled up to him. "Yes, sir?"

"I'm going up ahead to see what's there. You stay here with the others and cover me."

"You sure you don't want me to go with you, sir?"

"I told you that I want you to stay here. Bell!"

"Yes, sir."

"Come with me."

Duncan and Sam Bell stood and began walking forward through the thick brush. They were six feet apart, crouched over, moving stealthily. Bell's eyes scanned every bush and rock for sign of German troops in ambush. He looked up into the trees for snipers.

"Hold it!" Duncan said.

Bell stopped in his tracks.

Duncan pointed ahead with his forty-five. "Look!"

Bell looked but couldn't see anything. "What is it?"

"I think it's a clearing. Get down."

They both dropped to their bellies and crawled forward, inching their way along the forest floor. Something snapped to their left and they stopped suddenly, jerking their weapons around toward the sound. They waited a few seconds, but when nothing happened they resumed their crawl. Finally they came to the edge of the woods. They peeked through the branches and saw wheat fields ahead of them. To the left they could see German soldiers running down the hill and heading toward a small village.

Duncan decided he'd better not take his men into the village without orders to do so. He'd better find Captain Harrington and tell him that the village was there. Taking out his map of the area, he marked down the location of the village, then motioned for Bell to follow him back to the platoon.

Captain Harrington lay in a shellhole, wondering what to do next. His company was strung out all over the woods, he was low on ammunition, nobody had eaten for more than a day, and it looked as though the fighting in Belleau Wood might go on forever. His company had been making only erratic movements through the woods and he had no wire communications to battalion headquarters. Maybe he should go back to battalion headquarters to check in.

Lieutenant Dirkson, his new executive officer, was lying beside him in the hole. Dirkson was smoking his last cigarette. He needed a shave, and his eyes were bloodshot from lack of sleep. Harrington knew he himself must look just as bad. Worse than the filth and fatigue was the guilt he felt for not being closer to the front with his men. But he didn't even know exactly where they were.

He heard something crash through the underbrush and drew his forty-five. Lieutenant Duncan Hunter of the first platoon appeared, running with his head low and his forty-five in his hand. Harrington waved at Hunter, and Hunter headed for the shellhole.

"Boy," Duncan said, getting to his knees and crawling in. "It was harder to find you than a needle in a haystack, sir."

"A wonder you didn't get lost," Harrington replied. "What's the problem?"

Duncan unfolded his map. "We've come to the end of the woods and I don't know what to do next, sir. There's a village down there," he said, pointing to its location on the map, "and wheat fields over there. We saw Germans headed down into the village but I can't tell how many of them are down there. You think I should send down a patrol?"

Harrington pursed his lips. "I don't know. A patrol might get massacred. Maybe I should see about bringing some artillery down on the village."

Duncan shook his head. "I don't know about that, sir. There might be civilians in the village and the Germans might just be passing through."

"Sir," said Lieutenant Dirkson, "maybe I should take a run to battalion and find out what's going on. Maybe I can get some kind of wire communications back here."

"No, I'd rather keep you here with me. You never know what might happen." Harrington looked at Duncan. "I think you should go, Lieutenant. You're pretty good in the woods."

"Back to battalion, sir?"

"Right. Tell them our situation here. We need ammunition and food, and instructions on what to do about that village."

"Sir, maybe you should go," Duncan said, "so there won't be any questions about what the orders are.

And besides, nobody's going to pay much attention to a lieutenant who's asking for food and ammo."

Harrington groaned. "You're right. They'll just walk all over you up there. But the bastards won't dare give me any trouble." He looked at Dirkson. "You think you can hold everything down until I get back?"

"I think so, sir."

"All right." Harrington looked at his watch. "It's 1500 hours. If I'm not back in three hours, you can assume that the Heinies got me."

Harrington got to his knees, hitched up his belt, and checked his forty-five. Then he looked at Dirkson and Duncan. "See you later, boys," he said. "Hold the fort."

Duncan returned to his platoon and found the men huddled around Private Robert Whitewater, a pure-blooded Indian from Utah who had joined the company shortly before it came to Belleau Wood.

"What's going on here?" Duncan asked.

"He's making food," said Sergeant Tucker, "or at least that's what he said he's doing."

Duncan got down on his knees and watched. Whitewater appeared to be grinding something between two flat stones.

"It's wheat, sir," Whitewater said. "I'm making wheat berry mush."

He lifted up one of the stones, and everybody looked at the pastelike substance that it had covered. Whitewater dabbed some up with his fingers and put it in his mouth. "Not bad," he said. "Could use more water, but we don't got more water."

Private Winslow and Private Crawford showed up with more wheat. Whitewater passed out the batch of mush he'd been working on, then started on more.

Duncan tried some, putting a small bit into his mouth. It was sweet and chewy. He noticed Bell sitting nearby, licking the substance off the palm of his hand.

"Bell, can I speak with you a moment?"

Duncan walked back several yards from the other men, with Bell following him. The woods smelled like gunpowder and freshly cut lumber.

"Bell," Duncan said, "I forgot to tell you, but that was a great job you did back there in that Heinie machine gun nest."

Bell looked away from him and scratched his nose in a nervous gesture. "Which nest was that, sir?"

"The one where the Heinies were wearing the Red Cross armbands."

"Oh, that machine gun nest . . ." Bell fidgeted and looked embarrassed.

Duncan smiled, thinking back to the way he'd ridden Bell when they first met. He'd been wrong about Bell, given him too little credit. Or maybe Bell had changed in this damn war. For that matter, he thought, maybe I have, too . . . "I'm going to put you in for corporal," he said. "You're a helluva soldier."

Bell looked around as though he wanted to escape. "Yes, sir."

"You may rejoin the others now, Bell."

"Thank you, sir."

Duncan watched as Bell ran back to the group of doughboys. Then he sat on the ground and leaned against the trunk of a tree, closing his eyes and puffing on a cigarette. It was strange that he'd come to respect and like Bell so much, when he'd thoroughly loathed him at their first meeting. But that seemed like so long ago. And Duncan had been quite a different person then.

* * *

Captain Harrington made his way through the tangled and devastated forest, in search of battalion headquarters. Whenever he found soldiers he asked them directions, but most of them didn't know where they were themselves. He continued toward the rear, following his instincts and scraps of information he was able to gather. The forest was littered with dead bodies, many of them torn apart by violent explosions.

Finally, after an hour, he ran into Captain Shilansky of Company C, who said he'd been to battalion headquarters a few hours ago and told Harrington where it was. Harrington set out in the direction Shilansky indicated, and a half hour later saw a large group of officers in a clearing. Harrington walked toward them and saw that it was Colonel Malone, the regimental commander, with several of his staff officers. They all looked glum, disturbed. Harrington approached and saw that they were standing around an immense shell crater. Harrington looked down into the crater and saw a few scraps of canvas, some lengths of splintered wood, and a man's shattered leg.

"Looking for battalion headquarters?" asked Colonel Malone.

"Yes, sir."

Malone pointed to the hole. "There it is, down there."

Harrington looked into the crater, the hair rising on the back of his neck.

"A direct hit from a 155," Stone said. "Colonel Foster and his staff were all killed instantly."

"Oh my God," whispered Harrington, the color draining from his face.

"I'm glad you showed up," Malone said. "We were

just talking about putting you in command of the battalion."

"Me, sir?" Harrington asked weakly.

"That's right. There's no one else available right now. I'm told you've got more time in grade than any other company commander in the battalion."

"Ah, I don't know, sir."

"I do. From now on you're an acting major and the commanding officer of this battalion. I'll send you a few officers to serve as your staff. You might want to bring your executive officer along with you from your company."

"Then who'll command my company?"

"The best officer you've got. I'm sure somebody will be able to handle it."

"Yes, sir."

"Another thing, Harrington," Malone said. "Whenever you move, dig in right away." He pointed to the hole in the ground. "I don't want any more repetitions of this. Carry on."

Colonel Malone turned and led his staff away from the clearing, leaving Harrington standing alone beside the big hole in the ground. Harrington took off his helmet, crossed himself, and mumbled a prayer.

Duncan lay at the edge of the woods, looking at the village through his binoculars. He could see no movement down there; the Heinies had evidently passed through and set up a position farther east. Duncan thought he ought to take the village while he had the chance in order to prevent the Heinies from coming back to occupy it. Nearly three hours had passed and Captain Harrington hadn't returned. Duncan really shouldn't take the village without orders—but on the other hand, he didn't think he should let the opportunity pass by. Finally he decided to send a patrol into the village to find out for sure if any Germans were there. After all, they might simply be hiding, using the village to set a trap.

"Sergeant Tucker!"

Tucker came crawling over. "Sir?"

"Take a few men down into that village to see if anybody's there. Don't take any chances. If anybody starts shooting at you, get the hell out of there, fast."

"Yes, sir."

Tucker decided to take Bell, Whitewater and Gleason. They walked out of the woods, hunched over, holding their rifles ready for action and their bayonets in their scabbards.

Down the hill they went, passing through the field of wheat. Their eyes darted around and their mouths grew dry, for they knew that a German machine gun might suddenly open up on them and cut them down. Bell imagined German eyes looking at him in the shadows behind the windows of the village. The Germans were probably licking their chops, waiting for the doughboys to get closer.

They approached the village. It consisted of a dozen stone houses on either side of a dirt road. The houses looked eerie to Bell. There should have been children playing in the road and women hanging out their wash in the backyards, but there was not a soul about. Perhaps residents of the village had fled, but were there Heinies lurking about?

They slowed and drew their heads lower as they moved onto the road leading into the village. Sergeant Tucker held up his hand, indicating they should stop.

It was silent; not even the birds were singing. The only sound came from the distance—the too familiar sound of muffled explosions and the fire of rifles and machine guns.

Duncan was watching them through his binoculars from the edge of the woods, and on both sides of him were the other members of the platoon. They were ready to open fire if anybody took a shot at the patrol.

Tucker looked at the silent rows of houses. He decided that they'd have to break into a few of them to make sure there were no Germans inside. If he were a German he'd put his men in the houses facing the woods, because that's where the American attack would come from. He pointed toward one of the houses.

"Bell," he said, "see if anybody's in there. We'll cover you."

Bell walked up the path that led to the front door of the house. He looked at the windows but could see no movement behind them. Everything was weirdly silent—too silent, he thought. He stepped on the wooden platform in front of the door and reached to the doorknob, trying to turn it. But it wouldn't budge.

"It's locked!" he called back to Tucker.

"Kick the damn thing open!"

Bell kicked the door with all his strength, but his foot only bounced off it and stung with pain. He aimed his rifle at the doorknob and fired three times, shattering the wood. Kicking again, the door flew open. He dashed to the side, in case somebody inside was ready to shoot. But there were no shots. Bell cautiously entered the house and found himself in a kitchen. There was a sink, a counter top and an icebox, but nothing else. He opened the icebox and there was nothing inside except a puddle of water. Returning to the door, he cupped his hand around his mouth and shouted to Tucker, "There's nobody here!"

Tucker sent Whitewater into the house across the street, and it too was empty. He checked the third house himself, again empty. Walking toward the edge of town, he signalled to Duncan that the town was deserted.

Duncan led the platoon into the village and deployed them in the houses. His men rampaged through the houses, looking for food and liquor. One man found some rabbits in a cage in a backyard, and others found bottles of brandy and wine. Potatoes, carrots and onions were discovered in some of the cellars. The soldiers lit fires in the stoves and began to prepare feasts.

Duncan settled himself in the living room of one of the houses and wondered whether to send somebody after Captain Harrington. The problem was that he didn't know where to look for his company commander. Had he been killed? What was the big delay? Duncan decided to stay where he was until ordered to move. Captain Harrington would return sooner or later. And if not, somebody else would arrive with orders.

A soldier brought him a bottle of wine and he took a drink. In the kitchen, a rabbit stew was simmering on the wood stove. Sitting in the living room and smelling the aromas of dinner somehow reminded him of his wife, Patricia, who lived with his two children in Virginia. He wondered what she was doing right now. It was the first he'd thought of her in some time. He didn't really miss her. He didn't feel much of any-

thing about her. Just a vague regret. He thought of
Catherine Hawkins more frequently, and with more
feeling, than he ever thought of Patricia.

A soldier Duncan had never seen before entered the
living room. "You Lieutenant Hunter?" the soldier
asked.

"Yes."

"I got a message for you from battalion headquarters.
I'm supposed to wait for a reply."

Duncan held out his hand, unfolded the paper and
saw the unmistakable scrawl of Captain Harrington.

> *Colonel Foster has been killed in action. I am
> the new battalion commander, and you are here-
> with appointed commander of B Company, with
> the temporary rank of captain. Lieutenant Dirk-
> son is coming to battalion with me. Report your
> present position, and I'll have supplies sent to you
> along with wire communications. Good luck.*

Blake Hunter, his right arm in a cast, sat in the rear
seat of a Rumpler C.IV as it approached the AEF
aerodrome at Villenueve, and Captain Steinhardt of
the German air force sat in the front seat. Long trails
of white bunting flew from the wings of the plane to
identify it to the Americans as a truce aircraft.

Blake, wearing his flying hat and goggles, looked
down over the side of the Rumpler at the aerodrome
below. He could see people congregated beside the
hangars, obviously waiting for him. A series of radio
messages had set up the prisoner exchange. Blake had
been worried that he'd have to spend years in a
prisoner camp, but now, only two weeks after being

shot down, he was being returned and exchanged for a German aviator. He couldn't wait to get his feet on the ground.

He saw Steinhardt pushing the stick forward to bring the Rumpler down. The nose lowered and the big bomber began its descent to the runway. Lower and lower it flew, and Duncan could see the runway coming up quickly. Treetops whizzed by and the Rumpler touched down. Duncan felt like shouting for joy. The first thing he wanted to do was call Danielle in Paris. She'd been on his mind constantly.

The Rumpler taxied down the runway. Blake looked at the buildings and hangars, and realized he'd never known he would be so happy to see them. Villenueve was his home and now he was coming back. Just a short while ago he'd wondered if he'd ever see Villenueve again, and now here it was.

The Rumpler coasted to a stop. Aviators and mechanics rushed toward it. Among them was a young man in a German uniform with a bandage around his head. He was being helped by two American aviators.

The Americans crowded around the rear seat of the plane. Two of them climbed up and lifted Blake out of his seat. They helped him out of the plane, and when Blake's feet touched the ground everyone cheered. He turned and walked forward to Captain Steinhardt, who extended his right hand out of the cockpit. The propellor was still turning, sending back blasts of air and making it difficult to hear.

Blake gripped Steinhardt's hand. "Good-bye," he said, "thanks for the ride."

"Till we meet again," Steinhardt replied.

The Americans placed the bandaged German in the rear seat and strapped him in. Then they all stepped back from the plane. Steinhardt waved one last time at Blake, then crouched over his stick and pulled out the accelerator. The idling Mercedes engine snarled to life and the Rumpler moved forward. Steinhardt turned it around and looked down the long runway. He glanced at the buildings and hangars, thinking how strange it was to be on an enemy air base, then accelerated down the runway. When he came to its end he pulled the stick back and soared into the sky.

There was a lump in Blake's throat as he watched the Rumpler and its white bunting become smaller in the sky. He'd liked the Germans he'd met when he was a prisoner. He'd been distrustful of them at first, but now he hoped he'd meet them again someday, when the war was over.

The Americans crowded around and shook his hand. Captain Kenneth Marr, the commanding officer of the squadron, welcomed Blake back.

"We thought we'd lost you for good," Marr said.

"You're not that lucky," Blake replied with a laugh. "I wonder if you'd mind if I used your telephone now. I'd like to call Paris."

"Sure," Marr said. "Come on back to my office. How's your arm?"

"It's broken, but I'm sure it'll be all right."

"How'd the Heinies treat you?"

"Pretty well."

Blake told them the highlights of his experience with the Germans as they walked toward the administration building. They were astonished by his description of the dinner with Hermann Goering. Blake could see that they were viewing him with awe, as if he were a god or a hero, and he liked the feeling. They crowded around him, listening to him talk, and he imagined that newspaper reporters would be interested in the story, too.

They came to the administration building and Marr took Blake inside his office. "Just sit behind my desk and make whatever calls you like," Marr said. "I'll leave you alone for awhile."

"I don't want to make you leave your own office," Blake protested.

"Shaddup and make your calls."

Marr left the office and Blake sat behind the desk. He looked at the telephone and the papers spread out on the desk, thinking how nice it must be to command a squadron of aviators. If his luck held out, he'd command one himself before long.

He picked up the phone and asked the operator to connect him with the Paris exchange. When the Paris exchange came on, he told the girl Danielle's phone number.

The phone buzzed in his ear, and he prayed she was home. There was a click, and he heard a female voice. "Giraud residence."

"Danielle Giraud, please."

"Who's calling?"

"Lieutenant Blake Hunter."

"Lieutenant Blake Hunter!"

"That's right."

"Just a moment, please."

A pack of cigarettes lay on Marr's desk, and Blake took one and lit it up while waiting for Danielle.

"Blake?" Her voice was breathless, excited.

"Hi," he replied. "Well, I'm back."

"Oh Blake—I'm so happy to hear from you!"

"Believe me, I'm happy to hear you, too."

"We were afraid you'd been killed!"

"No, I've just got a broken arm. I'll probably be coming to Paris in a day or two. Can I see you?"

"Of *course* you can see me. I've missed you so much."

"I've missed you, too," Blake said. "In fact, I've been thinking about you a lot. I've decided that I'd like to marry you. How do you feel about that?"

There was silence on the other end for a few moments. Then: "I think it's a marvelous idea," she said, her voice tightly controlled now. "You see, I'm pregnant . . ."

Blake stared at the top of the desk. "Pregnant?" he asked.

"Yes."

"Oh . . ."

"Not changing your mind, are you?"

"No. I'm just a little surprised, that's all. Do your parents know?"

"Yes. They've been taking it rather well, all things considered. They'll be very happy to know you're back. They were going to send me to Switzerland."

"Your father probably wants to kill me," Blake said with a chuckle.

"Not anymore," she replied, relieved at Blake's reaction. It would be all right after all. Better than all right. "He did at first, I think. Now he's resigned to the situation. He'll be happy to know that you've proposed to me."

"Gee," Blake said. "I can't believe you're pregnant."

"Well, I am."

"I've got to get back to duty. I'll call you before I come to Paris."

They said good-bye, making kissing sounds and hung up. Blake stubbed out his cigarette and looked out the window at a Spad taking off. I'm going to get married, he thought. I guess it's about time.

3

22

"THE TIME HAS COME to counterattack," said Field Marshall Foch, standing at the map table in his office.

On the other side of the table were General Pershing, General Haig, Field Marshal Pétain and General Mangin. They knew that the German offensive had been stopped cold and the German troops were exhausted, their supply lines drawn taut. If ever there was a propitious time for the Allied armies to attack, it was now.

Foch planted his finger on the map in an area near Soissons. "We attack here," he said. "There are forty German divisions commanded by General Boehm in the area, and if we can take the high ground near Soissons, we'll place them in jeopardy. A lightning thrust will cut off their supplies and we'll be in a position to close in and annihilate them." Foch scratched his mustache and continued. "We will attack along the front from Rheims to Soissons, with the main effort on the west. I have selected General Mangin's Tenth Army for the task, with the Twentieth Corps as the spearhead. The actual assault divisions will be the First and Second American Divisions, and the First French Moroccan Division. They'll be supported by a full complement of artillery, and by approximately one hundred fifty light and heavy tanks. Two more divisions will be in immediate reserve." Foch looked up and smiled. "As you can see, this will give us overwhelming strength on a front only five miles wide. Each of you will receive more detailed orders within the next few days, but are there any questions now?"

No one said anything. They all preferred to see the specifics of the plan first.

"Gentlemen," said Foch, "I feel that we have come to the crucial moment of this war. Now at last we are in a position to deliver the boches a crushing blow when they are weak at the front and their government is collapsing at home. I believe that this war can be won by the end of this year, if this assault is successful." Foch gazed purposefully into the eyes of each officer before him. "Gentlemen," he said, "we dare not fail."

Blake, his arm still in a sling, climbed the steps to the building where Danielle lived. His heart beat rapidly for this would be the first time he'd seen Danielle since he'd been taken prisoner by the Germans. She had told him on the phone that both of her parents would be home, and he'd put on a freshly cleaned and pressed uniform for the occasion.

He knocked on the door. There was no response, so he knocked again. Glancing behind him, he saw that the sidewalks and streets were crowded again, just as they'd been before the war. The citizens of Paris who'd left when the German army was threatening the city had returned now that everyone knew that the Germans had been stopped.

The door opened and Georgette stood there, a nervous smile on her face. "Yes?" she said.

"I'm Lieutenant Hunter," Blake said, taking off his hat.

"Please come in, Lieutenant Hunter. Please give me your hat."

Blake had no sooner handed her his hat than Danielle appeared in the vestibule. She threw herself at him, and he drew her tightly against his chest and pressed his lips to hers.

"I love you," he whispered.

General and Mrs. Giraud entered the vestibule. General Giraud cleared his throat.

Danielle separated from Blake and introduced him to her parents. Her mother shook Blake's hand and smiled, deciding that he was every bit as handsome as Danielle had said. Even General Giraud was impressed by the dark handsomeness and self-confident manner of the young aviator. Perhaps, the general thought, everything's going to turn out all right after all.

There were a few moments of awkward silence as everyone looked at Blake, whose eyes were admiringly on Danielle.

It was Mrs. Giraud who spoke first. "We heard you'd been wounded, Lieutenant. I trust you're mending well?"

"Quite well," Blake said, flashing his irresistible smile. The living room behind the vestibule, he noticed, looking around for the first time, was nothing less than sumptuous. He was marrying into a wealthy family, probably, as wealthy as his own. He doubted his parents would have any objections to this match. And his marriage, unlike poor Duncan's, was for love. Who would have thought that Blake Hunter, that daring and frivolous young man, would marry for so serious a cause as love . . .

General Giraud looked at his watch. "I must get back to the front," he said in his gravelly voice. "I believe we have something to talk about, Lieutenant?"

"Yes, sir."

"Come with me, please."

Blake followed the general across the living room and down a corridor to a wood-paneled office. The general sat behind the desk and invited Blake to sit on one of the two green leather chairs facing it.

"Well," said General Giraud, "let's not waste any time. I understand that you want to marry my daughter."

"Yes, sir."

"Good. You appear to be a decent young man. I hope that you'll be good to her."

"I love her, sir. I'm sure that we'll be happy together."

The general gazed at Blake, trying to perceive a glimmer of falsehood. But he could detect nothing. The young man appeared to be sincere.

"You understand," the general said, "that marriage is very difficult?"

"Yes, sir," Blake replied, thinking of his mother and father and of Duncan's marriage. "But I believe—and you might think this silly—that Danielle and I are destined for each other, and that we'll have a successful marriage."

The general pursed his lips. "Let's hope so," he muttered. "Well, there's a problem, as I'm sure you know. Danielle—"

"I'm sorry about that, sir," Blake interrupted. "It was . . ."

General Giraud held up his hand. "It's too late for that now. We must deal with the problem at hand. You and Danielle must be married as soon as decently possible. Then, within a reasonable length of time, Danielle must leave for Switzerland to have the child. She has an aunt there with whom she can stay. When the baby is born, we'll make certain changes in the birth certificate. I'm sure you realize what I'm talking about."

"Yes, sir."

"Good. Then everything is decided. Let's go out and have a drink with the ladies."

They rose and left the office. As they made their way down the corridor to the living room, General Giraud looked sideways at Blake.

"What did you say your father does?" the general asked.

"He's in the railroad business," Blake replied.

The railroad business, the general thought. This marriage is looking better and better all the time.

They entered the living room. Danielle and her mother looked at them, hope on their faces.

"Everything is settled," the general said. "Let's drink a toast to the upcoming marriage. Then I must be getting back to the front."

23

EVERETT DEWITT WAS WALKING from the French War Ministry to General Pershing's Paris Headquarters at 73 Rue de Varenne. His briefcase was stuffed with papers, because he'd just attended a meeting with lower-echelon French officers concerning details of the attack at Soissons. Looking at the ground, his brow furrowed with thought as he considered asking General Pershing for a transfer to the front.

He'd begun to feel like a coward. So many of his friends and former classmates were serving at the front, while he was fighting the war far behind the lines, working in the comfort of spacious offices, sleeping on clean sheets every night and dining in Parisian restaurants. He was living such a soft life while others were attacking German machine gun nests daily.

When he returned to New York someday and people asked him what he'd done in the war, it would be embarrassing to say that he'd worked in offices far behind the lines. Even now when he spoke with his friends, he noted an attitude of condescension toward him; they were combat officers, after all, while he was basically a clerk.

"Everett!" called out a female voice.

He glanced up and was astonished to see Danielle Giraud, on the arm of none other than Blake Hunter.

"How are you, Everett?" Danielle asked graciously, holding out her hand.

"Very well, thank you," Everett replied. "How are you, Danielle?"

She touched her left hand to her face, but Everett was still too surprised to notice the engagement ring on her finger. "I'm fine," she said.

Blake held out his left hand. "Good to see you, old man."

"Good to see you." Everett awkwardly shook Blake's hand, noticing his right arm was in a sling. "Nothing serious, I hope?"

"It's only broken. They say it'll be good as new in a few weeks."

"Crash your plane?"

"I was shot down by the Heinies."

"Sorry to hear that," Everett said, becoming irritated. Everyone had wounds sustained in battle, wounds that were like a badge of nobility, and the worst thing that had happened to him was that he'd stubbed his toe while walking around barefoot in the dark in his room.

Danielle managed to wave her engagement ring in

front of Everett's face again. "I don't suppose you've heard the news," she said.

"What news?"

Danielle looked at Blake and smiled proudly.

Blake grinned. "Danielle and I are getting married."

"Congratulations," Everett said, feeling the irritation turn to anger. Blake the combat pilot had won the beautiful girl, while he was walking around in the dark stubbing his toes. "I hope you'll be very happy together."

Danielle touched Everett's arm. "You'll have to come to the wedding, Everett dear."

"That's right," Blake said. "After all, you're the one who introduced us."

"Yes, I did, didn't I?" Everett said, trying to be convivial.

Danielle opened her purse and took out a little leather notebook. "What's your address," she asked, "so I can send an invitation?"

Everett told her his address, then asked, "When are you getting married?"

"Sometime in mid-July," she replied. "We haven't set the precise date yet."

Everett thought it seemed awfully soon, but didn't comment on it. They continued to chat for awhile, then Everett glanced at his watch and told them he had to return to his office. They shook hands once again, Everett congratulated them and they parted.

Everett was angry as he walked toward the Rue Varenne. Danielle had preferred Blake to him, he decided, because Blake was a famous aviator and he was a mere clerk. Everett was more determined than ever to transfer to a combat unit. He resolved to ask General Pershing about it first chance he got.

On Bastille Day, the tricolor fluttered in the summer breeze from the rooftops of houses and public buildings all over France. The Second Division was billeted in the villages around Montreuil-aux-Lions, taking a well-deserved rest after having been withdrawn from the fighting on the Marne two days before. The men were spending most of their time sleeping and caring for equipment. There were rumors about a whorehouse in one of the villages, but so far the men had been too tired to investigate.

In the evening, Captain Duncan Hunter returned to his command post in a little white cottage and hung his tin hat on a peg on the wall.

"Tell the platoon leaders to report to me immediately," he told Private Whitewater, his runner.

Whitewater sprung up from the cot where he'd been sleeping and ran out the door. Duncan took a cigarette and looked at Sergeant Kersey, his new first sergeant.

"We're moving out first thing in the morning," Duncan said. "You'd better start getting everything together now."

"Where we going?"

"You'll find out at the meeting."

Duncan walked back to his office, opened his map case, and took out the maps they'd given him at battalion headquarters. He spread the maps on his desk and was studying them as his platoon leaders arrived one by one. They sat on wooden chairs around the desk and when all of them were there, along with the quartermaster sergeant and Sergeant Kersey, Duncan began the meeting.

"We're moving out first thing in the morning," Duncan said. "There's going to be an attack around Soissons, and we'll be in the spearhead as usual."

The sergeants and young officers groaned. They had thought they'd have a week of rest at least, but now it was back into the meat grinder again.

"I knew something was up," said Second Lieutenant Thorpe of the Third Platoon. "The artillery's been moving out all day."

Duncan pointed to the map. "We're headed for the forests around Retz," he said. "Once we get there, we'll travel by night to the jump-off point. We'll be part of a very big battle, much bigger than anything we've been in before. Speed will be very important— keep your men moving. At headquarters they think that if we can beat the Heinies at Soissons, we can win the war by the end of the year."

"Bullshit," said Sergeant Tucker.

"Maybe so," Duncan replied, "but I expect all of you to give this fight your very best. Any questions?"

"Where's the jump-off point?" asked First Lieutenant Dawes of the Second Platoon.

"I don't know yet," Duncan said. "I imagine I'll find out tomorrow and I'll pass the word along. Any other questions?"

Nobody said anything.

"Return to your units and prepare the men to move out," Duncan said.

General Pershing looked up bleary-eyed from the stacks of papers on his desk. "You wanted to speak with me, Everett?"

"I know you're busy, sir, but it'll just take a minute."

"Have a seat."

Everett sat in front of the desk and looked at the Iron Commander, whom he knew was buried under work connected with the big Soissons offensive. "Sir," he said, "I wonder if I might be permitted to transfer to a combat unit."

Pershing sighed wearily. "I knew you'd ask sooner or later, Everett. Everyone wants to go to the front and fight the Huns. But I'm afraid I need you here. I'm sorry."

"But sir," Everett protested, "you said once yourself that no one is indispensable in the army. It shouldn't be any problem at all to replace me. Why, I could find a replacement myself."

Pershing shook his head. "It's true that no one is indispensable, but I want you here. The AEF has a variety of needs, and your special skills are of more use in my headquarters than anywhere else in the army. I'm sorry, Everett, but that's the way it has to be. The army comes first. Also, to be blunt, I don't think you'd be good in the infantry. Although you're tall, you appear frail. Physical strength is an extremely important factor in the war that's developed here in France. There's been a great deal of hand-to-hand fighting, and the man with the greatest physical strength will almost certainly win. I think you can serve the army best with your mind, which is a very fine one, rather than with your body, which probably wouldn't last long at the front. That's my final decision. Anything else?"

"No, sir."

"You may return to your office."

Everett rose and walked out of the office. Frustrated

and disappointed, he made his way down the corridor to his office. I may not get a transfer, he thought, but someday I'll figure a way to get to the front, and then I'll find out what kind of man I am.

24

IT WAS the night of July 18 in the Forest of Retz. Lightning jagged across the sky and rain fell in torrents. It was so dark that the men of the Second Division had to hang onto each other's belts as they moved in long columns through the woods. They were soaked to their skins, tired and hungry. But they had plenty of ammunition and they thought they'd have the element of surprise on their side.

Men cursed as they slipped in the mud. They'd been on the move for two days, traversing twenty miles of roads congested with trucks, tanks and the Second Division Ammunition Train. The French troops they were relieving came from the opposite direction and added to the confusion. American officers didn't see how their troops could make it to the line on time. French officers were confident everything would go off like clockwork.

The Second Division doughboys hadn't eaten all day, and their canteens were low on water. Everything had been sacrificed to speed. They were moving into position at night so the Germans would have no inkling of the attack that would befall them in the morning. The attack would be German-style, preceded by a brief but intense artillery bombardment, and then a wild charge intended to cover as much ground as possible. The First Division would be on the left, the Second Division on the right, and the Moroccans between them. The assault troops had been ordered to move quickly and leave enemy strong points to be mopped up by the second and third wave of attackers. Their immediate objective was to seize the heights above the valley of the Crise.

Duncan marched at the head of Company B, along with Sergeant Kersey and Private Whitewater. Rain dropped onto his tin hat and he shivered underneath his soaking clothes. Bolts of lightning illuminated the woods for brief moments, and Duncan could see the men of the First Battalion all around him, spread out over a half mile of the attack line. He looked at his watch. There were two more hours to go before the attack began. He hoped they could make it to their jump-off point by then.

Wet branches slapped him in the face, making his scar sting. He pushed the branches out of the way and kept trudging along. The Forest of Retz was spooky and he wouldn't relish being here all alone at night. He'd read that the forest had been the site of a castle inhabited by Gilles de Rais, a fifteenth century nobleman who was reputed to have been the original Bluebeard. Duncan wondered if any women were buried under the earth where he was marching. He'd read that not all the victims of de Rais had been found.

Exhausted and confused, the Second Division moved through the forest. The doughboys heard tanks rumbling along the dirt roads, and they hoped their artillery was in position. They wondered how the attack would go. The old-timers among them had seen many comrades die at Château-Thierry, and more than half of the attacking doughboys were new replacements. Not a man among them didn't wonder if he'd be alive tomorrow night at this time.

As the hour of attack approached, the order was passed down to double-time. The doughboys ran through the woods, their gas masks and gear bouncing up and down. Some tripped and fell face-first into the muck, but their buddies helped them up and they kept going. Panic set in among some of the new replacements; they wondered what had gone wrong. The old-timers tried to reassure them and keep them moving along.

Finally they reached the edge of the woods. They stopped and lay panting on their bellies, checking their equipment and waiting for the barrage to begin. Duncan looked at his watch; it was nearly 0435 hours. They'd made it to their jump-off point.

The pitter-patter of rain and the thunder in the heavens were suddenly augmented by the roar of the artillery barrage. The ground trembled beneath them and they could see flashes on the horizon. Swarms of shells whistled over their heads and landed on the German lines straight ahead. Even through the driving rain they could see the orange and red shellbursts. Duncan took his forty-five out of its holster and licked his lips. He'd been through this routine many times already, but he still had the metallic taste of fear in his mouth. He knew he'd never get used to it no matter how many battles he was in.

An officer from battalion rode by on a horse. "Let's go, boys!" he shouted. "Up and at 'em!"

Duncan stood up and raised his pistol high in the air. "Forward!"

The doughboys couldn't see where they were going, but they got up off their bellies and went anyway. They emerged from the Forest of Retz and moved out across a grassy plain. It was still dark, and the German front ahead of them was aflame. The artillery barrage rained hell upon the Germans. French tanks were interspersed among the doughboys, and some of the tanks were already firing their machine guns to get the range of the German positions. As the French Moroccans screamed their battle cries, the doughboys realized this was the biggest show they'd been in so far. They became excited and more confident. Some shouted rebel yells; others made Indian war whoops. Duncan looked from right to left, shouting orders and trying to keep his lines straight.

"Dress right!" he yelled. "Keep moving!"

The barrage began rolling back. Duncan pumped his right arm up and down in the air.

"Double-time!" he bellowed. "Charge!"

He saw the barbed wire of the first German outposts straight ahead. The barbed wire had been blown apart by artillery shells, and there were huge craters everywhere. Duncan jumped over some barbed wire but one of the hooks caught his pantleg and ripped it open, cutting his skin. He landed on the ground, ran four steps, and saw a German aiming a rifle at him from inside the trench. Duncan screamed and jumped feet first at the German, who fired his rifle. The bullet whizzed past Duncan and he kicked the German in the face with both of his boots. The German dropped to the ground, half-unconscious, and Duncan rose to his knees and shot him through the heart.

He looked to his left and right and saw his men overpowering the few Germans in that forward outpost trench. "Charge!" he yelled. "Keep moving!"

They climbed up the rear of the trench and continued their drive. Tanks fired machine guns at the fleeing Germans. The attack had been easy so far, but the old-timers knew that German resistance would stiffen within the next mile or two. The Germans were falling back to build up a strong defensive position and marshal their reserves for a counterattack. The rain still fell, but the day was growing lighter. The sun was rising, although it was still heavily obscured behind the clouds.

The attacking troops swept across the fields in three waves. German mortar fire began to fall on them, but they kept on going. German machine guns opened fire on them but that didn't stop them either. Doughboys were blown into the air and cut down by bullets, but those still alive kept charging hard. They knew that their only salvation was to keep moving.

Duncan saw the next German trenches straight ahead. Again there was torn barbed wire everywhere and German helmets behind the rifles and machine guns in the trenches.

"Keep your lines straight!" Duncan called. "Go get the bastards!"

Duncan ran toward the trench, firing his forty-five wildly in front of him. The ground rocked with explosions and bullets whistled everywhere. Men screamed as they fell to the ground, trying to staunch the flow of blood from horrible wounds. The doughboys jumped into the trench with the Germans and the melee began. The soldiers stabbed each other and swung rifle butts around. They grunted and shouted as they fought shoulder to shoulder in the trench. Blood spurted into the air and in the darkness it was hard to see who was friend and who was foe. The soldiers soon found themselves fighting on top of the dead bodies of others who'd fallen.

A German soldier lunged his bayonet at Duncan, who fired his forty-five at the soldier's face. The bolt clicked; the pistol was empty. Duncan raised his left arm to block the bayonet, and it sliced him open from wrist to elbow. In the excitement of the moment, he barely felt the pain. Rearing back his right hand, he slammed the German in the face with his empty pistol. The German's nose split apart and blood squirted out. Duncan hit him again, shattering his jaw. The German fell back, and Duncan kicked him in the groin. Duncan snatched the rifle out of the German's hands, positioned it, and plunged the bayonet into the German's stomach. The German reeled and collapsed.

The killing of the German and the pain in his arm unleashed an animal wildness in Duncan. Bellowing like a crazed bull, he slammed the rifle butt into a German's face, breaking cheekbones and fracturing his skull. The German fell and Duncan stepped on his stomach to charge another German soldier. The German hesitated, fear on his face, and Duncan reared back, throwing his rifle and bayonet forward like a harpoon. The bayonet sank to the hilt into the German's chest, and his eyes rolled in his head. Duncan yanked the bayonet out and blood gushed after it. The German sagged to the ground. Duncan looked to his left and saw a German running a doughboy through with his bayonet. Duncan raised his German rifle, took quick aim and pulled the trigger. The German shuddered as if shaken by a giant, and a dark stain appeared on the back of his tunic. He fell face-first into the bodies lying at the bottom of the trench.

"Forward!" Duncan shouted. "Keep moving!"

The doughboys climbed out of the trench and charged farther into the German line. The Allied barrage still blanketed the landscape before them with shells. The doughboys followed it, their ranks greatly depleted. Duncan looked to his right and left and saw that his company had about half the men he'd started out with when the attack had begun. He heard hoofbeats behind him and turned around. Astonished, he saw French cavalrymen leaping over the trench he and his men had just taken. The cavalrymen stood in their stirrups and waved their sabres in the air.

"Make way!" Duncan yelled to his men. "Let them pass!"

The soldiers bunched together and the troops of cavalrymen thundered past. They wore bright blue uniforms with silver helmets and yellow plumes. They shouted battle cries and their sleek horses kicked clods of mud into the air. The men of the First Battalion watched in astonishment, for they'd never seen anything like it in their lives.

Duncan realized that the attack must have opened a

huge hole in the German front, and cavalry was being rushed in to exploit it. We're winning, Duncan thought. We've got the bastards on the run.

"Forward!" he screamed. "Dress right and follow me!"

There was a knock on the door. General Ludendorff opened his eyes. "Who is it?"

"Captain Beck, sir. General Boehm is on the telephone. He's under attack and he wants to speak to you."

"Under attack?" Ludendorff reached for his telephone. "What is it, Boehm?"

"Sir," said the anxious voice in his earpiece. "I have been under attack since four-thirty this morning, and I thought I'd better notify you."

Ludendorff turned on his lamp and looked at the clock on his dresser. It was fifteen minutes after five. "Who is attacking you, and where is their main effort?" he asked, trying to sound calm although his heart was pounding like a drum.

"They are Americans and French, and they appear to be concentrating on the high ground near the Crise Valley."

Ludendorff closed his eyes and saw the map of that area in his mind. He recognized immediately the threat to Boehm's Seventh Army if the enemy took that high ground.

"Boehm, can you maintain your position in those hills?" Ludendorff asked.

"I don't know, sir."

Ludendorff thought for a few moments, while trying to hold down the rising panic. He'd known that an attack would come from somewhere, and he'd been afraid that the Allies might inflict a humiliating defeat on him. But he could not permit that to happen. It would be better to give up ground than suffer a defeat.

"Can you hear me clearly, Boehm?"

"Yes, sir."

"Get out of there. Move all your troops back to our side of the Marne. I don't want to take any chances with forty divisions of good soldiers. Is that clear?"

"Yes, sir."

"You have your orders. Carry them out."

In his headquarters bunker near Reims, General Boehm hung up the phone.

"What did he say?" asked his adjutant, Colonel Hoepner.

"He said to retreat to the other side of the Marne."

Hoepner shook his head. "He's lost his nerve."

"But we must follow orders. Who knows, he may be right."

"He's not right," Hoepner replied, looking at the map. "He should bring in troops from another front and hit the Americans on their left flank. That would bring their big attack to a sudden halt, I can tell you that."

Boehm looked Hoepner in the eye. "Would you risk the safety of forty divisions on the success of a flank attack?"

Hoepner wilted before Boehm's stare. "I don't know," he replied. "I'd have to give it more thought."

"There isn't time for more thought," Boehm snapped. "The decision has to be made now, and the colonel-general has made it. It's easy to criticize, but much more difficult to make this type of fundamental decision." He looked down at the map. "We'll carry out our orders, but in our own way. My army will move back to the Marne, but the Americans will pay a high price for every inch of ground they get."

Carrying a captured Luger in one hand and a forty-five in the other, Duncan, bleeding from his arm and leg, led his company up the hill to the artillery emplacement.

"Keep moving!" he yelled. "Take those goddamned guns!"

The company had only eighty men left now, but they followed Duncan up the hill. The German artillerymen huddled behind the sandbags surrounding their big guns and fired rifles at the charging doughboys. But the Germans weren't front-line infantry soldiers and weren't accustomed to this kind of face-to-face warfare. Some of them broke and ran, while their officers screamed at them and tried to order them back to their positions. The Germans who stayed levelled their rifles at the Americans and pulled their triggers as quickly as they could.

Doughboys fell to the ground, but the mass of them kept running.

"Hand grenades!" Duncan shouted.

The doughboys dropped to their stomachs, took hand grenades out of their pockets, pulled the pins and hurled the grenades on the German position. The grenades flew up the hill like plump birds and landed behind the sandbags. A series of ear-splitting explosions rent the air, and German bodies were blown above the sandbags. Duncan leapt to his feet, brandishing both of his pistols.

"Follow me!" he cried. "Take the high ground!"

He ran up the hill and his remaining doughboys followed him. He saw a hole that the grenades had blasted in the sandbags and ran through, his pistols cocked, ready to shoot anything that moved.

But nothing moved. Blood and broken bodies covered the ground around the big artillery piece. The grenades had done their job. In the distance, he could see German soldiers running away.

"After them!" Duncan ordered.

His men chased the Germans around the bunkers where they'd lived, shooting some of them in the back. A few got away, but the rest surrendered. The doughboys invaded the bunkers, capturing more Germans and finding hot coffee on stoves and sausages on the fire. The doughboys hadn't eaten for a day and a half, and they fell on the food with orgiastic intensity. One group of doughboys found a telephone station in a bunker, but the German operators had thrown a hand grenade at the switchboard before they'd fled.

Duncan watched his men running around like maniacs, stuffing themselves with food. Fatigue overtook him and he leaned against one of the artillery pieces, taking off his helmet and wiping his brow. He felt the pain in his arm and leg, and knew he ought to find an aid station. But there wasn't time. He had to get his men moving again.

Private Whitewater brought him a loaf of bread and two boiled knockwursts. Duncan sat at the base of the cannon and began to eat. His men found the German water tank and were filling their canteens. Some had confiscated Lugers from German officers. A group of soldiers arrived wearing the ivy leaf patch of the Fourth Division, and they too joined in the feast. The German prisoners huddled in a circle, watching the mayhem around them, fearful that they'd be shot at any moment.

Private Whitewater pointed to Duncan's left. "What army is he in, sir?"

Duncan looked and saw a man with an upturned mustache, wearing the uniform of an officer in the French foreign legion. The Frenchman had a big smile on his face and shook hands with every doughboy he met. He spoke with one of them, and the doughboy pointed at Duncan. The officer strutted toward Duncan, who rose to greet him.

The Frenchman, his eyes glittering with joy, held out his hand. "It is an honor," he said in a thick French accent, "to serve on the field of battle with such companions as you!" Then he walked off, intoxicated with their victory, shaking hands and slapping backs.

Duncan gnawed at his knockwurst. Private Whitewater brought him a full canteen, and Duncan drank a few gulps. He felt exhausted and didn't think he could go on. Moreover, his men had been attacking all morning and they needed to be relieved.

An officer on a chestnut mare rode into the artillery emplacement. "Who's in charge here?"

Everyone pointed to Duncan, who raised himself off the ground. The officer dug his spurs into the horse and trotted toward Duncan.

"Are you in command?" the officer asked.

Duncan transferred the knockwurst into his left hand and saluted. "Yes, sir."

"What's your name?"

"Captain Duncan Hunter, commanding officer of B Company."

"Do you think you're out on a picnic, Captain?"

"No, sir."

"Then get your men together and move them out!"

The officer pulled his horse's head to the side, spurred it and galloped away. Duncan put his helmet on his head and walked toward the center of the artillery emplacement.

"I want a column of twos right away!" he shouted hoarsely.

It took awhile, but the men finally formed up. They carried bread and sausages, and one of them had found a bottle of brandy. Duncan ordered six of them to take the prisoners back to an internment camp and then marched his men forward toward the fighting again.

The half hour or so that they'd spent in the artillery emplacement had caused them to fall far behind their advancing front line. Duncan might be in trouble when the battle was over, because he should have sent the prisoners to the rear immediately and continued advancing with his men. But they were all tired and hungry, and he hadn't thought they could maintain the fast pace of the advance. Now, however, they were refreshed. Now he and they were ready to fight again.

They marched down the other side of the hill and saw the line advancing ahead of them. The rain had stopped and the sun was up, but the heavy cloud layer still blocked its rays. About a thousand yards ahead of B Company they could see the front lines advancing, moving up a hill and disappearing. Duncan wondered whether to double-time his men so they could catch up, but decided to take his time. They'd be back in the battle soon enough. A brief respite from the war would be good for them.

"Look, sir!" cried Corporal Bell.

He was pointing up to the sky, and Duncan saw a dozen tiny dots. Airplanes . . . He didn't know whose they were at first, but then he saw that they were diving toward his company. Soon the hum of their engines could be heard.

"Spread out and hit it!" Duncan yelled.

The men scattered in all directions and dived into shell craters or any other depressions in the ground they could find. The planes swooped down and opened fire. Their bullets kicked up mud and ricocheted off stones. Duncan pressed his face into the mud and imagined one of those big 50 caliber bullets blowing his back apart. The engines of the planes roared as they passed overhead. Duncan turned around and saw the black crosses on their wings. He was afraid they might turn around to make another pass, but they kept heading toward the American rear. He waited for a few minutes, then ordered his men back into formation and moved them out again.

They marched across the field and up the next hill. As they neared the summit they heard artillery falling to their front. Reaching the summit, they looked down and saw another field with rows of doughboys lying in the middle of it on their stomachs. In the distance, shells were raining down on what Duncan presumed were German positions. The Germans must be dug in pretty well over there if the advance had halted.

At the bottom of the hill he formed his men into a skirmish line and moved them toward the front positions. When they got there he told them to get down. They dropped to their stomachs and took out the sausage and bread they'd brought with them, finishing their meal.

Duncan left Lieutenant Dawes in charge and

crawled away to find out what was going on. He saw
a cluster of men toward his right and crept toward
them.

"Is there an officer around here?" he asked them.

"I'm an officer," said a young man with pimples on
his face.

"I'm Captain Hunter from B Company of the
Twenty-third Regiment, and I just got back on the
line. I'm trying to find out what's going on."

The pimpled young officer grinned. "I can tell you,
sir." He pointed to the line of hills ahead. "That there's
called the Vierzy Ridge and it's the Heinie stronghold.
We're gonna attack it before long."

Duncan wondered whether to look for his battalion,
but decided to keep his men where they were. He
could look later when things got quiet. Crawling back
to his company, he told Lieutenant Dawes what the
young officer had told him, and ordered that the information be passed along.

Lieutenant Dawes was the only other officer in the
company now, and Duncan had about seventy men
left out of the two hundred that had begun the assault
in the morning. They'll have to relieve us pretty soon,
he thought. We can't keep taking losses like this.

The shelling went on for twenty minutes before
suddenly stopping. Farther down the line, a man with
a pistol in his hand jumped to his feet and motioned
for everyone to follow him. Duncan saw that it was
Major Harrington, the new battalion commander. He
was going to lead the attack on the Vierzy Ridge
himself.

The doughboys climbed to their feet and followed
Major Harrington, screaming their enthusiasm for the
attack. They charged up the hill. When they were

halfway up the Germans came out of their holes and opened fire. It soon became evident that the Germans hadn't been damaged very much by the long bombardment. Their machine guns raked the advancing doughboys and their mortar shells rained down. German marksmen found plenty of targets, and doughboys dropped their rifles as they fell bleeding to the ground.

"Forward!" shouted Major Harrington. "Follow me!"

A bullet hit him and he went down. The attack faltered as the doughboys wondered whether to continue moving forward or fall back. The German fire was withering, and the doughboys began backstepping. Duncan thought he should run to the front of the lines and take over command of the attack, but he didn't think the doughboys could take the ridge without more troops. The doughboys turned and ran back down the hill, and Duncan found himself exposed and alone. His first instinct was to drop to his belly. German bullets whistled over his head and mortar rounds continued to rain down. Duncan looked ahead to where Major Harrington had fallen; his former company commander lay still on the ground. Duncan began to crawl forward as the German gunfire diminished. The attack by the doughboys had failed, and the Germans were going to conserve their ammunition for the next attack.

Duncan crept around dead and bleeding doughboys, making his way toward Major Harrington.

"Mother, I can't see," wailed one of the wounded doughboys.

Duncan crawled around him and reached Major Harrington, who was lying facedown on the ground. Duncan turned the major over and saw the bullet hole in his forehead. Harrington was dead. He felt the major's pulse to make sure, but there was nothing. The major's eyes were closed, his face expressionless, as if he were merely sleeping.

Duncan heard hoofbeats. Looking behind him, he saw a French cavalry troop in silver helmets and yellow plumes, pointing their swords straight ahead of them and charging up the hill. They spurred their horses and shouted battle cries, looking splendid and unstoppable in the gray morning.

When they were halfway up the hill, the Germans opened fire. Machine guns ripped into the horses and men, and mortar shells blew them to bits. Horses whinnied with fright and pain, and men fell from their saddles and crashed to the ground. Some kept charging, holding their swords in front of them and urging their horses on. Duncan ducked his head and one of the horses jumped over him. But the Germans maintained their fire, and blood spouted like geysers from the horses. The huge beasts stumbled and fell to the ground, pitching their riders forward out of their saddles. On foot, some of the cavalrymen charged up the hill with only their swords, but they were cut down by German machine guns. Finally the last horse and last cavalryman were shot down.

Horrified, Duncan looked at the carnage of horses and men around him. Blood ran in rivulets down the hill. Some of the horses twitched spasmodically in their death throes. A lone cavalryman stumbled about in a daze with his sword trailing behind him. His helmet had fallen off and blood trickled from the corner of his mouth. He appeared to be no more than twenty years old. A German rifle shot rang out, and the cavalryman fell to the ground.

The hillside became silent. Duncan covered Major

Harrington's face with his helmet, and then crawled
back down the hill toward his men.

The kaiser, followed by an entourage of aides and
staff officers, climbed the steps to Field Marshal Hindenburg's headquarters in Avesnes. The front door
opened and Hindenburg appeared, stately and digni-
fied. The kaiser and the field marshal shook hands.

"I know why you're here," said Hindenburg gravely.
"You've heard of the Allied breakthrough."

The kaiser looked him in the eye. "How bad is it?"

"It could be much worse. Come—I'll show you precisely, Your Excellency."

They went into the country mansion that Hindenburg was using for his headquarters and entered the
conference room, where Colonel-General Ludendorff
was poring over the map table. With Ludendorff were
general staff officers, among them Karl Ritter von
Beck, who had been promoted to major.

The kaiser handed his helmet to an aide and approached the map table. Hindenburg pointed to a
sector of the line. "I believe Your Excellency may de-
sire first of all our opinion as to how we got into this
critical position."

The kaiser nodded. Hindenburg described the dis-
position of German forces throughout the entire front
on the morning of the attack, and said that the attack
had taken them by surprise.

"It rained last night as you know, Your Excellency,"
he said. "The weather prevented us from seeing the
Allies move into their attack positions."

"But surely," replied the kaiser, "they didn't move
everything in one night. For an attack of this magni-

tude, there must have been troop movements for days. Surely someone must have seen something."

"There are always troop movements in combat zones, Excellency. We detected nothing unusual. Their main movements were covered by the weather. I don't believe that anyone can be blamed for not perceiving that the attack would take place."

The kaiser's eyes went cold. "We should not have been taken by surprise in this manner," he said in a deadly tone.

"It was unavoidable, Excellency."

"Show me the present line in the critical sector."

Hindenburg traced it with his arthritic finger. "It is here, Excellency."

"Can we hold?"

"We must withdraw, Your Excellency, because General Boehm's army is threatened by enemy troops infiltrating into the high ground here." He pointed to the vicinity of the Vierzy Ridge.

The kaiser looked at the map. "No," he said firmly.

"I beg your pardon, Excellency?"

"There will be no withdrawals."

"But—"

"I repeat, there will be no withdrawals."

"We have no choice, Your Excellency. If we don't retreat, we stand to lose forty divisions in an enemy pincer."

The kaiser shook his head and raised his chin in the air. "It is not politically feasible to withdraw at this time. The home front would not stand for it. They are suffering terrible deprivations, and a defeat would imperil their will to support the war effort."

"But Excellency," said Hindenburg, "it is not pru-

dent to permit political considerations to overrule
sound military procedures."

"No withdrawal," the kaiser insisted. "We must hold
the enemy and push them back."

Ludendorff, who had been bending over the map,
stood and squared his shoulders. Everyone turned to
look at him. His face had become flushed with anger,
and his eyes were bulging.

"Cowards and slackers on the home front shall not
dictate the course of this war!" he shouted. "It is
because of them that the Imperial Army lacks suffi-
cient supplies and manpower to turn back attacks like
this one. The Americans attacked with tanks, but we
have no tanks to oppose them. Why have we no tanks?
Because the cowards and slackers in Berlin have not
seen fit to supply the army with them. No, we shall
not stand and be slaughtered. We will withdraw, and
establish new strongpoints that the enemy shall *never*
penetrate!"

The room was silent. Aides and staff members looked
at one another, surprised and embarrassed by Ludendorff's outburst against the kaiser. The kaiser stared at
Ludendorff, aware that Ludendorff had the power of
the army behind him, while he, the kaiser, had only
his prestige and the royal family.

"Can we not," the kaiser said softly, "bring in reinforcements from another sector of the front?"

Hindenburg nodded. "That is a possibility."

Ludendorff drew himself erect again and glowered
at Hindenburg. "Anything of that sort is utterly un-
feasible—as I thought I have already made abun-
dantly clear to the field marshal! Any sector of the
front that we weaken will be attacked by our enemies!
We shall pull back in the threatened sector to a more

secure line. That is the only possibility left to us at present."

The kaiser felt old and tired. His army was being pushed out of France, and in Berlin there was talk of revolution. His wife was distraught and under the constant care of a physician.

Hindenburg saw the kaiser's depression. "The war is showing a hard face," Hindenburg said consolingly.

The kaiser sighed. "It is very strange that our soldiers cannot get used to tanks."

Ludendorff calmed himself now that he saw the kaiser knuckling under. Calmly, he described the new defensive positions that he thought would be impregnable. They would be located in the Argonne Forest, and would be heavily fortified. Nothing, not even tanks, would smash through them.

In a dark corner of the room, Major Beck listened and knew that if the German army had not been able to hold the Allies at Soissons and on the Aisne, they would not be able to hold them anywhere. Unless heaven sends us a miracle, he thought, this is the beginning of the end.

The Second Division howitzers subjected the Vierzy Ridge to another massive bombardment, but there were nooks and crannies where their shells couldn't reach, and where the Germans huddled, waiting for the attack that they knew was being prepared in the fields below.

In those fields, Duncan led his company back to the First Battalion and discovered that it too had suffered massive casualties. Of the six hundred men who'd jumped off that morning, less than two hundred were left. Some companies were being commanded by sergeants and corporals, and after a meeting with the other surviving officers he discovered that he had become the ranking man in the battalion.

He left Lieutenant Dawes in charge of B Company and tried to pull the battalion back together as a fighting unit. He reorganized the companies on the line and moved them together to make room for fresh regiments and battalions moving up. Nearly one hundred tanks were assembling for the attack on the ridge, which was wreathed in smoke.

Duncan's left arm was stiffening from the wound he'd sustained in the first German trench. Every time he moved it he felt a pain like a flaming torch. Medics roved through the line, bandaging wounded men and giving them pills. One of them noticed Duncan giving orders to the sergeant who now commanded Company D. The medic put antiseptic on the wound, then wrapped a bandage around Duncan's arm.

Duncan moved back and forth on his line, shouting encouragement to the men, asking them their experiences, slapping them on the back. Canteens full of water were brought up from the rear and exchanged for empty ones. The men took hardtack out of their packs and tore at it. Duncan was amazed to see that the battalion had shrunk to a unit barely larger than a full-strength company. He thought of all the dead and wounded men scattered over the fields and woods between the ridge and the jump-off point in the Forest of Retz. It was incredible that so many could have fallen, and for what? A few miles of ground? He looked up to the hill and found the area where Major Harrington had fallen. It was unbelievable that a man like Harrington could be struck down by the war, an old Regular Army soldier like that, risen from the ranks and a veteran of the Spanish-American War. Harrington had known every trick in the book; if he could be killed, so could anyone. Duncan began to think for the first time that he would not survive the war. The odds are against me, he thought. Perhaps this is my last day on earth.

Walking on the line, trying to give his men confidence by his manner and orders, he came back to Company B and saw Corporal Bell sitting on the ground, munching on his hardtack.

"How's it going, Bell?"

"I only got three men left in my squad, sir, but other than that I'm doing okay."

Duncan looked at Bell and saw him bleeding from a cut on his cheek. His pants were ragged where they had evidently been torn by barbed wire, and his face was covered with dust and grime.

Duncan knelt beside Bell, took out a cigarette and lit it. "Bell," he said, "if we had a few more like you out here we'd take that ridge without any trouble."

"If I were you," Bell replied, "I think I'd rather have more tanks. You can never have enough tanks, sir. They go right over everything. Why, back there, I saw a shell hit a tank, and the goddamned tank kept going as if nothing had happened to it. There was just a dent on it, that's all."

"Yes," Duncan agreed, "I guess you can't have enough tanks."

An officer on a horse appeared, holding his reins with one hand and waving with the other. "Get ready!" he yelled. "The barrage is going to stop in five minutes, and then we attack!"

Duncan took out his forty-five and checked it to make sure the clip was filled. He rammed a round into the chamber and clicked the safety off.

"Keep your head down, Bell," he said.

"You too, Captain."

Duncan jogged to the center of his battalion. He got out in front and looked at them lining up. His heart beat rapidly and he felt the rush of blood in his veins. He looked at the shells falling on the ridge and was surprised to realize that he was eager to get moving. He turned around and saw his men holding their rifles ready, waiting for the order to attack. He was light-headed and feeling the blood-lust coming over him again.

The artillery barrage suddenly ended, and the countryside became silent.

"Forward!"

Duncan raised his pistol high in the air and then pointed it at the ridge. "First battalion—follow me!"

He ran up the hill. Behind him he heard the boots of his men stomping on the ground. He felt as if electricity were running through his veins, and he screamed like a madman and waved his pistols in the air as he leapt over dead men and dead horses. His men shouted battle cries and war whoops. The Germans came out of their holes and rushed toward their fortifications. They fired their rifles and doughboys fell to the ground. The American tanks made a terrible racket as they rolled up the hill, crunching over the bones of dead men and horses, firing their cannons, blowing holes in the German fortifications. Their machine guns sprayed hot lead at the Germans, who were forced to keep low and fire without taking adequate aim.

Tanks are the key to everything, Duncan thought as he approached the barricades. A German raised his head and Duncan fired at him. The head disappeared, but Duncan didn't know whether he had hit him or not. He leapt over the barricade and saw the German on his knees, unmarked and terrified, holding his rifle like a shield. Duncan shot him in the face, and the German's head blew apart. Duncan spun around and shot another German in the chest. A third German ran at him and he shot him in the throat.

The doughboys poured into the German position, and it was clear to everyone that the Germans were hugely outnumbered. The Germans turned and fled, and the doughboys got down on one knee, taking careful aim with their Springfields and picking them off one by one. Tanks crashed through the barricades and levelled their machine guns at the retreating Germans, who stumbled and fell to the ground, never to move again.

The Germans ran across the ridge and down into gullies and caves. The doughboys ran after them, pausing every several feet to fire their rifles. The ridge became narrow and dropped off steeply, and the tanks couldn't go any farther. The Germans in the caves and behind rocks fired back at the doughboys, who dropped onto their stomachs and took cover.

Duncan hid behind a boulder and peered around it. The doughboys had taken the front of the ridge but there were still a lot of Germans in the caves and gullies. It would be tedious work to extricate them, but the work had to be done, cave by cave and gully by gully. They might as well start with the nearest cave and proceed systematically until all of them were cleared out.

He looked around and saw a sergeant he didn't know. "Sergeant—get over here!" he yelled.

The sergeant leapt up from the depression he'd been hiding in and ran toward Duncan, joining him behind the boulder.

"What's your name?" Duncan demanded.

"Levinson, sir."

"Can you round up ten good men?"

"Yes, sir!"

"Go get them and bring them here."

The lanky sergeant ran back to get the men. Duncan looked over the boulder at the first cave. It was down the side of the ridge and surrounded by bushes. Flashes of light could be seen where the Germans were firing from the mouth of the cave. Duncan licked his lips and tasted salty perspiration. His arm no longer ached. The tanks lined up on the ridge and fired their cannons at the German positions, but their shells exploded harmlessly on the rocks.

Sergeant Levinson returned with ten men, and Duncan was pleased to note that one of them carried a Chauchat machine gun.

"You know how to use that thing, soldier?" Duncan asked.

"Yes, sir."

Duncan told them that they were going to move out on his signal and take the first cave. He split them into two equal groups, one under his command and the other under Sergeant Levinson. They would attack in turn, each group covering the other. When they got close to the cave they would lob their hand grenades in and then charge.

"Everybody understand what we're going to do?" Duncan asked.

They all nodded, anxious to get going.

"My group will go first," Duncan said. "The rest of you get into position and start firing."

Sergeant Levinson deployed his men and they began firing at the mouth of the cave. The Chauchat gunner was in Levinson's group and their bullets flew into the cave and ricocheted off the rocks outside.

"Up and at 'em!" Duncan bellowed. "Take the damn cave!"

He jumped up and ran down the hill, and the five other men followed him. One of them tripped on a boulder, tumbling down the incline and rolling past Duncan, but he managed to get to his feet. Another soldier was hit and fell with blood streaming from his shoulder. They reached the bottom of the hill and went up the other side toward the cave.

"Hit it!" Duncan screamed.

They dropped to the ground and fired at the mouth of the cave. Sergeant Levinson ordered his men to their feet and led them in a charge down the hill. They reached the bottom, climbed the other side and passed Duncan's group, continuing for ten more yards and then flopping onto their stomachs. But the Chauchat gunner was a little slow, and before he could touch down a German bullet tore through his stomach. He shrieked and doubled over, clutching his bleeding gut. The Chauchat gun fell to the ground and Duncan took note of where it landed.

Duncan rose and ran up the hill, his men charging behind him. He headed for the Chauchat gun, picked it up and continued running past Sergeant Levinson and his men. Duncan aimed the Chauchat gun at the mouth of the cave and pulled the trigger. It bucked and stuttered in his hand as the bullets spat out of the barrel. He saw German helmets in the cave and figured he was close enough to throw grenades.

Duncan and his men dropped to the ground, raising their rifles and firing at the mouth of the cave. Sergeant Levinson brought his group up and they formed a skirmish line adjoining Duncan's group.

"Hand grenades!" Duncan shouted.

They took out their hand grenades, pulled the pins and hurled them into the mouth of the cave. The ground shook with the explosions and smoke poured from the cave.

At Duncan's command, his men jumped up and ran the remaining distance toward the cave, Duncan in the lead, firing the machine gun. Like a mountain goat he went up the hill and jumped into the cave. Dead Germans were lying on the cave's floor. Farther back German soldiers were waving white handkerchiefs in surrender.

"Get out here!" Duncan yelled.

The Germans moved forward cautiously, holding their hands high and still waving the handkerchiefs.

"Sergeant Levinson—take your men and search them for weapons."

Levinson moved forward with his four remaining men and surrounded the Germans, patting them down and poking hands into their jackets to see if they had any hidden pistols or grenades.

Suddenly one of the Germans shouted, and all of them dropped to their stomachs. Shots rang out from deeper in the cave, and the first one hit Sergeant Levinson, blasting out the side of his head.

"Hit it!" Duncan screamed.

The soldiers dropped to the rock floor of the cave

for cover. The Germans who'd pretended to surrender ran toward the deeper recesses of the cave, but Duncan aimed his machine gun at them, pulled the trigger, and cut them down.

Four men were left with Duncan, and they lobbed hand grenades deep into the cave. The explosions sent shrapnel whizzing around the confined area, ricocheting off the walls.

"After them!"

Duncan jumped up and ran into the cave. He saw movement ahead of him and fired his machine gun at it from the waist. The four remaining doughboys followed closely, firing into the smoke and shadows. They stepped over dead and shattered Germans and advanced more deeply, firing every step of the way.

"*Kamerad!*" called out a German voice. "*Kamerad!*"

"Come out of there," Duncan replied.

Germans waving white handkerchiefs emerged from the darkness of the cave and inched toward Duncan. The one in front had a nervously ingratiating smile on his face, but the others looked downright scared.

"Be careful," Duncan warned his men. "They might try something."

The Germans kept coming. Duncan held the machine gun tightly and pulled the trigger. The cave echoed with the sound of exploding bullets, and the German soldiers twisted and turned as they were ripped apart. They fell to the floor of the cave but Duncan kept firing at them until his machine gun was empty.

25

THE WEDDING RECEPTION was held at the Giraud home on the Rue St. Faubourg. Numerous dignitaries representing the worlds of government, diplomacy and the military were there. General Giraud had obtained a brief leave from the front to attend the wedding, and he stood proudly as the newlyweds entered the living room.

Danielle wore a white wedding gown with the veil pushed back over her head. Her hair was golden and her smile radiant. She held Blake's good arm tightly as she walked around the room, accepting congratulation. Blake's wounded arm was out of the sling but still somewhat stiff and painful. He looked very much the dashing young aviator as he flashed his winning smile and shook hands with the guests.

One old gossip hid her mouth with her fan and

whispered to her friend, "The bride's tummy appears a bit large. wouldn't you say?"

"The marriage *was* arranged rather hastily," her friend replied.

Everett DeWitt happened to be standing behind them, and frowned as he looked at Danielle's belly. Could she really be pregnant? No, it was impossible. Danielle wouldn't do anything like that before she was married. She had been one of the most straightlaced women Everett had ever known.

"I don't believe we've met," said a voice to Everett's left.

Everett turned and saw an officer wearing aviator wings. He was about Everett's age, had a ruddy complexion and appeared half-drunk.

"I'm Lieutenant Everett DeWitt," he said, holding out his hand.

"Lieutenant Hamilton Fuller."

"What outfit are you with?" Fuller asked. He was looking at Everett's left breast pocket, which was devoid of any combat ribbons.

"The General Staff. I imagine you're in Blake's squadron?"

"Yes, the Ninety-fourth Aero. I envy you, old man. Must be nice to be back where the bullets aren't flying."

"The grass always looks greener," Everett replied with a sardonic smile. "I wish that I could see some action."

Fuller's eyebrows rose in surprise. "It's really not much fun. You should feel lucky you are where you are."

"I feel like I'm not really in the war," Everett complained.

"To hell with the war," Fuller replied, taking a large swallow of his drink.

"That's what I say," said another aviator standing nearby.

Fuller pointed to Everett. "This feller here is on the General Staff but he wants to go to the front. Can you imagine?"

"He doesn't know when he's well off," said the other aviator.

Everett didn't like the two aviators, but smiled and chatted with them anyway. He thought they were condescending to him because they were aviators and he sat behind a desk. He doubted they really wanted to change places with him. Men like them were usually contemptuous of desk jockeys.

"Everett dear . . ."

Everett spun around and found himself looking into the lovely blue eyes of Mrs. Danielle Hunter, with Blake at her side.

Everett bowed slightly. "Congratulations to both of you," he said. "I hope you'll be very happy together."

"Thank you, old man," Blake said, shaking Everett's hand.

Danielle bent forward to kiss Everett lightly on the cheek.

A thrill passed through Everett's body at the touch of her lips. He looked at Blake and wanted to kill him. He was still crazy about Danielle, he realized. Or maybe he was just being a sore loser? Whatever, he was sick and tired of taking a back seat, whether in the war or in love.

"You must come to visit us when we get settled," Danielle said.

"I certainly shall," Everett replied.

The newlyweds continued their little stroll, shaking hands and accepting congratulations. A waiter walked by with a tray of drinks, and Everett took one, gulping down half of it. I can't stand him, Everett thought, looking at Blake's broad back. I wonder why it is that I can't stand him? Is it because he stole Danielle from me, or is it simply that I can't stand him?

Everett wondered how his dead brother Franklin could have been so friendly with Blake Hunter. He didn't seem to be the kind of person Franklin would like at all.

26

ON THE NIGHT of July 19, the Second Division was relieved and moved back from the front. In its two days of fighting at Soissons it had advanced seven kilometers, captured three thousand prisoners and seventy cannon, and had sustained five thousand casualties out of the eight thousand doughboys who had begun the attack.

It was placed in reserve for several days, and a special letter of commendation was sent to every command in the division from Mangin, the French general they'd served under at Soissons. Part of it said:

> *You went into battle as to a party. I am proud to have commanded you and to have fought together with you to deliver the world.*

On July 25 the division was marched to the Nan-
teuil-Le Haudouin area, where the doughboys were
packed like cattle into trains. Also on that day, Major
General John A. Lejeune, a Marine officer from Louisi-
ana, was appointed the new commander of the division.

The next stop for the doughboys was the beautiful
city of Nancy, considered by travellers before the war
to be a miniature Paris, and for centuries the capital
of the Duchy of Lorraine. The doughboys were billeted in homes throughout the city and began a period
of rest and recuperation. New replacements arrived
and leave was granted to as many men as possible.

Duncan wrangled a leave himself and immediately
set off to find Catherine Hawkins. A French doctor
told him that the 349th Ambulance Corps was stationed in Chalons. Carrying his field knapsack and
wearing a soft cap, Duncan hitchhiked north on roads
cluttered with troops, tanks, trucks and horse-drawn
artillery. He had no difficulty finding a ride, but the
going was slow. The scuttlebutt along the road was
that the Germans were falling back steadily all along
the front, and that the war was entering its final stage.
The sun was hot and dust rose in thick billows along
the road. The air swarmed with flies attracted to the
field latrines and garbage pits dug throughout the area.

Duncan reached the hospital in Chalons just as the
sun was setting. He found the headquarters of the
349th Ambulance Corps and was told that Catherine
Hawkins was on duty, but should be returning soon.
Duncan told the woman at the desk that he'd wait for
Catherine in the canteen, and requested that she be
told he was there.

The hospital reminded Duncan of the one in Paris where he'd been treated for the wounds to his face and scalp. It had dark, gloomy corridors and smelled of antiseptic. Nurses and doctors ran back and forth, and soldiers groaned in the wards. Duncan was glad that he wasn't a patient anymore.

The canteen was set up cafeteria style, and was nearly full. Duncan went through the line and received a slab of boiled beef and some vegetables, plus a few slices of bread and a cup of coffee. He sat at a small table for two along the wall and proceeded to dine. Doctors and nurses talked and laughed around him, and he thought of Soissons, the battle for Vierzy Ridge, and how Major Harrington had been shot through the head.

Duncan was troubled by the exhilaration he'd felt during the fighting at Soissons. It was true that he'd been tense and scared, but he also had to admit to himself that in a strange way he'd enjoyed the give and take of battle. He found pleasure in leading his men to the little victories they'd won. It gave him a tremendous feeling of accomplishment, and he thought that war had brought out the best in him: courage, leadership abilities, and a talent for sizing up a situation quickly and taking appropriate action. Maybe I should make a career out of the army, he thought. I almost think I'd rather be a professional soldier than anything else in the world.

He finished his meal and sipped his coffee. At around eleven o'clock, while still musing on the battle for Soissons, he felt a cool hand on the back of his neck.

"Hello," said Catherine.

Duncan stood and turned around. She wore a tan cotton dress belted at the waist, and she filled it out beautifully.

"Hello," he replied.

"Have you been waiting long?"

"A couple of hours."

She sat down with her cup of coffee, raised it to her lips and looked at him with her dark oriental eyes.

"I'm so happy to see you," he said, leaning toward her. "I think of you all the time."

She placed her cup inside the saucer. "I've thought of you quite a lot, too," she said softly. "Sometimes I thought I'd never see you again, because I knew that your division was taking heavy casualties at Soissons. I see your arm is bandaged. Are you all right?"

"Yes, it's fine."

She touched the bandage with her hand and smiled sadly. "You men go through such hell in this war. I really don't know how you do it."

He shrugged. "It's simple enough. We're trained to follow orders in such a way that we follow them automatically, regardless of the circumstances."

"That's crazy."

"I suppose it is."

"God, what a war . . ." She raised her cup to her lips again, then gazed into his eyes. "Oh Duncan," she sighed.

"What's wrong?"

"I wish you hadn't come."

"Why not?"

"Because you're only going to leave me again."

"I'll be back."

"But one day you won't be back, Duncan," she

said sadly. "The boches will get you or you'll survive the war and return to your wife in America."

He placed his hand over hers. "There's no point in worrying about what might happen. Neither one of us can say for sure we'll be alive tomorrow. We might as well make the most out of every moment that we can be together."

She shook her head. "I worry about you too much. I don't want to lose another man. I couldn't bear it."

He squeezed her hand. "Stop thinking about those things."

"I'd think about them less if I hadn't met you. I don't want to be attached to anybody. The separations are just too awful."

"Catherine," he said earnestly, "you've got to take one day at a time and not worry about tomorrow. We can't possibly know what will happen tomorrow, but we can make the best of today."

She touched her fingers to the scar on his face and smiled. "Duncan," she said, her voice becoming stronger, "I really don't mean very much to you."

"That's not true, Catherine!" he exploded.

Her gaze met his in challenge. "Would you divorce your wife and marry me?"

"I . . . ." He couldn't finish the sentence. Dropping his eyes from her, he reached into his shirt pocket and took out his cigarettes. He held the pack out to her, then lit both their cigarettes.

She laughed bitterly. "You just failed the acid test, my friend," she said.

He looked down into his empty cup of coffee and took a deep breath. "I can't divorce my wife," he said.

"You told me you don't love her very much." There was no bitterness in her voice, just weary patience.

Duncan couldn't look at her. "That's true, but it's a complicated family situation. I could never divorce her."

She touched her hand to his cheek. "At least you're honest, Duncan. Another man would lie and say that he'd divorce his wife, then back down when the time came. I want to be just as honest with you. If I can't have you completely, then I don't want you at all. I don't want to be anybody's temporary girlfriend. This will be our last night together, Duncan, and then I never want to see you again . . ."

General Pershing stood with his back to the map on the wall of his office at Chaumont. In front of him were his corps and division commanders, gathered for the meeting he had ordered. It was early in the morning and the bright summer sun shone through the oversized windows. Lieutenant Everett DeWitt and the other General Staff officers stood to Pershing's side.

"Gentlemen," Pershing began, "I have good news. I attended a meeting with Marshal Foch in Paris yesterday, and he has finally given permission for the AEF to function in the future as a unified army under its own commanders, answerable only to himself."

The generals smiled and some clapped their hands lightly. They'd been waiting for this opportunity for a long time: to fight as an American army instead of reinforcing French and British units.

Pershing held up his hand and they became silent. "This was a very difficult decision for the marshal to make, because the various British and French commanders don't want to give up their American divisions. They say that we American commanders are too inexperienced to control and direct an army far larger than any which has hitherto served under the American flag. Let me tell you that it took a great deal of persuasion to convince the marshal to give the AEF this chance, and that it would be a terrible blow to American prestige and the morale of our soldiers if we were to fail."

"We won't fail, sir!" said one of the generals.

The other officers nodded and sat straighter with determination. A shared sense of mission spread over the room. Pershing turned to the map and aimed his pointer at a section of the line.

"General Foch has given us a job to do," he said, "to test the effectiveness of the AEF as a unified fighting force. I'm sure that all of you are familiar with the St. Mihiel salient. It has been an ugly tooth sunk into the French line for two years. The time has come to flatten it out, and that is what we are about to do. As you can see, the enemy position runs along the Meuse River. The Germans have heavy guns inside it that have long interrupted the French railroad system and highways in the vicinity. The terrain is generally well wooded and rolling, with the highest points in the center of the salient and toward the east. We will have adequate artillery preparation and supplies. There can be no excuse for failing to take our objectives."

Pershing explained the attack positions of divisions and corps, and described the tactics and strategies of the operation. Eight American divisions would participate in the battle, and General Lejuene was pleased to learn that the Second Division had been chosen once again to be spearhead of the attack.

27

THE DOUGHBOYS MOVED into their positions around
the St. Mihiel salient during the night of September 11. At one A.M. on September 12 an artillery barrage of twenty-eight hundred guns began. The
Germans were taken by surprise and went deep into
their holes. The bombardment continued for four
hours, blasting apart the German fortifications and
driving many German soldiers insane. The sector became a hellish mass of exploding shells, burning supply dumps, star signals and obliterated villages.

At five in the morning the doughboys attacked
fiercely, and the Germans fell back. The doughboys
pushed forward throughout the day, and by nightfall
had captured all their assigned objectives. Nearly
sixteen thousand prisoners had been taken, along with

four hundred fifty guns. Casualties among the doughboys numbered about seven thousand.

The German army was on the run, and the doughboys stayed after them. The doughboys wheeled to the
northwest and charged into the Argonne Forest, where
the German army intended to make its last stand behind the Hindenburg Line.

The terrain favored the Germans. They organized
their defense along four lines of fortifications, each
backing up the other. On the heights of Montfaucaun,
Cunel, Romagne and Mont Blanc, they could see and
shell everything in front of them. The natural defenses
were augmented by concrete pillboxes, dugouts, and
machine gun nests containing as many as a hundred
machine guns. A dense network of barbed wire pro-
vided additional fortifications for every position.

By September 25, more than six hundred thousand
doughboys were fighting in the Argonne Forest. They
didn't know it, but they were in the biggest battle the
world had ever seen.

The doughboys threw the Germans out of their
first-line fortifications, and on the night of September
28, Germany's List Regiment found itself with a rag-
tag conglomeration of other units atop Mont Blanc.
They huddled in their bunkers and pillboxes as American artillery shells fell upon them, exhausted, hungry
and demoralized. There were rumors that revolution
had broken out in many German cities, that the civilian population was starving, that the empress had
suffered a heart attack and the kaiser was going to
abdicate.

"To hell with this war!" said Sergeant Lofhausen,

in one of the concrete bunkers. His uniform was torn and his face was covered by a thick growth of beard. He sat on an ammunition case and smoked his last cigarette. "We're only fighting for the millionaires anyway! They get richer and we die for them. What the hell's the point of it all? I tell you boys—I'm ready to throw down my rifle and go back home."

"I'll go with you!" said Private Steiner. "The war is lost anyway."

Private Kiesel grunted. "Where's the goddamned kaiser?" he asked. "I'll tell you where the goddamned kaiser is. He's back in Berlin living in the lap of luxury, while we don't have anything to eat."

Lofhausen puffed his cigarette to the final half-inch. "The hell with the kaiser," he snarled. "The hell with Hindenburg and Ludendorff! To hell with this war! Why should we die in a war that's already lost? Let the kaiser, Hindenburg and Ludendorff die. They're the ones who want this war."

"That's enough!" said a murderously low voice in the corner.

Everyone looked and saw a gaunt figure with an upturned mustache and eyes burning like embers.

"I will not tolerate that treasonous talk," the soldier said, standing up. He pointed at Sergeant Lofhausen. "You be quiet, or I'll see that you're silenced for good."

One new replacement, only sixteen years old, turned to one of the old veterans and whispered: "Who's that?"

"That's Private Hitler," the veteran replied. "He goes crazy when people say the kind of thing Lofhausen was saying."

Sergeant Lofhausen, a brawler from the riverfront

of Bremen, got to his feet and threw his cigarette to the floor. "Let's see you shut me up," he said, raising his fists.

Hitler dashed across the room and leaped on Lofhausen, knocking him to the floor of the bunker. As soon as Lofhausen landed on his back, Hitler began punching him hard with both hands in the face. Lofhausen managed to block a few punches, but most of them got through. His nose bled and his lower lip split open. Heaving with his belly, he pushed Hitler off him. Hitler tried to regain his balance, but Lofhausen reached up and grabbed Hitler by the throat, squeezing with all his strength until Hitler's eyes bulged. Hitler joined both his hands together in a massive fist and brought it down on top of Lofhausen's head. Lofhausen was stunned and he loosened his grip. Hitler hit him again the same way, and Lofhausen sagged to the side. Hitler pulled Lofhausen's hands from his throat and punched him in the mouth, splitting his upper lip split open. Lofhausen punched back wildly and landed a blow on Hitler's eye. When Hitler fell back, Lofhausen got out from underneath him, scrambling to his feet.

Hitler got up too. They charged each other, throwing punches from all directions. Lofhausen was stronger but Hitler was faster, able to duck Lofhausen's blows and land more of his own. A hard overhand right from Hitler dazed the burly sergeant, who began to backstep. Hitler went after him, punching with all his strength. He jabbed Lofhausen in the stomach and Lofhausen lowered his guard. Hitler slugged him twice in the face, and as Lofhausen dropped to his knees Hitler reared back his leg and kicked Lofhausen in the face. Lofhausen went flying and landed on his back, out cold.

Hitler stood in the middle of the bunker, his breathing hard, his hands balled into fists at this sides. "Anyone else want more of the same?" he cried, spittle flying from his lips.

No one moved or said anything.

"This war is not lost," Hitler said, "unless we think it's lost! The will to win is everything. We may be retreating, but the army is still intact and capable of winning battles. Cowards and weaklings should keep their mouths shut and do their duty. If they did, the army would not be in the situation it is in today!"

Hitler returned to his seat in the corner and looked about him defiantly. Two soldiers bent over Sergeant Lofhausen and tried to revive him. The bunker was silent except for the explosion of shells overhead.

The next day the Second Division arrived by camion at the foothills of Mont Blanc. General Lejeune called a meeting of all brigade and division commanders in a section of the forest that afforded a clear view of the mountain. It was a sunny day with a few puffy white clouds in the sky, and in the background the continuous sound of artillery bombardment could be heard.

General Lejeune was short and dark, of French Creole parentage. He had fought in the Spanish-American War, in the Phillipine uprising and in Mexico. Prior to assuming command of the Second Division, he had led the division's Fourth Brigade, composed entirely of marines.

He pointed to Mont Blanc and told his officers: "The Second Division has received orders to take that mountain. On it is located the enemy's main line of resistance. When we take it, a principal segment of the Hindenburg Line will be broken and the enemy will be compelled to evacuate the surrounding territory. We don't think they'll ever be able to reform after that." Lejeune pointed down to the map table that had been set up on the ground. "Our assault will consist of a frontal attack by the Fourth Brigade on the left half of the objective, and a simultaneous oblique attack by the Third Brigade on the right half. As you can see, this plan utilizes fully the salient position on our right and avoids an attack on the Bois de la Vipère and several other strong points."

Lejeune continued to describe the details of the attack, mentioning the artillery bombardment, supply problems, and procedures for handling prisoners. Then he looked up at his officers. "I have told General Pershing that I feel no doubt whatever about the ability of the Second Division to overcome any resistance on that mountain. Are there any questions?"

No one spoke.

"Return to your units and prepare for battle," said Lejeune.

At three o'clock in the morning, as doughboy artillery pounded Mont Blanc, Duncan stood with his B Company in the wooded foothills, preparing for the big attack. He looked up at the fireworks on the crest of the mountain, thinking that there was always one more hill to take, and then a river, then a forest, and after that a village and then another hill. Would there be no end? he wondered. Colonel Malone had said that if they took Mont Blanc they could throw the Germans out of the Argonne Forest, but Duncan didn't believe it. He was beginning to think that the war would go on forever.

A star shell was fired into the air, the signal for the attack to begin. The Third Brigade moved up the left face of the mountain in a vast wave. At first the going was easy, the men leaning forward and trudging up the rocky incline, carrying their rifles with bayonets fixed. American artillery continued to shell the crest until the doughboys were halfway up the side. Then, suddenly, the artillery stopped and the doughboys double-timed in their mad dash to reach the German fortifications before the Germans could come out of their holes to man them.

Duncan held his pistol in his right hand and ran at the head of B Company. The doughboys surged up the hill and the Germans dashed to their barricades, opening fire with rifles and machine guns. Some doughboys dropped and rolled down the hill but others kept going because they knew their only hope was to get inside those fortifications and engage the Germans hand-to-hand.

Duncan had read enough military strategy to know that the attack wouldn't have been ordered in the first place unless the doughboys outnumbered the Germans by almost three to one. The experts believed that's what it took to overwhelm a strong defensive position. So the Second Division would probably take Mont Blanc sooner or later and a third to half of its personnel would be wiped out. Those were the mathematics of the game that the people on the General Staff played.

"Keep rolling!" Duncan shouted. "Over the top!"

Like an ocean wave the Third Brigade crashed over the sandbag fortifications and landed behind them to grapple with the Germans. Duncan found himself standing in front of a boy who was no more than sixteen years old. The boy lunged at him with a bayonet. Duncan shot him between the eyes, and the top of the boy's head and his helmet flew into the air. Duncan shot another German, fired at a third German and missed, and fired again, the bullet finding its mark this time. The German soldier fell bleeding into the bottom of the trench.

It was the usual bloody chaos inside the trench, with men grunting and trying to kill each other by any means possible. Soon the bodies of dead doughboys and Germans began to fill the bottom of the trench. But there were many more doughboys in the fight, and they prevailed. Duncan decided that the time had come to move forward to one of the more heavily fortified positions.

"Forward!" he yelled. "Follow me!"

He scrambled out of the trench and ran into no-man's-land again, holding his pistol tightly. The rest of his company followed him, but some of the new replacements were slow. Sergeant Tucker kicked at them and slammed them on their arms with his rifle butt. "You heard the captain!" he bellowed angrily. "Get the hell going!"

The frightened soldiers climbed over the sandbags and followed the rest of the company. Ahead of them the Germans opened fire with rifles and machine guns. Tucker threw one leg over the sandbags and looked ahead at the charging company of doughboys. It was the last thing he ever saw. A bullet sliced into his chest and he toppled backward, like a rag doll, landing on his back in the mud and blood at the bottom of the trench.

On the chalky ridge Duncan was aware that huge numbers of his men were falling before the intense enemy fire. If he and his men continued their charge they would be wiped out in the next fifty yards.

"Hit it!" he screamed. "Get down!"

The men dropped down on the flat rock at the top of the ridge. The rim of the sun appeared like a red line on the horizon, and a hail of bullets flew over their heads. Duncan was trying to figure out what to do, but the first few mortar rounds that fell made up his mind for him.

"Back to the trench!"

The men turned around and crawled back as mortar shells exploded all around them and machine gun fire ricocheted off the rock. Some of the new men panicked and jumped up to make a mad dash for the trench, but the machine guns cut them down.

The rest slithered over the rocky crest of the mountain and when they came to the sandbags they vaulted over to the safety of the trench. As soon as Duncan landed he called out for Private Whitewater.

Whitewater came running over the dead bodies at the bottom of the trench. "Yes, sir!"

Duncan pointed to his right. "Battalion headquarters is over there. Tell Colonel Malone that we need some machine guns and mortars over here. Tell him what we're up against. Got it?"

"Yes, sir."

"Get going!"

Whitewater climbed up the rear of the trench and ran off in the direction Duncan had indicated. Duncan marched down the center of the trench, pushing his new reinforcements against the sandbags. "Fire back!" he ordered. "What the hell do you think you've got those rifles for!" He saw a soldier kneeling in the middle of the trench. "Hey—what do you think you're doing!"

It was Private Bell. "Sir," he said in a strained voice, "Sergeant Tucker is dead."

Duncan moved toward Bell in huge strides and dropped to one knee beside Sergeant Tucker, whose eyes were wide open and glazing over. His chest was a mass of blood.

Bell shook his head in wonderment. "I never thought he'd get hit," he mumbled.

Duncan looked at Tucker's face and fought hard to restrain the rising scream inside him. He bit the inside of his cheek as he bent over and closed Tucker's eyes. Good-bye you crusty old bastard, he thought. You taught me how to be a soldier and I'll never forget you.

28

WAKE UP, BLAKE!"

The voice sounded far away, down a long tunnel. Blake rolled over to get away from it.

"Come on—let's go!"

Blake felt himself being shaken. He opened his eyes and saw Lieutenant DiPietro looking down at him.

"What's going on?" Blake asked sleepily.

"We've got to go up."

Blake looked at his watch. "So early?"

"Yes. Are you awake?"

"Not yet. But if you keep talking I will be."

"Hurry up."

DiPietro left Blake's room. Blake pushed the covers away and swung his feet around to the floor. It was six o'clock in the morning and the sun was just coming up. He reached for his package of cigarettes and lit one, hoping it would help clear out his head. He'd been flying missions every day for nearly two weeks, often twice a day. His hands sometimes trembled uncontrollably and he never seemed to have any energy.

He put on his clothing and boots, grabbed his flying hat and left the room. He walked down the corridor to the latrine, took a leak, washed his hands and face and rinsed out his mouth. Then he went outside and saw mechanics pulling the airplanes onto the field. A cool autumn breeze was blowing and Blake buttoned up his sheepskin-lined jacket. He made his way to the briefing hut and went inside, seeing most of the pilots from the squadron already there. A cook was serving coffee and buns, and Blake got some, then sat on a rickety wooden chair next to Lieutenant Fuller to eat.

"How do you feel, Blake?" asked Fuller.

"Like shit."

"I know what you mean."

The other pilots arrived and sat on the chairs. They munched buns and sipped coffee, waiting for Captain Eddie Rickenbacker to show up. Rickenbacker had become commander of the Ninety-fourth Aero only three days before.

When Rickenbacker arrived the briefing began. He told them that they were going on a strafing mission in the Meuse-Argonne sector and pointed it out on the map. The Germans were holding onto fortifications on some critical high ground, and the squadron had to attack them. Blake was half-asleep and missed a lot of the details, but he'd been on plenty of missions already and knew what to do.

The briefing ended and the pilots gulped down the remainder of their coffee, then left the briefing hut and went out onto the runway. As they approached the planes they shook hands and wished each other luck. Separating, they climbed onto the wings of their planes, strapped themselves into the cockpits, put on their long-eared hats and adjusted their goggles.

The sun was a big red ball hovering above the horizon. The wispy clouds in the sky were tinged with pink. A mechanic turned Blake's propeller a few times and Blake flipped on the ignition. The engine sputtered and roared to life, making the Spad tremble. Blake tested the engine and all his controls. Everything seemed all right and the coffee he'd drunk seemed to be taking effect. Two by two the planes were taking off already. Blake waited for the signal and then moved onto the runway with Lieutenant Fuller. The two pilots straightened their planes out and blipped their engines. When the ground officer gave them the high sign, they pulled out their accelerators, roaring down the runway in tandem and lifting into the sky.

The planes circled and formed two vee formations in the air above the field, beginning their journey to the Meuse-Argonne sector. Blake sat hunched in his seat, both hands on the stick, listening to the monotonous drone of the engines. He looked over the side of his cockpit at farmland and trees. The flight was supposed to take about an hour and Blake, like the other pilots, was anxious to get the mission over with so he could go back to bed.

It was a beautiful morning and the sun gleamed on the metal fittings in his cockpit. He thought of Danielle, who was now in Switzerland with her aunt. He hadn't seen her for a month, and often found himself yearning for her. He thought of her lying in bed, her golden hair tousled and her nipples pink and in-

viting, and he wished that the war would end quickly
so that he could be with her always. There had been
a time when he'd loved the war, but now there was
nothing in the world that could compare with his love
for Danielle.

He looked around the sky to see if there were any
German planes up there, but he couldn't see anything.
Unfastening the top button of his jacket, he took out
the gold locket and chain that she'd given him and
opened it up. Inside was a picture of Danielle with
a demure smile. What incredible beauty, Blake
thought. And she's all mine.

He closed the locket and buttoned up his jacket. He
gripped his stick with both hands again and the
squadron continued to make its way toward the
Argonne Forest. Soon they heard the faint rumble of
artillery, which became louder as they drew closer to
their objective. They saw smoke on the horizon and
in the open fields below were columns of soldiers
marching toward the front. The roads were choked
with vehicles and troops. Vast quantities of soldiers
and supplies were moving forward in never–ending
streams to engage the Germans.

Finally they reached the battleground and saw long
thin lines of doughboys charging German trenches and
fortifications. The shell explosions looked like white
mushrooms covering the landscape. Blake couldn't
help thinking how spectacular it all was, that war had
a way of dwarfing everything else in human existence.
He remembered how the war used to thrill him, but
that was before he'd met Danielle.

The squadron changed course and headed for a
range of mountains. Soldiers could be seen advancing
up the sides in long skirmish lines and the top of the

mountains were covered with smoke from their fire. The squadron flew to its objectives and saw networks of trenches and fortifications. They circled as Captain Rickenbacker pinpointed targets, and then formed up for their first strafing run.

They flew away from the mountain and then turned around, forming one long straight line. The lead plane dived toward the trench below, the other planes following at fifty-yard intervals. German antiaircraft batteries opened fire, and machine gunners swung their barrels around and fired at the Spads descending toward them.

Blake eased his Spad down, keeping the wings and tail stable. He winced whenever an antiaircraft shell landed close by, but his hand was steady and the engine screamed as he dived toward the trench. He could see the German soldiers in the trench scattering in all directions to escape the machine gun bullets of the American planes. When Blake was in position he pressed his trigger lever and his twin Vickers machine guns barked viciously. The hot lead spit out as Blake kept firing into the middle of the trench. German bodies lay everywhere and he saw running Germans ripped apart by his guns. He passed a bunker, fired into another length of trench, fired into a mortar squad, and at the end of the trench dueled with a German machine gun nest. German bullets rippled through the fabric on his wings and he pulled the stick, lifting the nose of the Spad and climbing into the sky.

The formation was breaking apart, with individual pilots selecting their own targets and doing their best to dodge the antiaircraft and machine gun fire. Blake spotted a howitzer emplacement and angled toward it, making a loop in the sky and diving toward the ground. He saw the German soldiers scrambling madly to hide behind the sandbags, and he opened fire and saw some of the Germans flung onto their backs by the bullets. Yanking back his stick, he climbed away from the howitzers, turned around in the sky, and came back for another pass. He opened fire on the emplacement again and saw the Germans run for shelter to the other side of the howitzers. Again his bullets caught some of them and sent them flying.

Soaring into the sky again, he decided to make another pass at one of the front-line trenches. He levelled off and looked around to make sure that no other American planes would be in his way and that no German planes were anywhere around. Antiaircraft shells exploded nearby, but he simply bit his lower lip and continued his dive toward the trench. The German machine gun fire ripped through his fuselage, and he knew he should get out of there, but he was committed to the dive now and could see the German soldiers in the trench dashing in all directions for cover.

He pulled his trigger lever and the Spad trembled as its machine guns fired. The bullets ripped open sandbags and cut down the fleeing German soldiers. Some of the Germans lay down in the center of the trench but the bullets descended on them like angry bees and punctured their backs. They writhed and screamed as Blake roared over them and climbed into the sky again.

He levelled off at two thousand feet and looked around for more targets. The sky had become darker with antiaircraft fire, and German machine gunners on the ground were spraying bullets all over the sky.

Blake saw a huge machine gun nest with forty or fifty machine guns in it. Again the little voice told him to get the hell out of there, but he had been on so many missions his responses had become automatic. He angled his Spad to the left and dived sideways toward the machine gun nest, opening up with his twin Vickers.

The German gunners swung their weapons around, but Blake was a fast-moving target coming at an unusual angle. His bullets zipped across the machine gun nest, and many of the Germans fled from the on-slaught. But some of them stayed, firing back at the Spad.

Blake heard bullets whistling by him. Some of them sliced through the canvas of his wings and fuselage. He saw German soldiers leaping away from his bul-lets and running to trenches nearby, while other German soldiers fell bleeding around their weapons.

Blake came to the end of the nest and gripped his stick to pull it back and climb out of there. Suddenly his plane was jolted by a bullet that tore away part of his propeller. The splinters flew back toward him and he ducked as he pulled the stick. The Spad began to climb, but without its usual speed. The German machine gunners who hadn't fled kept Blake's plane in their sights and kept their triggers depressed.

The bullets ripped apart Blake's wings and fuselage. One of the bullets hit him in the back and flung him forward against his dials. His body pressed against the stick and the Spad carved a big circle in the sky, pulling out of its climb and beginning to dive.

Blake felt as though his back and chest were torn apart. Blood burbled out of his mouth and the earth spun around underneath him. He tried to sit erect and bring the Spad under control, but he knew he couldn't do it. He tried to take a deep breath but the blood clogged his throat and he started to cough. Oh my God, he thought. I'm going to die . . .

He looked at his dials but saw only blurry images. Bullets continued to rip into his plane and the engine sputtered. A bullet hit him on the shoulder and would have knocked him out of the cockpit if he hadn't been strapped in.

The sky and earth became dark. Blake could feel the wind on his face and heard humming in his ears. He tried to think of something to do but his mind was fading out. His lap filled with blood and the fierce pain sent him into convulsions.

"Danielle," he whispered, as his plane fell out of the sky.

The Spad crashed into the side of a mountain and burst into flames, the wreckage cascading down the slope, a mangled and burning body trapped inside.

29

O N OCTOBER 6, Everett DeWitt, recently promoted to first lieutenant, was returning to General Pershing's field headquarters in the Meuse-Argonne sector after attending a meeting with French officers of the Fourth French Army. Everett's mission had been to deliver in person General Pershing's complaint that the French soldiers were not keeping up with the doughboys, and the American left flank was becoming exposed.

"We have been in this war much longer than you," the French general had told Everett, "and we have learned to be economical with our men."

Everett told them that General Pershing believed the attack could succeed only if the Allied armies moved quickly, before the Germans could adjust their tactics and fight back. The French officers argued that rapid mass attacks had been too costly in terms of casualties, and they preferred to move more deliberately, outmaneuvering the Germans in a series of pincer movements.

Now Everett was returning to General Pershing with the results of the meeting. He figured that Pershing would use one or two of the new divisions coming into the battle to cover his left flank.

The battle in the Meuse-Argonne sector was costly, but it appeared to be going well. The Second Division had finally taken Mont Blanc Ridge, although it had suffered terrific casualties, and the rest of the AEF was assaulting the fourth line of the Hindenburg fortifications. The General Staff believed that once the third line was broken, the German army would either retreat into Germany or surrender.

Everett drove over a narrow dirt road that cut through the middle of a forest. In the distance he could hear an artillery bombardment, and the sound brought a bitter smile to his face. The war would probably be over by the end of the year, he thought, and he wouldn't have fired a single shot.

He drove out of the woods and saw rolling fields and hills. A large group of doughboys comprising perhaps two battalions were moving across the road ahead in columns of twos, heading for the front. Everett slowed down and stopped twenty yards from the column nearest him. Some of the soldiers looked at his little Renault blankly. They were tired and dirty. On their shoulders were the insignia of the First Division, also known as the Big Red One because that was what the patch looked like. The Big Red One was one of the original Regular Army divisions and had seen some of the toughest fighting in the war. Now it was evidently going to the front again. It looked as though the First had been pulled out of one sector and was being transferred to another.

One of the doughboys from the Big Red One pointed at the General Staff license plate on Everett's little car, and his buddies smirked. Everett knitted his eyebrows together and took out a cigarette. There it is again, he thought, that goddamned contempt. Even the buck privates detested him. Everett felt his cheeks becoming warm. He wanted to give the doughboys a talking-to, but he'd never commanded any troops since he'd been in the army and wasn't even sure of how to bawl them out. Besides the doughboys' commanding officer would probably tell him to get the hell out of there. None of the combat soldiers, be they privates or officers, had any use for staff officers.

The troops passed over the road and moved across the field toward a forest in the distance. The road was clear now, but Everett kept looking at the soldiers. I wish I were going with them, he thought. I'd like to be a real soldier at least once before the goddamned war is over.

He looked at his watch. It was one o'clock in the afternoon. He ought to return to General Pershing's headquarters and get some lunch, but he kept looking at the soldiers from the Big Red One. A dangerous thought began to glimmer in his mind. Why don't I go with them? he asked himself. Who's to stop me?

He knew that his presence wasn't vital at headquarters. When the Iron Commander received more reports, as inevitably he would, that his left flank was still unprotected, he'd take the appropriate action. Sooner or later Everett would make it back, and he'd tell them that his car had broken down or that some other calamity had befallen him. They were in a war zone, after all, and anything could happen. There was no reason they wouldn't believe him.

The doughboys were moving farther away from him. This might be my last chance to see some fighting, Everett thought. What the hell—I might as well do it.

He pulled the keys from the ignition of the Renault and dropped them into his pocket. Taking off his soft cap, he put on the helmet he always carried with him in case of trouble. He also carried a forty-five that he'd last fired a few months ago. Opening the door of the car, he got out and looked at the doughboys from the Big Red One. Here goes, he thought as he went after them.

He double-timed, sucking in huge breaths of air. The grass on the ground was yellowing and the leaves on the trees were turning red and gold. It could have been just another sunny autumn day, entirely normal, but far in the distance there was smoke and the sounds of battle.

Everett reached the end of the column and fell in, adjusting his helmet. One of the doughboys turned around and looked at him curiously. The doughboy evidently wanted to ask who he was, but when he saw Everett's rank he decided to keep his mouth shut.

Everett tagged along at the end of the column, thinking of his few weeks at training school, when he'd gone on maneuvers in the fields and forests of Georgia. A city boy, he'd always felt out of place in the woods. The country had always felt as alien to him as Mars.

They entered a forest and continued marching along. The trees muffled the sounds of the artillery bombardment ahead. Huge portions of the forest had been ravaged by a previous bombardment, and Everett figured the area had probably been hotly contested a few days ago.

Somebody shouted for the column to halt and take a break. The doughboys sat in old shellholes or leaned against the trunks of trees. They opened their packs and took out cans of beans and packages of hardtack. Everett sat with his back against a boulder and wondered what he should do to get something to eat. He was awfully hungry. The doughboys moved away from him and looked at him as if he were a ghost.

A buck sergeant examined Everett for a few moments, then walked ahead and disappeared behind the trees. A few minutes later he came back with a young first lieutenant. The sergeant sat and rejoined his men, but the lieutenant advanced toward Everett, squinting at him against the bright sun. Everett stood up and smiled.

The lieutenant grinned. "Hello there," he said. "I didn't know you were with us."

Everett grinned back. "My car broke down on the road back there and then I saw your outfit. Hope you don't mind if I tag along for awhile."

The lieutenant looked at Everett's collar insignia, which marked him as a staff officer "Headquarters is that way," he said, pointing to the rear.

"I know, but I thought I'd take a look at the front. May I know your name?"

"Lieutenant John Simpson, sir."

"I'm Lieutenant Everett DeWitt."

Simpson hesitated for a moment, as if undecided as to what to do. Then he said tentatively, "You don't look as though you've got anything to eat with you."

"As a matter of fact I don't."

"Well . . . I've got a few extra things. Why don't you come up to the head of the column with me?"

"Thank you very much."

Everett followed Simpson to the front of the company column and sat down with him and two other young officers. They gave Everett beans and hardtack, which he ate with gusto. He learned that the units weren't two battalions, as he'd thought, but the remainder of a regiment, and that it was moving to the front to take a village up ahead.

When Everett was almost finished, the order came down to get moving again. He gulped down the remainder of his food, threw the empty can away and returned the fork to the sergeant who had lent it to him. The brigade resumed its march and Everett took his position with Lieutenant Simpson at the head of Company G.

Everett was exhilarated to be moving into battle. He'd always wanted to do this. In fact, when he'd signed up for the army in Washington he'd wanted to be in the infantry, but the procurement officer, who was a friend of the family, told him he'd be of more use as a staff officer. But now it was going to happen at last. Under his enthusiasm there was a shimmer of fear, but he told himself that he'd be careful, that nothing would happen to him.

The brigade came out of the forest, crossed a field and entered another forest, this one the scene of widespread destruction. Every tree was bare of leaves and most were shattered. Trenches and shellholes were everywhere and Everett had to watch his step so that he wouldn't fall. There was a terrible odor and then in one of the trenches Everett saw the bloated, greenish body of a German soldier. Everett's eyes bugged, and he gagged and looked away quickly. But his eyes fell on another dead German.

"What a stink," said one of the sergeants.

"A dead heinie is a good heinie," said another soldier.

The woods looked like a nightmare landscape. The sounds of fighting came closer and Everett's fear increased, the sudden reality of war bringing thoughts he had never before considered. It was easy to imagine the gruesome fighting that had gone on in these woods. What a terrible way to die. And for what? He wondered why soldiers fought so hard. Why didn't they just pull out and to hell with it?

"Skirmish line!" somebody shouted.

Lieutenant Simpson turned around and cupped his hands around his mouth. "Let's go, Company G—skirmish line!"

The brigade spread out in a long skirmish line in the woods. There was pushing and confusion, with officers running back and forth, giving orders. Everett was surprised at how docile the men were. They did what they were told as if resigned to their fates.

"Forward!"

The skirmish line moved through the woods, which was strewn with fallen trees and pocked with holes. Instead of a straight line the regiment broke up into numerous smaller lines. They saw a large number of doughboys ahead and squeezed closer to fit in among them. Officers ran around shouting at the men to form three skirmish lines. Everett and Company G were part of the second line. The mass of men moved through the woods again and after a while arrived at

a field beyond which was a town under bombardment.
The doughboys lined up at the edge of the woods and
waited for the bombardment to stop.

Everett lay on his stomach and looked at the town.
It was quite large and had evidently been an important commercial center at one time. Several roads led
into it, and Everett remembered something his friend
Georgie Patton once told him. *The key to victory is
control of the road net.* But then Georgie was a tank
officer and roads were very important to him.

The town was covered with smoke, and shells were
bursting everywhere inside its perimeter. Many buildings had been destroyed but a surprising number of
them were still standing. Everett figured that a thousand people or more had lived in the town, but now
the population was decimated.

The bombardment lessened in intensity and a few
minutes later it ceased entirely. Whistles were blown
and the doughboys got to their feet. Officers appeared
in front, waving their pistols.

The first wave moved out, running toward the town.
After a brief interval the second wave followed, and
then the third. Everett was wild with joy—at last he
was a real soldier. The men around him whooped and
cheered. Their battle cries echoed across the fields
and Everett shouted along with them, holding his
pistol tightly in his hand, and thinking that one day
he'd tell his grandchildren about this magnificent
charge.

The first German mortar shells began to fall, but
they landed too far back. Then more mortar shells
fell, and they were too far forward. Only three hundred yards separated the doughboys from the town

when the full weight of the mortar barrage rained down on them. Groups of men were blown into the air but the soldiers kept moving. Everett became frightened, disoriented. The German machine guns opened fire and doughboys were cut down like wheat before a scythe. Everett was horrified; the picture was suddenly changing. Instead of a heroic charge he found himself in the middle of a slaughter. He wanted to run back to the woods, but he'd have to fight his way through the doughboys behind him and the shame of having them see him in retreat was too much to bear. Now he understood why everybody followed orders; it was too humiliating not to. Better to be dead than branded a coward.

His whole body was shaking with terror and he was afraid his knees would give out. The German fire increased in intensity and doughboys were falling to the ground everywhere. One of the sergeants with whom Everett had eaten lunch an hour ago was shot through the throat, and as he fell to the ground his blood spurted out and streaked Everett's pants. Everett thought he'd faint, but somehow he kept going.

"Keep moving!" shouted Lieutenant Simpson. "Into the town!"

I know what I'll do, Everett thought feverishly. I'll fall down and pretend I'm dead. Then, when things quiet down, I'll sneak away.

Doughboys screamed all around him as they were hit with bullets, and the mortar rounds continued to blow other doughboys to pieces. Everett took a deep breath and fell down. He skinned his knees and hurt his elbows but he managed to get to the ground and make himself still except for his trembling legs. It looked so false, he thought, aghast at what he'd done. What if somebody noticed? I can get court-martialled . . . My family will be disgraced . . .

But in that wild, headlong charge, nobody noticed. The doughboys ran past him and Everett peeked up at them. The German fire was ripping them apart but still they kept driving toward the town. He wondered how they did it.

He closed his eyes and buried his face in the grass, trembling all over. I'm a coward, he sobbed. Whatever made me think that I'm a soldier? I'm nothing more than a clerk. I was a fool to come here today.

He looked up again and saw dead and wounded doughboys all around him. Some of them moaned and tossed convulsively on the ground. If only I had been shot, too, Everett thought. Then at least I could have kept my honor.

He raised his tear-stained face to the sky and saw puffy gray clouds. He knew that he'd never be able to live with himself again, that he might as well take out his pistol and shoot himself then and there. I'm a disgrace to my name and my family, he thought, I'm yellow, a coward. He closed his eyes and sobbed bitterly into the grass.

He imagined his ancestors looking down at him sniveling on the ground. His father and grandfather had told him stories about the generals and colonels and captains who'd been in his family and had fought for America ever since the French and Indian Wars, and the military lore of his family had filled his childhood fantasies. He could see them all now, as clearly as he had as a boy, in their strange uniforms, representing all the armies that the United States had ever put into the field. His own father had been with the Rough

Riders on San Juan Hill, and Franklin too had gone into battle, his death tragic but heroic. They had made the DeWitt name a proud one in America, and now he was letting all of them down.

Trembling, still terrified, Everett forced himself to stand. He wiped his eyes with his sleeve and ran slowly at first and then with more purpose toward the shattered skirmish lines. He raised his pistol and pointed it at the sky, firing once to give himself courage. Then came a savage cry tearing up from deep inside him, wrenching him free of all restraints of any thought of fear or safety. "Take the town!" he screamed, racing forward across the bloody and ravaged land.

The skirmish lines were faltering under the withering fire. Officers and men fell to the ground in huge numbers, but more than half of the original thousand in the regiment were still on their feet.

Everett ran at top speed through skirmish lines that were slowing down. "Forward!" he bellowed, oblivious to his chattering teeth and the tears pouring down his face. "Always move forward!"

Somehow he found himself in front of everybody. He imagined all his ancestors looking down at him from the heavens and smiling in satisfaction. He waved his pistol wildly in the air and ran toward a brick wall behind which German soldiers were firing.

"Keep moving!" he cried again. "Always keep moving!"

He levelled his pistol and fired toward the stone wall. German helmets bobbed around in back of it, and he shouted: "Kill me, you bastards—I don't even care . . ."

He jumped over the wall and German soldiers

swarmed all over him, but he spun and dodged, firing his pistol as quickly as he could pull the trigger. A German bayonet slashed his chest and another cut his shoulder, but none of the wounds were deep and he barely felt them. When his pistol was empty he hurled it into a German soldier's face and yanked the man's rifle and bayonet away.

The rest of the brigade stormed the wall and joined Everett, who had become crazed with the violence of the battle, stabbing and butting every German who landed in his path.

"Kill them!" he shrieked. "Kill them all!"

He had the added strength and sharp instincts of a madman; no German could stand before him for long. One German officer fired a Luger at him but Everett was a fast-moving target and the bullet missed. The officer fired again and this time the bullet hit Everett's helmet and ricocheted off. It was like being hit over the head with a hammer, and Everett dropped dazed to his knees. The German officer was going to fire again, but a doughboy charged him and ran him through with his bayonet.

Everett tried to clear his head as the doughboys pushed the Germans back. The doughboys were charging into the buildings and cellars and Everett tried to get up to go with them, but his legs buckled and he fell to the ground. He tried again, but he couldn't make it.

Somebody was bending over him. "Are you all right, son?"

Everett looked up into the face of a middle-aged officer. "I think so."

"You just lay still there, and a medic will be with you directly. What's your name?"

Everett was aware that the side of his face was wet. He touched it and looked at his fingers. It was blood.

"I said to lay still now," the officer said. "Who are you?"

"Lieutenant DeWitt . . ."

"You're not in my battalion. What are you doing here?"

"I don't know, sir."

The officer smiled. "Well, whatever it is, welcome to the Big Red One. I saw what you did just now, and I'm going to put you in for a Silver Star."

30

THE LIST REGIMENT was among the German units falling back from the third line of defense in the Hindenburg system of fortifications. Private Adolf Hitler ran through the smoke and explosions, searching frantically for cover. Then he saw a shellhole and dived into it, only to become aware of a fierce burning in his lungs.

"Gas!" somebody shouted.

Hitler panicked when he realized that he'd already inhaled the gas. He tried to hold his breath and reached for his gas mask. A shell exploded nearby and shook the ground so hard that he was stunned for a few moments. When his head cleared he found that everything was blurred in front of him. With shaking hands he managed to free his gas mask and put it on, but he already felt faint and everything around him was dissolving into a uniform grayness.

I've been gassed, he thought. I'm going to die. Terrified, he jumped out of the hole and ran in the direction of the German rear. He couldn't see anything and his chest felt as though a firestorm was inside. Shells burst around him and bullets flew in all directions. He tripped and fell, got quickly to his feet again, but dropped his rifle as he ran to safety.

His mind was filled with tumultuous thoughts and he was becoming nauseous. His legs wouldn't hold him up anymore and he fell to the ground. He tore off his gas mask and screamed: "Help—I've been gassed! Help!"

He walked a few steps forward on his knees, then fell over a dead soldier. I should have kept my gas mask on, Hitler realized. He held his hands in front of him to feel the way. Everything had become dark now.

"Help!" he shouted. "Help!"

He heard footsteps, and somebody grabbed his arm. "I've got you," a soldier said.

The soldier helped Hitler up and dragged him back to safety.

In Zurich, Danielle sat in the bedroom of her aunt's home, reading a newspaper. She'd been following the war avidly and knew that the American divisions were breaking the back of the German army in the Argonne Forest. She especially searched for news of the air war; she worried about Blake and thought of him constantly. In the back of her mind was the nagging memory of the first night she'd met him, when she'd had the premonition that he was going to die.

There was a knock on her door.

"Come in."

Her aunt entered, her face pale. Danielle saw that there was a telegram in her hands, and a wave of fear passed over her. "What's wrong?" she whispered.

Her aunt silently handed her the telegram. Danielle read it, and then simply stared at it for a few moments. She rose unsteadily to her feet, her look of disbelief turning to anguish. "*Noooo!*" she screamed, and with the cry still dying on her lips she crumpled to the floor in a faint.

Her aunt called the servants and they tried to revive her, but to no avail. After putting her to bed her aunt called a doctor, who arrived a half-hour later. The doctor gave Danielle an injection to relax her and keep her asleep. He stayed with her throughout the afternoon and evening, examining her repeatedly because he feared she might miscarry. When he finally took his leave after midnight, he said he'd return in the morning to check the patient again.

Danielle woke before he arrived. The injection had worn off somewhat, and her soft sobs were interspersed with Blake's name.

The doctor returned at nine, and after giving her another sedative he told her aunt that he was much encouraged. The mother and baby would most probably survive the tragedy.

In Berlin, the kaiser sat behind the desk in his office. Seated across from him were Field Marshal Hindenburg, Colonel-General Ludendorff, and Foreign Minister Paul von Hintze. The atmosphere was solemn and tense, for they had been discussing the catastrophes at the front.

Hindenburg's face was chalky-white and he looked twenty years older. "Your Excellency," he said wearily, "the western front is about to collapse. If we do not get an armistice, the army will be destroyed."

"It's true," Ludendorff said nervously. "The only way to save Germany is to appeal to President Wilson at once. An armistice *must* be arranged within twenty-four hours."

Hintze, a former rear admiral in the Imperial Navy, couldn't believe his ears. "An armistice?" he asked. "In only twenty-four hours? I had no idea the situation was so bad."

"It's worse than you can possibly imagine," Hindenburg growled.

"It would be impossible to obtain an armistice in only twenty-four hours," Hintze protested. "An armistice is an enormously complex matter."

The muscles in Ludendorff's face twitched. "You must do it!" he said. "The fate of the Fatherland hangs in the balance!"

"But gentlemen," Hintze said, outraged at the demand, "such a move would be tantamount to unconditional surrender. The German people wouldn't stand for it. There would be revolution and possibly the overthrow of the imperial dynasty. You must give me a few days to work this out, gentlemen, so that I can obtain better terms from the Allies. If we appear too desperate, the Allies' demands will be severe."

Ludendorff shot to his feet. "We *are* desperate!" he screamed. "What must I do to make you understand that *we are desperate!*"

The kaiser, who'd been the calmest man in the room, raised his hand. "Kindly return to your seat, General Ludendorff."

"Yes, Excellency."

Ludendorff sat again. The two officers and the foreign minister waited for the kaiser to speak. The kaiser looked at each of them and sighed.

"I never dreamed it would come to this," he said softly, "but this is my decision. We will ask for an armistice, but we will not beg. The Fatherland may be in dire straits, but we're not a nation of beggars yet. The foreign minister will take as much time as he deems prudent to obtain the most favorable terms possible for the Fatherland."

"We don't have much time!" Dudendorff said, his voice strident, close to hysteria. "The front is collapsing even as we speak!"

"The German soldier knows what his duty is," the Kaiser replied. "I have made my decision and it is final. All of you may return to your stations."

31

O N THE MORNING of November 11, the Second
Division was deployed in a forest near the banks
of the Meuse River. The Second Field Artillery
Brigade was shelling the German side of the river,
and the Second Engineers were building a pontoon
bridge so the doughboys could cross later in the day.

Duncan sat in a shellhole with his new executive
officer, Lieutenant Crandall from Little Rock, Arkan-
sas, eating canned willie and hardtack. They and the
other men in the Second Division were eating their fill
now; they expected to attack before noon and didn't
know when they'd get a chance to eat again.

The woods they were in had been a bloody battleground only two days ago. The Second Division had
managed to push the Germans across the river, but the
woods had been nearly destroyed, with holes and

broken trees everywhere. The smell of gunpowder was still in the air.

There had been a change in Duncan ever since he'd found out that his brother had been killed in action. He talked and joked with his men less, and arranged to be alone as often as possible. He often appeared distracted. The men were worried about him.

Now, sitting in the hole, he munched hardtack and thought of Blake. His heart was heavy and he found himself unable to accept the fact that Blake was dead. Blake had been so dashing, so full of life. If there were any sense and order in the world, he thought, Blake would have lived and he would have died, for he was the dull and plodding one, the brooding fellow always hidden in the shadow of his more spectacular brother. Duncan realized that he loved his brother more than he'd ever loved anybody else, despite Blake's many faults. With Blake's death he felt that a part of him had died, too.

The shelling on the other side of the river suddenly stopped. Duncan perked up and turned toward the river. Through the broken, twisted trees he could see the engineers on their half-built pontoon bridge, looking toward the German side of the river. The other officers and men in B Company were also looking at the other side of the river, wondering why the shelling had stopped.

This turn of events was quite curious. A sudden halt in a barrage in progress had never occurred in Duncan's experience on the front lines. He stood up, his can of meat in his hand.

"The war's over!" somebody shouted.

Duncan spun around in the direction of the voice.

He saw some soldiers from his Fourth Platoon coming through the woods, surrounding Major Berry from battalion headquarters. The major carried his helmet in his hand and was smiling.

No, it can't be, Duncan thought, walking toward the major. The other men in the company came out of their holes too. They'd heard the cry and wanted to know what was going on.

Duncan saluted Major Berry. "Do you know why the shelling's stopped, sir?"

Berry returned the salute, his smile broadening. "I sure as hell do—*the war is over!*"

Duncan and the other men from B Company stared at him in disbelief.

"Are you sure?" Duncan asked.

"Yep," said Major Berry. "The armistice was signed this morning. The war is over, boys! General Lejeune wants us all to stay in position and keep our heads down just in case, but the fighting is finished."

There were a few moments of silence, and then the doughboys began to cheer. They ran around like madmen, slapping each other on the shoulders and jumping up and down. A few of them fell down on their knees and prayed. Some cried shamelessly. Duncan, however, was stunned and stood still as a statue.

"Carry on here," Major Berry said, "I've got to pass the word along to Company C." Berry turned and walked away.

Duncan took off his helmet. If only Blake could have lasted a few more weeks, he would have made it through the war. But Duncan suddenly realized that he himself had made it. *I don't have to fight anymore,* he thought.

Corporal Bell ran toward him, his face flushed with emotion. "Sir!" he shouted. "The war is over! The war is over!"

The two men looked at each other, and all they'd been through together passed between them. Bell lurched forward and embraced Duncan, pressing his face against Duncan's chest.

"The war is over!" Bell said, as the tears flowed down his cheeks. "The war is over!"

Bell turned Duncan loose and ran off, waving his hands, his cry repeated among the other men. "The war is over! The war is over!"

Duncan stumbled through the woods toward the river, where his men rushed up to him to shake his hand. The engineers on the pontoon bridges ran back and forth screaming at the top of their lungs. There was chaos and jubilation everywhere. Duncan made his way to the bank of the river, kneeled, scooped up some cold water and splashed it on his face. Then he looked up to the clear blue sky.

My God, he thought. *The war is over.*

THE END

NINTH IN THE DRAMATIC
FREEDOM FIGHTERS
SERIES:

Shellfire
on the
Bay

by Jonathan Scofield

What the Cubans saw lying off their coast was
the answer to a decade of prayers and
deprivation. Most of them had been living like
animals in the hills. They had seen their families
die of starvation or fever and watched the ever-
lengthening arm of Spanish authority tighten its
grip on all their lives.

Among the Americans who had come to their
rescue were the idealistic Charles Bell and the
dashing, deceptive Lowell DeWitt. Locked in an
intense rivalry for the love of a young nurse, they
fought bravely side by side to defend their
nation's honor in the explosive Spanish-American
War.

BE SURE TO READ
SHELLFIRE ON THE BAY—
ON SALE NOW FROM DELL/BRYANS

TWELFTH IN THE DRAMATIC
FREEDOM FIGHTERS
SERIES:

Armageddon in the West

by Jonathan Scofield

In the cause of liberty, American Airborne
Division 101 joins the allied battle to crush the
seemingly unstoppable power of Nazi Germany.
For Lieutenant Logan Hunter, war draws a thin
line between friend and foe, lover and enemy, as
an American officer plots his countryman's
doom—and a beautiful Dutch lover is revealed as
an enemy spy. A war-hardened hero loses his
heart to a lovely young war correspondent whom
he may never see again, and an army of
greenhorns prepares for its final confrontation
with Hitler's awesome forces as the battle rages to
its bloody climax.

BE SURE TO READ
ARMAGEDDON IN THE WEST
COMING IN FEBRUARY FROM
DELL/BRYANS